Lapse

Lapse

Alex Rodriguez

Quantity Purchases:
Companies, professional groups, clubs, and other organizations may qualify for special terms when ordering quantities of this title. For information, email info@ebooks2go.net, or call (847) 598-1150 ext. 4141. www.ebooks2go.net

Published in the United States
by eBooks2go, Inc.
1827 Walden Office Square, Suite 260, Schaumburg, IL 60173

ISBN: 978-1-5457-5458-0 (Paperback)
ISBN: 978-1-5457-5419-1 (Hardcover)

Library of Congress Cataloging in Publication

If you came to me,

with a face I have not seen,

with a name I have never heard

I would still know you.

Even if centuries separate us,

I would still feel you

Somewhere between the sand and the stardust,

through every collapse and creation,

there is a pulse that echoes of you and I.

—*Lang Leav*

Table of Contents

Chapter 1
A Broken Team

Nora waited outside the science building sitting on the thick branch of a barren oak tree. Most of its leaves were scattered along the lawn of the quad below. At the base of the tree was her schoolbag, full of assignments she ignored for the past several days. Two additional textbooks lay beneath the worn-out beige knapsack. A rough, cold breeze made her lose her balance. It tousled her dark brown hair over her eyes. She tugged at her sleeves, covering her palms, then brushed aside the wandering strands. Nora shifted in her spot before resuming her gaze at the double doors.

Shadows danced behind the small window. Students freshly released from their lectures moved through the corridors, eager to leave for a short break. The doors burst open, and college kids of every variety trotted down the steps. They split in different directions—some toward the pavilion for a late lunch, and others darted to the parking lot.

Nora craned her neck quickly, studying each incoming wave of new faces. Nothing. She jumped down from her perch, plucked her bag and books off the ground, and started toward the building. An inkling of worry crossed her mind, but she pushed the doubt to the back corners.

Self-consciously, she reached for the black sundial dangling around her neck. It was second nature to have it in her grasp when she couldn't find what she was looking for. The sundial was small, not much bigger than a dollar coin. She felt it humming in between her fingers as if it recognized what Nora sought. It yearned to jut forward and lead the way. She pressed her thumb against the flat surface of the sundial plate, trying to soothe the timepiece. Nora opened her hand letting it lay flat in her palm. Its engraved hour lines gleamed white, and the thin shadow of the gnomon almost touched the two mark. The sundial didn't move.

She made her way up the steps, wondering if he had indeed managed to thwart her yet again. He had done an excellent job of doing so for weeks now, but Nora was determined not to let him get away. They were meant to be on the same side, yet he acted as though she were his enemy. She could never be against him. On the contrary, she was doing what she thought was in his best interest.

Only recently he accepted the fact he needed her protection. That didn't mean he wanted her around. That was also a new development Nora had to grow accustomed to. It was something she anticipated sooner rather than later, if she was being quite frank. The texted updates stopped coming, and the unexplained disappearances posed infuriating challenges for her. It forced her to keep him on a tighter leash, whether it was with or without his knowledge. What made her want to pummel him to oblivion was his complete disregard for the danger that loomed over him—the way he would scoff and discredit her warnings.

Nora reminded herself daily to be patient. *He hadn't suffered yet,* she reasoned. Loss wasn't a part of his life. He could try and avoid her—a game he often never won. He just didn't know it.

A tough shoulder hit her arm. The pressure of it made Nora sidestep back and drop her bag. She glanced down the stairs to look for the culprit who bumped into her. Somehow she knew already who had done it. At the bottom of the steps, Mason Lyle glanced over his shoulder as if to claim his wrongdoing. She picked her books up and rushed back down the steps.

He noticed her advance and tore off in the direction of the soccer field. Nora's heartbeat quickened. This was her chance. She clutched her sundial, muttering a prayer. Suddenly, she was a few feet in front of Mason. No one noticed her travel twenty yards without crossing the grass. Mason only rolled his eyes in annoyance and picked up his pace.

"Nice parlor trick," he scoffed, shouldering passed her again, harder than the first time.

"Mason," Nora called after him.

He kept his walk brisk, making Nora run to keep up.

"I know what you're going to say," he said flatly.

"Good," Nora huffed. "Because I hate repeating myself!"

"I told you to keep away from me," Mason hissed. He avoided looking at her, as if she were a younger classman he couldn't shake. "Go home and wait for me there."

"You know I can't do that. It isn't safe. I'm staying. I'll be in the library like always, and I'll be back before practice ends. If you leave, I'll know," she said, slowing down to let him walk off. Nora watched him part from the sidewalk to take the dirt path leading to the locker rooms.

He emerged a few minutes later in a university-issued jersey and sweatpants. His teammates whistled and greeted him with enthusiasm. He jogged onto the field, where they passed him the ball. He juggled the ball on his knees with ease for a moment before passing it on to the next.

Mason was built like the athlete that he was—tall and lean with short black hair and deep, calculating brown eyes. He had a good smile, too, enough to get him out of trouble. Coupled with the right words and a shift in his gaze, Mason charmed his way through school just fine. But none of that was for Nora. His tone with her often wavered between anger and razor sharp sarcasm. It was easy to mimic his mannerisms when he was so openly hostile with her.

The shrill sound of a whistle made Nora jump. The coach walked onto the field, making the team gather around him for instructions, only to have them scatter a moment later as the old man barked out orders for the warm-up drills. She watched Mason move down the field to his position with one of his teammates. He looked around, checking who made it to practice, then his eyes left the field, wandering toward Nora's direction. Their eyes locked. He raised his head at her in a stiff nod, whether in cool acknowledgment or some kind of warning telling her to leave. Nora couldn't quite tell. She offered him a weak smile before turning and heading back up to the school.

Nora walked to the library above the lunch hall. She purchased a cold sandwich and chips, courtesy of the vending machine, then headed to the quiet third floor. A lonesome table near the window where she could see the soccer field became her nest for the next three hours.

Her long-awaited neglected homework was itching to be done. Nora pulled open her metaphysics textbook. She began to read the first paragraph and then a bit more until she caught herself scanning words without taking in the meaning. Although it was her favorite course, her heart wasn't in it that afternoon. She decided to leave the reading for another time.

Instead, Nora opted for her astronomy homework. She enjoyed the study of the planetary system and stars—the history of the known universe. It also involved plenty of math. Calculations. Nora could do numbers as easily as she breathed. They were uncomplicated, full of equations, facts, and less abstract theories. The facts and numbers would chase away the thoughts that ran circles in her brain for days now.

Facts were also the reason she was able to take college courses ahead of schedule. When Mason graduated, so did she the following summer as a sophomore. There was no point to remain in high school when he was a town over attending college. Her superb grades and desire for more challenging course work made the transition easy. Though it had been a ploy to watch Mason during his sessions, she had done her fair share of tutoring to the struggling upperclassmen. The school lamented to see her go.

Aside from those two courses, she was taking a physics course as well. Nora was unsure *which* one, since she stopped attending the class two weeks ago. She lost interest when the professor geared the class toward the subatomic and mechanics. The only bit that interested her was already briefly discussed in the first weeks of school: optics and quantum mechanics. If she was dropped from the class, it suited her fine.

After her assignments were complete, Nora checked the time. It was still early. Mason would not be pleased to see her back, but she didn't have anywhere else to go. All the eating areas on campus were bound to be empty with full students poring over notes and textbooks or gathered around for company. And there weren't familiar places for her to go. It was hard to piece together a social life when Nora had a round-the-clock job that required her undivided attention. She decided to head to the soccer field.

The campus looked emptier now as it progressed into the early evening hours. Cliques of students gathered in different areas of the campus. Those most anxious about midterms sat indoors, their noses deep in their textbooks, while the more relaxed sat outside chatting with friends and listening to music. Here and there study groups congregated to complete projects outside the classroom. The chill of the mid-October day offered little discomfort because most had warm sweaters and drank hot coffees. Lights flickered on along the campus as the sun began to sink toward the west.

When Nora reached the field, she saw a small audience had gathered to watch the practice game. Practice was well over, but the players stayed behind for a game. It was a good call she happened to wander down when she did. Mason may have left without her. She went to stand near a pile of duffel bags.

Back in his day clothes, Mason was in control of the ball. An opponent was right on his tail, trying to take possession of the ball. He made a grab for Mason's shirt, but he managed to slip through the player's fingers and kicked the ball to another teammate. Mason and his guard slowed to a walk.

From what Nora could tell, he was a fantastic soccer player. Mason would score one or two goals in a practice game and usually make at least one in an actual game. His successes on the field translated to the student body. Mason gained popularity fast, especially once he made the team last autumn, his freshmen year. After a particularly good game, his jock status catapulted him to more parties and other places Nora struggled to watch from afar.

Mason moved around, trying to make himself available for a pass. He watched the other players fumble around, inching the ball closer to the goalpost. Out of sheer luck, one of the guys with dyed blue curls managed to kick it away from the chaos.

The ball went soaring back to Mason's side of the field. His opponent tried to block him, but Mason overpowered him with ease, jumping high into the air and making a spectacular header. The goalkeeper dived to no avail. The ball flew passed him, hitting the net.

The whistle blew to indicate the game was over. Mason jumped in the air, punching the air before receiving well-earned fist bumps and claps on the back. Nora smiled a little, proud of his accomplishment. Amused, the coach hollered at them to get off the field and go home.

The team finally dispersed, some drawn to the attention of the crowd that gathered, while others who were more in a hurry headed for the stockpile of belongings. He saw her waiting. Mason's lips almost curved upward as if to smile, but he stopped himself.

"I thought I told you to go home," he muttered, shouldering his bag.

"That's not how this works," Nora replied.

"Look," Mason said, stepping forward so their conversation wouldn't be overheard by his friends. He grabbed her arm and pulled her along. "The guys want to meet up at Gio's. I'll drop you off at home. I'll report in every hour on the hour if you let me go alone."

"How do I know you'll actually do it this time?" she asked. "You've gotten me—no, both of us—killed like that before!"

In what is now present-day Hong Kong, 1372, she wanted to add, but instead kept her mouth shut. She didn't need to blurt that out on campus for all to hear.

"You're gonna have to trust me."

"Well, I don't," Nora said and wrenched out of his grip. She headed to the trail that led up to the darkening campus. "You pull this crap on me over and over again, Mason. Like hell I'm going to trust you to go anywhere."

"So you're gonna keep stalking me?" he snapped.

"Believe me: it's not because I enjoy it," she countered.

Mason followed unhappily.

"Nothing's going to happen to me," he said, taking on the tone of angry exasperation she knew so well. "I'll be fine. I'll be out in public; whoever's out there won't be dumb enough to attack with so many witnesses. Come on, Nora."

They cut through the grass over to the parking lot and crossed the still very full lot to his silver Nissan.

"I've told you already: I'm not taking any chances with you," she told him. Mason popped open the trunk and put his things in the back. Nora did the same. He shut the back, and they got in his car. "What would you do if an anachronism—a time traveler—catches you? I'm the only one with a time key here. Have you forgotten? You jump into a time warp straight into the Passage, and you can say goodbye to *your* time. And all of what you know, for that matter! Doesn't that mean anything to you? Your lies put you in danger, Mason. Don't you see that? Once I can trust you, you're free to wander!" She buckled herself in.

"That's another thing," he shot back, truly annoyed starting the car. "Why the hell don't you take the train home like the good little college girl you're pretending to be? I'm not your personal taxi service."

"You're not listening to me!" Nora scoffed.

She heard him retort something back under his breath, but she didn't bother to ask him to repeat it. Instead, she clenched the sides of the seat to keep her from landing a swift blow to his head. He was really testing her patience today.

They took their usual route home.

Mason wasn't always so difficult. Up until recently, they got along well these last several years. They were more friends than acquaintances. Nora knew he saw her more as the girl next door than his personal bodyguard. He had over a year to adjust to the information she confided in him—who he really was. He was complacent and open to Nora's wealth of information; then the lines began to blur when she tried to reform the boundaries that changed everything. Now she was left facing the backlash.

The thirty-minute drive past the valleys and ridges led them into the small town of Torch Crossings. Mason took the main road to head toward their neighborhood. Torch Crossings was nestled among the hidden valleys in Oregon's mountain range. Only six other towns were nearby before reaching the reasonable-size city of Valo. Torch Crossings itself was average in size and population. It was equipped with a school district, shops and stores, parks, restaurants, and everything else in between to be a fully functioning community. It even had a decent-size theme park near the interstate. It took them about another fifteen minutes to reach their street.

Mason and Nora lived on Wells Drive in the older part of town. The aging, rusting houses stood tall and proud, with brightly lit porches. The meticulously cut lawns looked wet with mildew. Mason drove slow to the end of the street and parked in his driveway.

They got out of the car.

"Is that really where you're going, then?" Nora asked as he opened the trunk. She hauled out her things and shouldered it. She looked up at him expectantly.

"What does it matter?" he replied coldly. "You won't believe me. If you really want to know, I'm not going." He grabbed his things, slammed the trunk, and tore off to his house. Nora watched him cross his lawn and slam his door on his way in, making the wind chimes jingle.

Then it fell silent.

She pinched the bridge of her nose, letting out a heavy, irritated sigh. She longed for the day when they weren't enemies on the same team. She hated being estranged. Nora turned to her own home next door to his, waiting a moment before entering. His bad temper would bring out the worst in her soon enough.

Chapter 2
Time Quake

Nora walked toward the back end of the house to enter her room. On her way through the gate, it let out a loud creak. She glanced at the windows. Surely it announced her arrival if anyone was listening. It swung shut behind her as she fished out her house key from her bag. The glass French doors were covered with thick white blinds, just how she left them that morning. Nora unlocked the door, opened it a partially, and wiggled past the blinds, sliding the door to a gentle close.

As she stepped into the large remodeled living room, Nora turned on the lights. The large space that was once a secondary living room now served as her bedroom. Her unmade bed, nightstand, clothes rack, and pile of laundry were in the farthest corner of the room diagonal of the television and an old teal recliner. Across was her desk and empty bookshelf. For the most part, it was a clean space, except for the stray pieces of newspaper and articles of clothing. Nora didn't spend much of her time here, but it suited her needs when she wasn't trailing after Mason.

She kicked off her shoes on the rug and set down her bag. Her sweatshirt came off too, landing in a heap on the wooden floor. Nora walked further into her room, running a hand through her windswept hair. She stepped over to her cluttered desk to rummage for the tablet she left earlier in the day.

It blinked on when her hand hovered over the screen. There were no new alerts, only junk mail from her school email. Nora swiped her fingers across the display, tapping her way back to the home screen.

A knock at the door made her jump, pulling her hand away from the tablet. The screen went dark once more. Nora quickly buried it under a stack of papers. She turned just as the door opened.

Nadine Hartley's familiar blond pixie cut poked into her room. "Hi, I heard you arrive next door with the neighbor boy again," she said, letting herself in.

"Oh yeah, Mason gave me a ride home."

"Good, sometimes I worry how you will get home from school. The train at this hour can be sketchy," Nadine said. "You two get along well?"

Nora shrugged a little. "Yeah, sort of. I mean, we're friends, I guess."

If only Nadine knew she got on his last nerve.

"I'm glad," she said with a smile. "I left your dinner in the microwave to reheat if you're hungry."

"Thanks, I'll be out in a second," Nora said. She waited until Nadine closed the door to exhale. With her gone, Nora rifled through her desk again. She grabbed the tablet and shoved it into her schoolbag. She dumped her assignments on the bed. Those were unnecessary and didn't need to be carried around anymore. The tablet on other hand needed to be with her at all times. The possibility of Nadine or anyone else getting a hold of it was dangerous. It revealed all her secrets as well as Mason's.

After supper she intended to finish the metaphysics reading she began at the library. Nora liked the idea of turning in early for the night. It was a rare event when she did so.

Nora opened the door to peer down the hall. There was no sound coming from the rest of the house, meaning the Hartleys were in their room for the night too. She hurried out of her room and walked down the hall, passing two closed doors. The pair of empty rooms used to belong to the two Hartley boys, Andy and Michael, before they moved away for good after college. Nora met them once three months ago, when they came to visit during the summer.

Further along she passed their bedroom followed by the bathroom. The hallway led to the formal living room, with a well-maintained modern beige sofa and the fifty-inch flat screen television hung from the wall. The faint glow of the lamp and book on the end table told her Nadine had been up reading.

To the right, the kitchen light was still on. The counter-height table was clean as well as the sink and stove. Nora opened the microwave door to see what was inside. A plate of mashed potatoes, a short ear of corn, and pulled pork sat waiting for her to devour. She shut the door and pressed the on button. In two easy stretches, she grabbed a glass from the cabinet over her head and opened the refrigerator to search for the carton of orange juice.

As she waited, Nadine strode in dropping off an empty mug in the sink. "Will you be going out with Mason tonight?" she asked.

Nora coughed into her glass, the juice burning the back of her throat when it threatened to make its way through her nose. "I don't think so."

"I know he's a friend of yours, but do be careful," Nadine went on. "He is slightly older than you, and Anna says he can be a tad reckless—"

"I know, Nadine. I know."

Even his mother and Nadine recognized he was a bit of a wild card.

"And you come home so late," she finished.

"Sorry, I'll try not to make so much noise."

Nadine grinned, amused by her apology. "I don't want to see you in trouble."

"You won't," Nora promised.

Nadine padded back to her room, and the door shut a moment later.

A seed of doubt planted itself in the pit of Nora's stomach. Nadine's sudden interest in her activities made her nervous. Why did it matter if she stayed in or out that evening? More so if she hung around Mason or not. Nora tended to come and go as she pleased; then another seed of doubt followed after.

Nora rushed to the front window to check if Mason's car was still parked in the driveway. Her heart pounded against her chest as if she already knew the answer.

It was gone.

The microwave behind her beeped, announcing her food was ready. The aroma made her mouth water, but she was no longer hungry. Nora clenched and unclenched her fists in red-hot anger. It was the only thing keeping her from punching a hole through the window. He dared to lie to her again.

Nora ran over to the foyer to snag a pair of keys off the line of hooks on the wall, then ran back to her room. She reached for the sundial. Just as she suspected, it hung suspended in front of her neck, directing her fury in the right direction. It pulled her along like an angry leash. As quickly as she could, Nora retied her shoes and tugged a sweatshirt over her head. She picked up her bag, taking that too. She darted out of her room.

"Heading out!" she hollered as she passed the Hartley's bedroom. "I'm borrowing the car."

Nadine shuffled out of her room. "Is something wrong?"

"Yes," Nora said in a rush.

"Nora—"

"I'll be back soon."

Nora ran out the door. The blue Honda blinked its lights as it unlocked. She hopped into the vehicle and readjusted the seat to fit to her stature. Once she got herself situated, Nora tore out of the driveway and down the road.

There were no words to describe how angry she felt. Nora clutched the wheel so tightly her knuckles turned white. She let it go briefly to slap the wheel with her palm as hard as she could. If he were within her grasp, she didn't know what she'd say to herself to not strangle him like a filthy rag. It was like everything she warned him about didn't matter. On the contrary, he did the complete opposite. If he didn't care for his own fate, Nora could fix that. It was a problem she ran into before. If he was doing it out of spite, they were in trouble.

The sudden rumble shook her out of her thoughts. Everything around Nora began to quiver and shake. The streetlights trembled in place. Stores and streetlights crackled madly as if an earthquake threatened to tear them in two. Parked cars along the streets rumbled without lurching out of place. A billowing darkness erupted like a firework causing one grand shake.

Nora yelped and slammed on the brakes.

The quaking came to an abrupt stop. She looked around to make sure everything had truly settled. No sirens wailed in the distance; no one came out to question the bizarre tremor. Nora calmed her breathing and continued driving until she reached Gio's Restaurant on Julius Road.

She pulled into the parking lot as two men in gray wool coats crossed the pavement. One clutched a bowler hat to his head as if afraid it would fly away. The second pocketed a small, dark item into his coat. Nora's heart tightened at the sight; it finally found something to be concerned over. That had not been an ordinary earthquake; it was a time quake. Someone had arrived in this time period.

Nora parked next to Mason's car and darted toward the entrance. She searched for the two men in wool coats that walked in only a minute ago. She saw them sitting up by the bar talking silently. Up close, the time travelers didn't look so intimidating. They looked out of place like foreigners lost on a trip. But that didn't mean they were any less of a threat.

Next, she looked for Mason. He wasn't hard to find. Gio's was full of college students—namely, the soccer team, their fan club of freshman girls, and others who gravitated toward that circle. Mason was walking back to the table with a large, meaty pizza balanced in his hand. The people gathered at the table applauded at his arrival. They cleared a path for him and a chair. He took a seat beside a pretty blonde sipping her drink. She offered it to him, and he took a portioned swig.

Anger flared again, briefly clouding Nora's cohesive train of thought built on strategy. She was so mad she almost wanted the time travelers to take him; he deserved it after he ditched her like that. But her instincts told her otherwise. She had to protect him.

She stood near the door to keep watch over Mason and the time travelers at the same time. She caught glimpses of the conversation going on inside. Combined with her skill of lipreading, Nora thought she had a decent picture of what was being said.

"He's here," she managed to make out. The bowler hat man pointed to the table for emphasis. He had taken the hat off indoors to mop his balding head with a napkin as if it cost him a great deal to sit. He was thinner than his companion.

"Which one is he?" his partner asked, glaring around. He looked around, not sure where to begin their search. His eyes were sunken in, and his complexion was gaunt. Nora thought they looked sickly or like newly released prisoners of war.

The time travelers stuck out like sore thumbs among the youngsters in the pizzeria. Their ragged clothing under their coats contained layers of patches, and their worn-out shoes looked like they would need to be stapled together soon. Nora couldn't exactly pinpoint from where or when they came from, yet she knew how they were going back.

They clearly didn't know who they were looking for. They pointed and stared, but they didn't move right away. The thin man put on his bowler hat with a harsh string of words. He reached into his pocket, and the other joined him. Deciding she didn't want to find out the hard way what was in his pocket, Nora straightened and grabbed the handle.

Nora stepped into the warm building. The smells of leather, old paint, and pizza filled her nose. The vintage music box was spewing out an old tune she only caught bits of. She watched the pair stride over to a booth of kids. With their backs turned, she made a beeline for Mason's table.

"Mason."

He looked up with dread and shock. "Nora—"

"Come on, we have to go," she pleaded. "Now."

"I'm not going anywhere with you."

She looked over at the two men. They were wading from table to table, glancing at a device in their hands. They pointed at the customers, who glared at them in suspicion. They would move to their section of the diner soon and spot them. Nora moved fast. Ignoring the disdainful glances of his friends, she yanked Mason out of his seat and pulled him to the back exit near the bathrooms. Nora forced him out the door, shoving him along the parking lot.

"You're a lunatic!" he snapped. "What is your problem?" He jerked away from her angrily.

"You!" Nora shot back. "You are my problem! You lied to me!"

"I had to. I can't go anywhere without you following me!"

"Because you refuse to listen!" She forced herself to focus. "We can't argue here in the open like this. You need to go."

"Forget it." Mason turned to leave.

"You aren't going anywhere except home," Nora almost shouted. She caught him by the arm and flung him around.

He glared at her, his eyes full of fire.

"Mason, please, you have to go," she tried again, gentler this time. She let go of his arm. "Right now, you're not safe. Anachronisms made it into our time. They came here to look for you." Nora waved over to the men still inside. "Do you want to be killed in front of your friends? Or swept out of time? This is why I insist on going everywhere with you. They keep getting closer to you."

"How do you know they're even time travelers?" Mason challenged.

"Look at them," she demanded. "Do they look like they belong here? I've been fighting them in every life cycle—the eighties, fifties, twenties, and hundreds of years before that. You really don't think I know how to spot them by now?"

The men hovered over the college kids Mason was with seconds ago. Nora pushed him toward their cars down the parking lot. His weight against her hands didn't help. "And there was a time quake. I felt one on my way here."

Mason stopped dead in his tracks. "A time quake?" he asked, a tinge of curiosity in his voice.

"It's a giant tremor shaking our time," Nora replied, pushing him along again this attempt much easier. "It's the effect time travelers have when they arrive in a new time period."

"Like a loud explosion rattling everything?"

She stopped shoving. Her eyebrows came together in surprise, then stepped beside him. It had been a long time since he could feel time quakes. "Yeah. You felt that?"

Mason nodded. "It only lasted a second. I blinked, and it was over."

"Did anyone see you react to it?"

"I don't think so, no."

Mason pulled out his keys from his pocket.

"Go straight home and stay there," she urged. "I'll take care of this."

"You?" Mason asked, his tone thick with skepticism. "What are you going to do?"

It didn't surprise her that Mason questioned Nora's ability to protect him; he always did. Much of what she did was without his knowledge. She kept him safe in more ways than she could count.

Nora opened the trunk to Nadine's car and reached under the mat of the wheel well. Years ago she hid instruments in case an emergency like this ever surfaced. She pulled out a dagger and small black film container.

"Mason, I'm a time guard," she told him, stuffing the container in her back pocket. She nodded over to his car to indicate it was his cue to leave. The faster he left, the better. "I'm just sending them the way they came."

"Which means?" he pressed on, looking nervous for the first time.

"It means I got this, so go."

Mason looked past her to the restaurant, then back at her. She did her best to make her expression serious and determined. Slowly, the anger in his eyes faded to something else she recognized: worry.

"Okay," he agreed.

Chapter 3
Time Warp

After Nora made Mason promise he would text her when he got home, she continued to insist he leave. It took all she had not to open the door and shove him inside his own car herself. Once his taillights turned the corner at the end of the block, Nora turned her attention to the restaurant. The time travelers emerging from the bathrooms showed no visible sign that the person they were seeking managed to slip away from right under their noses.

To prevent a scandal, Nora decided to wait outside. They were clueless as to who they were looking for, but that didn't mean they weren't wrong either. Something brought them to Torch Crossings. Nora leaned on the bumper of Nadine's car as a van parked two spots away. The time travelers inside made their way to the doors. She stood a little straighter, waiting. They weren't going to get far the moment they stepped out.

Time travelers were drawn to Mason because he wasn't a regular person. He was the physical incarnation of time, a time marker. Time wasn't solely hours, minutes, and seconds. It was the past, present, and future. Together they marked time as an ongoing force—the most absolute order of time. Mason in particular was the time marker of the present. If he and his counterparts were to disappear out of existence, time would collapse upon itself, unable to coexist without its essential components. There would neither be a future to look to nor a past to reflect on. And if his soul was pulled out of time, time would be severely damaged. His death would trigger a new cycle. All of Nora's hard work to keep the natural order would be in vain.

Nora found Mason eight years ago, but revealed her identity as a time guard over two years ago. She moved in with Nadine and Isaac Hartley when running aloof on the streets endangered her freedom. Social services wanted her in a home. In order to avoid being put in the system, Nora sought out an alternative. She coaxed the unsuspecting couple into believing she was their long-lost niece who lost her family in a boating accident. Since then, Nadine took Nora in and treated her like family. Isaac Hartley never much cared for her unless she ran into trouble; it was then that he reminded her how ungrateful she behaved. Nora wasn't fond of using them to be close to Mason, but it was the only way in this time to stay hidden and to keep an eye on the present time marker.

Finally, the time travelers moved to the exit. They looked frustrated. The first man scolded the other as he shoved the device he carried in his pocket. The thinner, balding man shook his head in disbelief. He was certain they were in the right place, the right time. They crossed the threshold, and Nora straightened completely.

She felt jittery just watching them. Her entire body was itching for a fight. All the pent up anger over the last several days would finally receive an appropriate outlet. She waited for them to notice her, unsheathing the dagger.

"Let's go," the time traveler grumbled. "He's not here."

"He's here. There is no mistake," the thin man replied.

Brits—she noted their accent before calling to them. "He fled," Nora said aloud. "He's long gone."

The men walked under the light of a streetlamp to get a look at her. Nora took a few steps to let them have a better view of who told them of their failure. Both their faces turned ashen out of fright. They saw what she wanted them to see—the black sundial around her neck that confirmed her identity.

Nora clutched the dagger in her hand and ran to them.

The man in the bowler hat swung first. She dodged his fist. Then, with hilt of the dagger, Nora hit him hard in the ribs, briefly disorienting him. She kicked him out of the pool of light into the empty parking space.

The second man took his turn. Nora sidestepped him and smacked the hilt across his face. He staggered back, shouting in pain. A long, thin cut on his cheek appeared where the blade grazed him. Angry, he tried a kick. She caught him by the heel and shoved him away.

The man in the bowler hat returned with a vengeance, twisting Nora's arm behind her back. She maneuvered out of his hold by lunging forward quickly, forcing him to move forward with her. She doubled over, letting him sail backward and land faceup, no longer moving. Her arm now free, she turned her attention to the other time traveler.

Doubt crossed his face. He advanced with a false bravado. He threw a halfhearted combo, backing her out of the light in the direction of the streetlamp. Nora dodged a few more blows before slamming him against the light post. The time traveler took to the ground just as fast as his friend.

Breathless, Nora looked around to make sure no additional eyes caught the quick brawl. She tucked the dagger carefully out of sight, took both men by the ankles, and dragged them off toward the alley between Gio's and the neighboring laundry mat.

She propped them against the wall, exhausted. For men who looked like they survived a famine, they sure held some weight. Nora crouched down and reached into the time traveler's pocket to get a proper look at the device they carried. It was a flat chrome square pad no bigger than a cell phone. She ran her thumb across its surface, wondering what it could be. It had a single pin-size hole at one side. It flashed a blue light. Nora flinched, but it didn't do anything. It kept flashing every five seconds. She took the time key in his other pocket and decided to keep the strange chrome device to examine it tomorrow.

"Can't have you ruin my safe spot," Nora told them as she pulled out the film container. Pills rattled inside. It opened, and fragments of lavender capsules fell in her palm. She picked up a nearby flat stone. With the flat surface, Nora crushed the remaining pieces of the amnesia pills into powder to pepper the fine dust onto their tongues. Once they regained consciousness, in what she hoped was inside a time warp, she couldn't have them remember where and in what time period the present time marker was located.

Nora raised the sundial and pointed it down the alley. A second later, in midair, the fabric of time started to unweave itself, revealing an unexplained darkness that whooshed and whistled like a tamed tornado. Dust and dirt flared away from the opening. The dumpsters rattled lightly, feeling the impact of the time warp.

One by one she rolled the time travelers unconscious bodies closer, as if to present them to the hollow black hole as a peace offering. The man in the bowler hat went first, the dark nothingness carrying him away from Torch Crossings. The second man followed. They whooshed away before the time warp let out a sharp gust of wind.

She stumbled back, careful to not get sucked in. The time warp, sensing that its purpose was done, stitched itself closed without a sound. Nora hurried back out of the alley to the safety of the car. By the driver's door, her eyes double-checked the scene. The alley, restaurant, and parking lot looked the same. She checked her phone.

There was a new message from Mason.

Made it.

A spark of relief hit her.

Nora got in the car, started the engine, and drove off. She circled Torch Crossings to make sure no other time traveler hid in her town. She drove slow, monitoring all the secret crevices and sketchy characters on the street. It was easy to tell when something was amiss. Her gut usually told her when a job wasn't finished. At that moment the threat had passed. The adrenaline evaporated the longer she drove. By the time she returned the car to Nadine's driveway, the sundial read midnight.

She sneaked in through the back, careful not to let the gate make any noise. On her way in, she noticed Mason's window was dark. The absence of light told Nora he was in bed texting like most kids his age or fast asleep. She tiptoed to the foyer to return the keys, then shuffled back to her room.

The softness of her bed sheets were comforting. Nora buried her face in the cool pillow. She tossed and turned, only bothering to kick off her shoes. Her clothes could wait until tomorrow. With five blinks of her eyes and a big yawn, Nora fell asleep.

Nora woke up the next day with her alarm going off at seven thirty on the dot. She stretched like a cat, then curled further into her blanket. She loved the few glorious moments between sleep and waking. It was in that limbo state where she didn't feel the weight of time on her shoulders. Grudgingly, she rubbed the sleep away from her eyes, then hopped out of bed.

She combed through her hair with her fingers, smoothing it into a simple braid over her shoulder. She changed out of her wrinkled clothes into plum-colored leggings and a loose gray sweatshirt. The quiet house was easier to move in when Nadine or Isaac weren't home. They left early for work most days and didn't return until late in the evening, giving Nora much of the freedom she enjoyed. The few occasions that the three of them sat together, as if they were some sort of family, felt uncomfortable.

She grabbed a granola bar and slipped out of the house. The cold morning brought a blanket of fog. It clung low and dense, making it hard to see ten feet ahead. Nora began to walk to the direction of the park ten blocks away, where she climbed trees while Mason was home. It was one of the habits she carried with her for as long as she could remember. Climbing was her way of cleansing her mind from the previous day and start a new. Every foot she took higher off the ground forced her to think of the next place she would reach—where her next foot placement ought to be. Nora loved the feeling of bark under her touch, the satisfaction of being above it all, and the challenge of finding a way down.

Nora hoisted herself up to the first branch with ease, then the second and third. She climbed until the branches became too frail to support her weight. A cozy spot under bristled branch gave her a view of the surrounding streets. As the morning progressed, the density of the fog began to lift. Traffic lights and signs shined through the mist. Nora spotted the rooftop of Gio's Restaurant behind a billboard.

No one would ever suspect that time travelers entered the sleepy little town. Torch Crossings wasn't a place where many time travelers managed to find. Nora could count on one hand how accurate they tended to be. Slim to none. Her encounters with time travelers in the past ten years were spotty, whisking away trouble from dozens of miles away.

It startled her how narrow Mason's escape was. This time they *knew* where Mason was. On the first try. And the device they had? It was new to Nora. It also didn't look like an object they picked up in any London shop.

Around nine o'clock Nora climbed down and jogged home. She spotted Mason at the end of the driveway, taking in the empty trash bins. He noticed her approach and waited for her with crossed arms.

"Morning," she greeted.

"I heard you get home last night," Mason said. "Why didn't you text me on how things went?"

At least he didn't sound angry, Nora noted. "Sorry, I was tired," she apologized.

He nodded to the Hartley's house. "I stopped by earlier to see if you got home okay, but no one answered the door."

"Everything went without a hitch," she told him. "What about you? No one followed you?"

"Don't think so."

"Good," she said with a nod. "What does your day look like?"

"Uh, mowing the lawn, taking Priscilla to dance practice, and work from noon to eight," he told her. "I'll keep you posted if I go anywhere else."

"Thank you," she said and smiled. Nora turned and headed to the house, wiping her forehead with the hem of her sweatshirt. She couldn't help but feel a little wistful. She wondered if at last Mason was going to listen her again.

Chapter 4
Down to Dusk

Minutes later, in the sanctuary of her room, Nora kicked off her shoes as the unmistakable sound of a lawn mower began next door. Her heart fluttered in relief—he didn't lie to her. While undoing her braid, she walked to the double doors, brushing aside the blinds to get a look at Mason.

Nora spotted him at the far end of his backyard, pushing the loud contraption. With one hand, he texted effortlessly, then pocketed his phone. He worked his way beside the fence in a perfect line. Watching him do something so mundane and ordinary made Nora feel a little less angry at him. Everything else paled in comparison if that meant he remained hidden and safe. She wanted to keep it that way as long as possible.

Mason must have felt a pair of eyes on him because he looked around the yard, searching for the culprit spying on him. Hastily, Nora backed away from the door, hoping he didn't catch her behind the blinds. The last thing she wanted was for him to throw this in her face too. She pulled herself together, sucking in a breath.

Instead, she neared her messy desk. The untouched textbooks from the previous semester piled high beside her trash bin. She intended to return them months ago, but things had gone astray from the beginning of this semester. The only purpose they served now sitting in her room was keeping her ambitious schoolgirl cover intact.

She picked up her bag to pull out the tablet. The screen burst on. The initial screen showed her dozens of locked icons labeled with different years: 2031, 2056, 2077, 2091. Nora tapped on the only available option: 2017. The interface changed to the familiar home.

Her mailbox was still empty.

She suspected it would be. No one wrote to her. The minimal chance someone would contact her were low. Nora and the two other time guards were under explicit instructions to not find each other by any manner. Eight summers ago, right before Nora found Mason, was the exception. They spent three summers trying to figure out their identities and piecing together the fragmented past that united them. Armed with knowledge and the discovery of their purpose, the time guards journeyed alone to find those they were sent to protect. Nine-year-old Nora took the separation pretty hard. Angeline and Hogan had been older, their memories sharper and able to redevelop their skills at a faster rate. She didn't feel ready to venture off without them, yet she did.

Nora swiped back and pressed another icon, a black broom and dustpan. It activated her homemade scanner program that safely and discretely scrutinized the internet for any trace of Mason's name or picture. The software eliminated it and bugged the source. It proved to cause a lot of trouble at the campus newspaper office since it would wipe their sports articles. They were constantly calling the poor IT fellow to resolve the problem. A window popped up to inform her it would take several minutes for the process to complete. Nora watched the revolving gear turn.

As she waited, Nora threw herself over the mattress and listened to the lull of the lawn mower draw closer. Staring up at the ceiling, she wondered how things got so complicated. A cold, sinking sensation passed through her. The fault was almost all hers. Nora had done everything right, and things were going well. It took minutes to tarnish all that she worked for—years of gaining Mason's trust went down the drain. There was little she could do to make things right;

he made that point clear. His refusal to patch things up stung, but it was the least she deserved after hurting him the way she did.

She jumped off the bed, shaking the thoughts from her head. Nora forced herself to think she had done the right thing. It was her duty to guard him, after all. The best thing for Mason was to put a stop to that confusing path.

A muffled ring a second later meant the hardware finished. She cast a glance at the double doors. The lawn mower sounded closer now. With a growing nervous pit in her stomach, Nora opened the door and walked over to the fence. Mason didn't notice her right away. She waited until he turned to see her tucking a strand of hair behind her ear. He shut off the lawn mower and approached.

"Can we talk?" Nora asked.

"I'd rather we not."

When he didn't dash off, she went on. "I didn't mean for things to get this way."

"Yeah, I'm sure you didn't," he said and took a step back. Mason moved to the lawn mower to unhook the full plastic bag of grass clippings. "I need space. It's hard to think clearly when you're always around." He walked to the tall paper bag and dumped the grass inside.

"After last night you expect me to back off?" Nora snapped. "I need to be near you. If that means we can't be friends, I understand."

A mixture of annoyance and anger crossed his eyes.

"We can't afford to do whatever it is you're doing. This isn't a game."

"I know that," he protested, nearing the fence again. Mason leaned his back on it with crossed arms.

"Do you?" Nora went on. "Because you've been killed this way before, putting distance between us. You run off without me and never come back. Trouble finds you, Mason. Leaving you unprotected—"

"You won't be leaving me unprotected."

She studied his face for a hint of a challenge or sarcasm. There was no sign of either. His eyes were on her, searching for something in Nora's features while he leaned in close. She held his gaze for a few seconds before stepping back. Despite the fluster rising in her cheeks, she managed to get angry.

"Don't look at me like that."

His smirk almost reached his eyes. Mason knew he could get under her skin. "Like what?" he asked.

"Like you aren't listening to me!" she said, exasperated.

The sound of a car door closing made them jump and look over to the front yard. A car was in the driveway, and the light thud of shoes on concrete told Nora that either Nadine or Isaac were home early—a rarity, as they were supposed to be at work. She threw Mason a contemptuous look and hurried back into the house.

Nora cracked the door open to listen. The sounds of drawers opening and undistinguishable muttering came from one of the bedrooms. It had to be Nadine; she tended to be more forgetful on occasion.

The backyard remained quiet. She double-checked the blinds. Mason was gone. It was fifteen minutes until noon. Nora expected him to drive to the high school to pick up his sister, take her to the dance studio several blocks over, and arrive at his job five to ten minutes late. She prepared to leave, shoving a textbook, her tablet, the spare time key, and the flat chrome device into her bag, then headed out the door.

She pushed past the side gate, reaching for the sundial around her neck.

"Nora?"

She yelped, pulling her bag close to her body like a shield. Her pulse raced, and her heart punched her in the sternum. The dull roar in her ears faded as Nora looked around to find Isaac by his car. He watched her cross the lawn in mild confusion. She was shocked to see him home. He was a straight nine-to-five man since the day she moved in.

"Isaac," she breathed. "You scared me." It was an extraordinary feat; Nora wasn't easily startled.

"Nadine said you didn't have class today," he said. "Where are you going?"

"Oh, um, out, I guess."

He stared at her with a weary expression. "How are you getting there, kid?"

"Walking, I suppose," she replied, approaching. "I'm going to Crossing's Square."

"Get in. I'll take you."

Nora hesitated, then hopped into the sleek black Toyota. He moved his briefcase and laptop bag to the back seat. He pulled out of the driveway, and they drove off in silence. She rode with her eyes set on the passing streets of Torch Crossings. The ten-minute drive felt longer than she anticipated. Isaac wasn't paternal, at least not with Nora. He made it crystal clear he was not her father, nor did he plan to raise her. It suited her fine; however, it did make things strange when they crossed each other. They had nothing to talk about or share. Their exchanges happened less now that she was nearing eighteen.

He dropped her off in front of the furniture store of all places. Nora thanked him anyway for the ride and watched him speed away. She was still some ways away from the hardware store where Mason worked. Hopefully he didn't notice Isaac's car drive through the square. He didn't need to know she was hovering.

Half of the town's shopping was done at Crossing's Square. The hardware, furniture, and grocery store were the largest stores in the vicinity. Smaller shops branched out down the strip like gravitating satellites.

Her first stop was the bank, in case she needed some spending money. Then she headed to the electronics outlet to browse what she could potentially use in the future. Nora bought two burner phones and a handy battery-powered radio. The furniture store wasn't as promising. There was nothing she could purchase unless she had her own home.

She ducked in order to avoid the windows of the hardware store when she scurried passed to reach the cozy bakery café on the other side. It was where she spent most of the hours Mason worked. Paired with the free internet and trendy food, Nora hid in a corner, pretending to read on her tablet. She ordered soup and a sandwich before taking a seat near a window. From there she watched costumers leave the building with carts full of tools, drills, or plywood.

Stirring her soup, Nora took the time key she confiscated from the time travelers. It was a dark wooden hourglass no bigger than the size of her pinky. As soon as she touched it, the pulse of time tickled her fingertips. It shot up her arm like an addictive current. The white sand inside swirled down the funnel. It wasn't a time key of her making, she always kept to more discrete pieces. She forced the hourglass to relinquish its fraction of power. The brilliant, unearthly, ageless shimmer of a time seal left the timepiece in a dark cloud, then evaporated into the air.

Nora set it aside, fished out the chrome device from her bag next, and weighed it in her hand. The strange, flat piece of metal was surprisingly light. It couldn't be heavier than a juice box. She brought it to her ear next, wondering if something was inside. Rattling? Gears? Circuitry? Nothing. She turned it over slowly in her hand, studying the sleek surface with her thumb.

She couldn't make heads or tails of it. Nora never saw anything like it before, present or past. An idea grew in her mind. She had been going about it the wrong way. Her assumption that the time travelers had come from the past was incorrect. They were from the future.

Nora rested her chin in her palm. "What are you?" she muttered to herself.

She gently stroked the little porthole with her thumb. A sudden flash erupted from the opening caused Nora to flinch and just about drop the thing in her hand. A holographic map of the area unfolded over the table. Nora straightened at the sudden development. She moved aside her bowl and plate to get a clear view of the image.

It was a detailed map of the area she was precisely in now. Every feature like the sidewalk, countless buildings, trees, and street benches were visible and perfectly scaled. Heart racing, Nora swiped her fingers grazing the surface as if it were a touch pad. Under her touch, the focus shifted, moving even closer or farther away from her position. Soon she was peering at a three-dimensional image of a baseball-size globe imitating the earth's rotation around an invisible sun.

It was a tracker. It would explain the time traveler's precision. Somehow this thing led them straight to Torch Crossings—to Mason. How they managed to get their hands on it was another mystery. Well, not so much so if they really had come from the future. Now it was in her hands. Nora thumbed over the port, and the globe faded away. She stuffed it in her bag for safekeeping.

She checked her sundial to see it was fifteen minutes until six. Mason still had two more hours left in his shift, which meant it was her time to go. Nora needed to get home in order to create the illusion that she stayed put all evening. Two hours was the most she trusted with him alone. She got to her feet, walked to the trash can to throw away the remains of her meal, and hurried out of the café.

The walk home was twenty minutes—fifteen if she took a short cut. She planned to cross the parking lot in the direction of the intersection, behind the post office and train station. Nora sneaked by the hardware store once again. Midway through, a gray SUV pulled up to the curb. A man, not much older than her, rolled down the window and exhaled the smoke of his cigar.

The driver wore a crisp white shirt, leaving his sapphire eyes to gleam. His jet-black hair was neatly combed back. The man looked like he belonged in an executive office, not in a hardware store parking lot.

"You waiting on someone, sweetheart?" he asked.

Nora glanced around, making sure he was speaking to her. "No, I was just leaving actually," she told him, readjusting the strap of her bag over her shoulder. He drove beside her, keeping his speed to match her pace.

"Where are you going? I can give you a lift."

"Don't need one."

He cast a glace at her, then ahead, trying to figure out where she was going. "Yes, I'm sure. You look like the independent type."

Nora stopped walking to look at him. "I am. And you're not from around here. Something tells me you're not about to ask me for directions, am I right?" she asked.

The man smiled, pleased that she had caught on. His smile made Nora feel uneasy. His unusual friendliness was unpleasant. Nora wished he would drop the act if he was a time traveler. She checked his wrist and torso for a visible sign of a time key, but didn't find one on either location. There was a fair chance he also wasn't a time traveler. She couldn't afford to be wrong in such a public place.

"Clever, very clever," he praised and blew out another ring of thick smoke. In one quick movement, he reached out and gripped her arm tight. Nora tried to pry him off, but it was useless. He was much stronger than her. He only tightened his grip when she resisted. "No need to be alarmed, sweetheart. Get in."

Nora stopped squirming to reply. "I'm not afraid." She landed a swift punch to the bridge of the nose to make her point clear.

He let her go. She backed away, massaging her knuckles. A rough hand yanked her even further away from the man's reach. Mason rushed to the SUV and pulled him to the window by the collar, slamming his body to the door. The cigar in his hand toppled onto the concrete, fizzling out. Mason hurtled a punch straight to the man's eye.

Horrified, Nora tugged Mason back.

"I see you anywhere near her, and I'll—" Mason seethed, trying to break free of Nora's hold.

"Stop it!" Nora demanded. "Enough!"

When she made it clear with her body that he wouldn't get another good hit, Mason took Nora by the elbow and dragged her back to the exit doors of the store. He didn't let go of her until they were safely inside by the cash registers. She glanced over her shoulder to get one last look at the stranger. The window had rolled up. Behind the tinted glass, she thought she saw a new cigar appear in his hand. With a screech of the tires, he tore out of the parking lot into the early evening.

He wrenched off his work issued vest. "Don't move," he ordered. "I'm getting my things, and we're out of here."

Nora nodded. She watched him head to the back of the store. He waved off a concerned coworker who asked if she ought to phone the cops, but he barked out a no, saying he would handle it. Mason returned minutes later, shouldering passed her, meaning she was supposed to follow. She did, trotting along to keep up.

"I've told you hundreds of times not to come," he said loudly so he wouldn't have to look over his shoulder at her.

"You leave me no other choice—"

Mason stopped walking. Nora almost ran into him, but she stopped midstep. "No, don't give me that crap," he said, turning to look at her. "That guy—"

"Hey!" Nora snapped defensively. She pulled herself to her full height, glaring at him dead in the eyes. "I could've handled him! I had this until you jumped in."

"Up until the point he tried to haul you in his car!"

She scoffed. "You don't think I could've taken him, do you?"

There was a long pause. Mason studied her for a moment as though he was choosing his next words wisely. "I never said that," he replied and continued the walk to his car.

The drive home was silent. It was worse than riding with Isaac. She knew he was angry. At what, she wasn't even sure of anymore. He only broke the silence at the end of the drive, when he cut the engine. He was staying home for the rest of the night to finish homework. They parted ways, crossing lawns. He went to the front door, and she to the back gate.

Nora turned in early too. She lay in bed, finally reading her metaphysics textbook. The endless paragraphs felt like she wouldn't even catch up. Terms and names swam across the pages, making it hard to focus. What kept her entertained was her trade of picture messages with Mason. He sent her frequent images of himself studying, looking as displeased as she felt.

A knock on the door tore her attention away from the textbook and phone in her hand.

"Come in."

Nadine popped her head in first, then entered. "Hey, I didn't hear you arrive," she greeted.

Nora sat up. "I had a long day and jumped straight to bed hours ago."

"You do look awfully tired," Nadine agreed, walking over to the bed. "I brought you an extra blanket. I hear the temperature is supposed to drop tonight. I'd rather you fry than die of frostbite." She smiled at Nora, handing her the peach-colored blanket.

"Thanks," Nora replied, taking it. "Night."

She caught the brief moment Nadine's face fell. She expected the visit to last longer, but Nora cut her off quickly. She preferred to be alone. Nadine took the hint, bid Nora goodnight, and walked out of the room.

Nora lay down again, pressing her palms to her eyes until she saw stars. Nadine was too good to her, offering kind gestures Nora didn't deserve. It was evident that all she wanted was a daughter, and since Nora came into the picture she unwittingly treated her as such. She couldn't let her get close. All this was an act. The Hartleys were part of her cover, and her priority was to keep Mason safe.

She sighed heavily, letting her arms drop to compose one last message of the night.

See you in the morning.

He responded back with incredible speed. She didn't even have time to set down her phone.

Sweet dreams.

Chapter 5
Hot and Cold

Nora threw her legs over a branch to look at the empty park below. The over night rain left puddles splattered across the grass and the playground slick with water. With the increasing drop in temperature, it began to lightly frost over. A woman walking her dog paid no attention to the girl who had scaled the moist trees overhead. Nora hoisted herself down, finding a branch for her legs to land on.

She and Mason were scheduled to appear in their respective classes. In order to squeeze some climb time in, Nora knew the morning was the best time for it. Today it also gave her a chance to look for the mysterious SUV with the man who had approached her. The way he held his cigar, the arrogant gaze in his eyes, and the way he spoke as if he knew her was painfully familiar. When and where Nora met him challenged her memory. She remembered how he was the downfall right before Mason's deaths: he was the Englishman in Hong Kong, the treacherous shaman in South Africa, and most recently he was the Bulgarian who promised safe passage. He was the dark omen that haunted Nora every chance he got. Their first encounter was a fog in her head. If he was significant at all, she would have remembered.

At first light, the last wave of children walked to school. They meandered through the neighborhoods, moving east to the elementary school. An hour ago, when it was still dark, she watched the older kids drive to the white brick building on Elmwood Road. It was nearing eight o'clock, which meant she ought to return home.

As soon as she hopped down, her phone chimed from within her bag. Nora tied on her boots and took off back home. Her loose ponytail came undone the faster she walked. By the time she turned the corner, Nora brushed away fragments of wet bark from her leggings and flannel shirt.

Mason was already out by his car, shoving his schoolbag and soccer duffel into the trunk. She saw him catch the time on his phone, then shake his head. Nora rushed forward to do the same. He took her schoolbag, placed it in with the rest, and shut the trunk.

"You're late," Mason noted.

"I know," Nora replied breathlessly. "Sorry."

"Where do you go every morning?" he asked, crossing his arms.

"I go to the park," she told him.

"And what do you there? Picnic every morning?"

Nora rolled her eyes. "Only if you count a granola bar as breakfast."

"Hardly."

They moved to the front of the car to get in their seats. "I don't know how you do it," he said, eyeing Nora before darting his attention to the rearview mirror. Mason pulled out of the driveway. She pulled the seat belt over her shoulder and secured it in place. "I'm not even fully awake until noon or without a cup of coffee."

"I guess I just have strict self-discipline," she said with a shrug.

"Hey, I have self-discipline," he shot back.

"I never said that."

Mason smirked, but with a shake of his head the almost deliberate smile disappeared. He drove out of Torch Crossings in silence. Nora bit down a grin of her own. Somehow her words brought forth a smile out of him, even if it was a contemptuous one. All was not lost, not yet. There was still a chance to fix what she broke.

The sudden jolt of the car made Nora lose her thoughts. Mason weaved through the interstate traffic as if he were on a racetrack. He had little patience to wade through the sea of cars like the rest of the morning commute. Nora gripped her seat belt, wondering what had come over him. He drove like a madman. She shouted once in terror as he narrowly missed hitting a semitruck. When they made it to school, Nora was grateful the ride from hell was over. She checked the time to see they had more than twenty minutes before their first class. Mason pulled into the south parking lot on campus and parked the car in the final lane near the back.

"Next time you think of killing us both, do it without me in the car!" Nora called after him in anger as he got out of the car. "I should have taken the train!" She did the same and shut the door behind her. She hurried to meet him at the trunk. She shouldered her bag so he could gather his things.

"I'll drive you to the train station myself."

"What is with you today?" she asked.

"I forgot I needed to be somewhere this morning," he muttered and picked up his schoolbag.

Nora crossed her arms in disbelief. "Really? And you're just telling me this now?" she demanded.

"I said I forgot," Mason said, sounding a little annoyed himself. "I have an appointment with my advisor. That's it. I didn't think it'd be a big deal."

"You know I don't like surprises."

He shut the trunk and took a long pause, keeping his eyes away from her. "It's not a surprise. I'm still on campus, a floor away from my first class. I'll be fine," he said. "You should go get a proper breakfast." With that, Mason backed away from his car and headed toward the building.

Nora watched him go. The fallout between them made understanding Mason frustrating. His rough exterior was a layer of protection—that much was certain. And she didn't blame him for it. What perplexed her were the cracks in his defenses. When he let down his guard for an instant, she suspected a part of him still wanted her around, still cared for her. It was too soon to say how long his uplifting mood would be willing to stay.

Once he was a good distance away, she headed toward the pavilion. The entire campus was a flurry with students who arrived just in time for the morning rush. Forcefully, Nora made her way to the breakfast booth. The line moved fast, and she arrived to the order window in just five minutes. She purchased a steaming cup of hot chocolate, a giant oatmeal cookie, and a biscuit sandwich to go.

She headed to her first class of the day, metaphysics. Nora took a seat in the back of the lecture hall and scarfed down the meal, listening to the professor enthusiastically speak about the reading material she crammed last night. Unlike most subjects, those that fell under the broad scope of philosophy displayed little progress to produce new theories worth sharing. Paired together, distance and time tarnished most ideas, dwindling them to reduced, misinterpreted bits of information. The aged, boggled-down theories were widely accepted as a legitimate theory studied by the most excellent minds. It was a shame man would never know that the past was so much closer to the truth than the future would ever be. The revolving set of questions about existence and the universe were never answered.

Ten thirty came around fast. Nora gathered her things and trailed after her classmates out the lecture hall. She had a long wait ahead of her until her second class of the day. And Mason was stuck in two more classes until he had a free hour. She found an unoccupied seat in one of the hall tables to do more homework for her online Latin course.

"Hey."

Nora looked up to see Mason and his longtime friend Diego standing before her. She scowled at his choice of company. Diego was arrogant, proud, annoyingly witty, and narcissistic. It was no secret that he didn't like her either. Nora saw it in the way he mocked her through out high school. Regardless of their silent hostility toward one another, he winked at her.

The bustle of students coming and going meant they were in between classes. "Hey," she said.

"You have any plans for lunch?" Mason asked.

"No," she said, tapping her pen on the table top. "Why?"

Diego snickered and nudged Mason as if he was in on a joke Nora wasn't. Mason shot him a look to quiet down.

"Look, I'm trying to do you a favor," Mason said.

Nora shifted in her seat. She didn't understand what he meant. Was he asking her to lunch because he knew she'd show up in the food court? Or was his invitation disguised as an apology for their constant bickering? Whatever the reason, she knew she had to proceed with caution.

"She's stalling," Diego jeered. "I think she's trying to find a way to let you down easy, man."

"Shut up, Diego," Mason said sharply, jutting him hard in the ribs with his elbow.

A surge of annoyance flashed within her. "I'm sure you can speak from experience," Nora said to Diego, resting her chin on her palm. She dazzled him with an innocent smile. "Rejection can't possibly be a new concept for you."

Diego took a step forward, trying to intimidate her, but Mason gripped his shoulder, then gave it a soothing pat. "Easy," he warned, steering his friend away from the table.

"I'll meet you by the Arbor building around noon," Mason said to Nora over his shoulder.

"Okay."

He clapped him on the shoulder, laughing hard. "I told you not to mess with her." His laughter found its way to her. It was like running water, crisp and clear and rippling. It had been weeks since she heard him laugh with such gusto and openness.

She looked back to the screen. Languages came easy to Nora, but Latin was one of the few she brushed up on every now and then to keep it fresh in her brain. The nearly extinct dialect would've grown hazy in her head if it weren't for modern languages. She spoke its descendant languages so frequently Nora could pick apart certain words with old Latin roots. The paragraph she was supposed to be translating was half finished. She caught maybe every fourth word. Her fingers poised over the keyboard spewed a few more words into English, then hovered still.

The cursor blinked up at her. The more she waited for the spark of recognition to continue, the more her mind wandered back to Mason. The thought of having lunch with him made her insides squirm. Nora let out a shaky breath, pushing her tablet away. She didn't want to think about him or the evening things went wrong. The night and day leading up to their current dismay flooded in.

Weeks earlier, just as the semester started, Mason kissed her at the soccer team's annual fundraiser. They hosted an outdoor movie for the student body and the local community to attend. He invited her to go, as friends, of course. Nora was hesitant to go, although he promised to take her home if she lost interest. The evening was innocent to begin with: She helped him sell last-minute tickets and prepare several dozen buckets of popcorn. Further into the evening, they didn't do much watching. Nestled in the back of the amphitheater, Nora and Mason talked for hours, hashing out the tangles and kinks of their troubled past, since they met eight years ago. Somewhere along the night, or rather well into the morning, he kissed her. And there was a high likelihood she kissed him back. The thought of his lips on hers made her heart sink further.

When she recognized the gigantic error she made, Nora put an end to whatever was going on between them. She was his time guard and nothing more. No matter how she felt, she pushed those feelings to the furthest, darkest areas of her mind. Locked away, her emotions couldn't interfere with protecting Mason. That night something opened in her. He found his way into her heart with very little effort. When it came to letting him down easy, she damned herself over and over again for putting him through the worst kind of turmoil. The look in his eyes of fading love turned to bitter hurt and resentment.

As a time guard, Nora was obligated to follow time's three most absolute rules: keep apart, keep a distance, and keep the time markers safe. She broke the second rule early on. It was the only way Mason would trust her, to let her be near enough to protect him. Not only did she reveal who she was but Nora also exposed many of time's mysteries in order to have him understand what they were both a part of.

Thinking of the trouble she caused made Nora fidget in her seat. Abruptly, she jumped out of her chair, shaking the memory out of her head. She shoved all her belongings in her bag and bolted down the corridor.

Nora arrived early to her astronomy class. She sat in the empty lecture hall. The dim lights exposed the starry night screen saver shimmering on the blackboard. Paired with the cool room, it almost reminded her of a time warp. Eventually, students and the professor trickled in. Nora pulled out a notebook when notes flickered on across the board. The graphs, numbers, and formulas soothed her. It brought Nora's tousled head back to the ground. She wrote diligently, copying words onto paper for the next ninety minutes. Disappointment washed over her when the lights came on and the professor dismissed the class. She picked up her things and headed toward lunch.

The midday lunch rush was as worse as the morning commotion. While few students left campus for a hot meal, the majority moved in the direction of the Arbor building. Nora trotted down the stairs of the science building. At the bottom of the landing, she made a sharp turn and crashed right into Mason. He caught her by the arm, steadying her.

"Watch where you're going," he scolded.

"You were in *my* way," Nora shot back. She jerked out of his grip, annoyed all over again. Her thoughts from earlier were long gone. When he was cold with her, it was easy to forget she felt anything for him.

Nora threw him a dirty look and led the way. They trotted down the last two flights of stairs. She ushered Mason out the door toward the Arbor building. The three-story brick building was nestled between the dorms and the performing arts building. The first floor was open space, reminiscent of a food court, providing a variety of meal options. The large glass windows let natural light flow in from every direction. Tables of all sizes and heights scattered the dining area. The upper floors were dedicated to the well-organized library.

They briskly crossed the grassy square. Mason shoved his hands in his pockets, avoiding eye contact. He didn't seem to mind her guidance for a change. In the crowded food court, lines weaved together, forming a mesh of students.

She squeezed by a group of pretentious English majors with effort. Noticing her struggle to maneuver through the horde, Mason sidled up next to her. His fingertips grazed hers, making Nora's wrist twitch away. He stepped forward, offering to take over. She followed him, staying close to not get lost in the hungry rush.

He had a particular way of going about the crowd. Mason strode forward with confidence, assured that people would move ever so slightly to provide enough of an opening when they saw him coming. When no one bothered to shift aside, he excused himself after passing motionless bystanders.

Mason found his finish line at the end of the pasta cart line. It seemed to be moving the fastest.

"Sorry about Diego," Mason said at last. "He can be—"

"A spineless bonehead?" she offered.

"I was going to say an idiot."

"He's not worth apologizing for," Nora replied. "You've had plenty worse friends than him."

Standing on tiptoes, she squinted to read the menu. The tiny board crammed a half dozen pasta options. Reading each one made Nora's stomach squirm in anticipation. By the time they made it to the counter to order, she decided on the cajun alfredo penne with grilled lemon pepper fish. Mason ordered a triple-meat macaroni and cheese bowl with a side of soup and salad.

"Don't you athletes have a strict diet to follow?" she japed, looking up at him.

"What?" he demanded, nudging her with his shoulder. "I'm as fit as an ox."

"That'll be twenty-four dollars even," the cashier said.

"We're paying separate," Nora said, fumbling with her bag, looking for her wallet.

"No, we're not," Mason told the hesitant cashier. "Eric, just take the damn card." He took the card, giving Nora a sheepish smile. She threw up her hands in surrender, took the bag of food, and turned on the spot to look for a place to sit. She left Mason behind to claim a tall table hidden away in a corner from their nosy peers.

Nora hopped onto the stool, pulling her food toward her. A moment later Mason caught up and took a seat in front of her.

"Don't do that," she muttered, stabbing at the pasta on her plate. "Don't pay for things hoping this will solve anything."

He pulled out a bottle of Gatorade from his backpack. "That's what you're supposed to do when you ask someone to lunch," Mason snapped. "Or is that not allowed too? Or am I hitting some sore spot in that guard ego of yours?"

"That was hardly an invitation," she shot back. "You assumed I would show up."

"Well, you did, didn't you? You were on your way here."

"I would've come here anyway."

"Following me."

"You know I have to," Nora fired away. "I don't know what kind of favor you thought you owed me, but this sure as hell isn't repayment."

"Whatever," Mason said, shaking his head at her.

He poked at his soup first, then tackled his hefty pasta and salad. Nora stabbed at her own pasta some more before eating. She kept her eyes down to avoid one less petty argument. They ate together in silence as if they were strangers. Every now and then she felt Mason's eyes on her like he wanted to keep arguing, but he remained quiet.

"I need to get to class," he said, wiping his hands on his jeans as he got to his feet. He threw his schoolbag over his shoulder. "Later."

"Later."

Nora got to her feet too. Unlike him, her lectures ended for the day. She wove easier through the crowd this time. Mimicking the way Mason moved among large group of people helped. Once she made it to the narrow hallway, the commotion of the cafeteria faded away. She headed to the second floor of the Arbor building. She shuffled to her usual spot by the pair of tall windows in the back, taking the tattered couch to finish the incomplete Latin paper saved on her tablet.

Chapter 6
Before the Brink

I'm late, Nora thought. *Damn it, I'm so late.* The unexpected nap disoriented her, thinking she slept right through the entire day. A wave of relief hit her when she saw it was almost six. Her day wasn't quite over. She rushed down the stairs two at a time. The food court was far from vacant; new meals were being prepared for those students who poured in for an early supper. Nora rushed to the exit, shouldering past two football players without much trouble.

"Hey!" they shouted after her.

She ignored them.

Nora hated being late. It didn't settle right with her, like a bad taste in her mouth she couldn't shake. Tardiness was becoming a recurrent problem for her in this life, along with a few other distasteful qualities. Her entire life this go-around seemed to be out of whack, as if the usual flow of time wasn't aligning with her life cycle. Because of it, less subtle differences caught Nora's attention, like Mason's ability to feel time quakes. It was rare gift time allowed him.

She consulted her sundial to see that the last fifteen minutes of soccer practice were almost up. She swore to kick herself if practice was cut early and Mason went home, leaving her stranded on campus. It wouldn't be the first time he'd done it. The day right after their heated mess of a breakup, he flew off the handle for days. He needed time to cool off. Nora understood and gave him space. With their recent time-traveling visitors, she wouldn't be as lenient.

She half walked, half jogged across the campus to the soccer field. The sound of a whistle echoed up to her ears when she reached the point where the sidewalk met the dirt path, cutting through the grass right down to the field. Nora let out a sigh of relief before making her way to the commotion ahead.

The team was in the middle of a quick game both refereed and coached by a much younger man Nora recognized as the assistant coach. He hollered orders from the sidelines to the players. The coach from the other day trailed after him, jotting down notes on his clipboard. He seemed to be focusing on studying the team rather than dictating them.

Nora reached the bleachers as she scanned for Mason among the players. He stood impatiently on the other side of the field, watching the ball's every movement. She made her way up the bleachers to watch the final minutes of the game. As Nora took a seat, she pulled out her phone from her bag, checking for messages. She found one from Mason sent an hour earlier.

Where are you?

She looked up to find him again. Mason's patience went to waste; his teammates weren't all too invested in the game. They were mostly playing keep away until their time ran out. Mason caught on, letting his tense shoulders drop. He placed his hands on his hips, trying to hide his disappointment that his teammates didn't share the same enthusiasm. Although he looked passive, Nora saw the bit of him that craved action. He wouldn't stand there for long. When the ball found its way to Mason, the game picked up.

He navigated the ball down the field to the opposite goalpost. The defense, now alert, went after him. But they were too late. Mason weaved around them with ease, making it directly in front of the goalkeeper. He aimed a kick just as the final whistle blew. The soccer ball soared over the goalpost, declaring no winner to the game. The game ended with a draw.

The team broke into excited chatter, ready to go home. They gathered around the coaches for a few last-minute pointers and instructions. The habitual smokers a few benches below Nora dispersed, while the girls at the bottom jumped to their feet, hoping to catch the eye of the soccer team. Some of the players drifted toward them, happy to indulge their fan club for a few minutes.

Mason walked off the field and picked up his duffel. Nora got to her feet as he searched the bleachers for her. Once he saw her descending, Mason walked over. Instantly, two girls dashed over to him, flipping their hair, dazzling smiles and all. He readjusted the strap on his shoulder and muttered a few words to them. Nora was too high up to read his lips to figure out what he said to them, but whatever it was it did the trick. They backed away looking glum, disappointed, and pinched in the face with an emotion she couldn't guess.

He climbed the bleachers to meet Nora halfway. For a moment she understood what the girls saw in him. Her heart picked up its pace, thumping hard against her chest. Mason was attractive, especially after putting in some hours on the field. The dirt, grass stains, and sweat didn't bother Nora. Any guy who could have something to show for all their labor was well worth noticing. She shoved those thoughts out of her head, knowing very well those kind of thoughts got them in trouble in the first place.

Mason came to a stop a few bleachers below her. "Are we making this a habit?" he teased.

The jab at her delayed arrival hardly stung. "It wasn't on purpose," she said, trotting down passed him.

He followed her down.

The girls who approached Mason moved their attention to the goalkeeper and midfielder, but glanced over their shoulders to look at Nora. Their eyes moved to Mason and back, then threw wicked knives in her direction. The girls shared a whisper among each other, giggling.

"Mason?" she asked, reaching the last bleacher and turned just in time to see him step beside her.

"What?" he asked.

Nora hopped down to the grass. "What did you say to get rid of them?"

"Nothing," Mason said with a shrug.

"It didn't seem like nothing."

"Well, it was. You coming or what?"

She followed him off the field and back up the campus to the parking lot. She chewed the inside of her lip, deep in thought. The way the girls looked at her made Nora nervous. Did he tell them about her? Or rather that they were something more? Whatever he told them, it did more than send them away this once—it kept them away for good. If their gazes could kill, Nora would be dead in the next two or three life cycles.

Mason reached the car first and waited for her to arrive. "You have that look on your face again—"

"What did you say to them? To those girls?" Nora demanded.

"Why can't you just let it go?" he shot back, his voice losing its cool right away. The walls he built around himself went rigid and cold. "I needed to get them out of my hair, and I made up a stupid excuse."

"Did it involve me?"

"It did. Happy?"

"Far from it."

"Good. That makes two of us."

Mason popped open the trunk with a push of a button. The car's doors clicked, and the trunk opened with a pop. He threw his things inside, then stormed to the driver's seat, slamming the door shut. Nora did the same, then took her place in the passenger's seat. They drove home in agitated silence.

Nora shifted in her seat. She couldn't exactly be mad at him for this one. For the most part, it was true. He was meeting up with her. But what that excuse meant to Mason and those girls held a different meaning than her own.

She stole a glance at Mason. He gripped the wheel with one hand while his other hand massaged his temple like he did every time he got frustrated with her. Nora sank back in her seat and closed her eyes for a moment. What was wrong with her? Why was she prying? Why couldn't she just let things go? What he told the girls shouldn't matter to her. Overthinking things landed her nowhere. All it did was send her in a spiral of doubt and anxiety.

Opening her eyes, Nora decided to let it go. She had to choose her battles, and this one wasn't worth fighting. She blinked into the early evening, recognizing her street. Mason finally loosened his grip on the wheel as he pulled into his driveway.

"You know, today was my last day of practice before the game this weekend," he told her, cutting the engine.

The game on Saturday was all her classmates spoke of the entire morning, placing bets and making predictions.

She nodded. "Yeah, I know."

"Will you be there?"

"Yeah, I'll be there," she replied, almost amused. It was silly he even had to ask. Did he really believe she would stop looking after him just because of their usual dry banter?

"I'll be at work tomorrow morning. I'll be home before noon."

"Okay."

He eyed her suspiciously. "All right, well, night."

Nora hopped out of his car, grabbed her things, crossed the lawn, and scurried off to the back entrance. The door shut, closing off Mason and the whole world behind her. She kicked off her shoes and set down her things. The light flickered on, revealing her usually messy room clean. She groaned, which meant Nadine had been in her room picking up after her. What worried her was that Nadine would stumble upon something she shouldn't. Nora couldn't have her cover blown. Just as she opened the door leading to the rest of the house, the tablet in Nora's bag dinged.

She ran over, diving for the ringing tablet. She wrenched open her bag to see the screen flashing, meaning someone was trying to reach her in an encrypted video call. Holding her breath, Nora punched in the code to accept the call.

The application took a moment to open. Static filled the screen for several seconds before the image began to clear. An attractive man not much older than Nora stared back at her. His dark blond hair was just above his piercing light brown eyes. He sported short stubble along his cheeks and chin. His lips curled into a brief smile when he saw her but kept to a tight frown soon after. Nora was drawn to the hint of anxiousness in his expression.

"Hogan," Nora said. He looked much older than she remembered. "I wasn't expecting your call."

"Nor did I expect to make one," he replied. "Things have been real shaky. We're on the run. Too many time travelers are on our tail." Nora crossed her legs, still sitting on the floor. "Anything at your end?"

"There were two, but I managed to get rid of them," she reported. "What about Angeline? Have you spoken to her?"

"No, not yet," he said. He momentarily shifted his attention beyond the camera, but looked at Nora again. "We'll be on the move to see if we can shake them."

"Then I should leave where I am too."

"No, stay where you are. You still have a safe place to hide. I'll report in once I'm settled and out of danger."

Hogan ended the call. The screen turned black and returned to the home screen.

Nora slumped further on her spot on the floor, the tablet sliding out of her hands. The magnitude of Hogan's call was major. He wasn't one to call in a warning—he never had. If he was on the run from time travelers, it was only a matter of days before she followed his example. How would she break the news to Mason? How could she ask him to pack up and run off with her? She always let him leave on his own terms—a tiny gesture to let him have some control.

What worried Nora more was Hogan said he would speak to her soon. Time guards were never allowed to communicate unless the circumstances were dire. They were never to disclose compromising information, like their location or who they protected. She wasn't too worried about him, though. He was more than capable of outrunning his enemies and lying low. For the past two hundred years, he was the last of the three time guards to die. He wouldn't let that streak end anytime soon.

On the other hand, Nora worried about the third time guard, Angeline. Out of the three time guards, she was the pacifist. She'd rather run than stay put and fight. Angeline was an excellent hider. When she didn't want to be found, it was nearly impossible to trace her. Nora had yet to find any hint of her by all mediums, not even the smallest sign. They hadn't seen each other since they were children, but Nora knew Angeline was well versed in the art of taking care of herself and her time marker.

Nora scrambled to her feet to look out her window over to Mason's house. His bedroom light was on. She'd have to keep a tighter security on him. He wouldn't appreciate it, but that didn't matter. His safety—his life—was above everything else. Anachronisms were out there hunting down time markers this very moment. Nora would have to be vigilant of wary drifters rolling into the Pacific coast, especially time quakes.

She shut the blinds.

The loud rumble of her stomach meant it was dinnertime. Nora walked to the opposite side of the house for a bowl of cereal. She sat at the table, listening to the muffled voices of Nadine and Isaac talking in their bedroom. She wondered if he bothered to tell his wife that he gave her a lift to the shopping center the day before. Nora checked her phone as the clock blinked to eight on the dot. Her phone vibrated in her hand.

Nora almost dropped it in the soggy half-eaten cereal. It was a message from Mason to inform her he wouldn't sneak off.

She put the phone to her lips thoughtfully, debating if she should tell Mason what was going on. Nora dismissed the idea. She couldn't do that to him. He needed to focus on tomorrow's game—that's what mattered to him. After all she put him through, the least Nora could do was give him this. Nora typed back a response.

Give 'em hell.

A second later he answered.

Always do. Sweet dreams.

Nora felt herself smiling at the text. The butterflies in her stomach began to flutter. She hated it when he sent sweet things like that over the phone. It made everything else around her melt away.

She set her phone facedown on the table.

Chapter 7
The Game

After her morning climb, Nora crawled back into bed with a plateful of pancakes. Nadine always cooked a big breakfast every Saturday morning before heading to the community center where she did volunteer work. It was a routine she picked up from when her sons were still in the house. Spread out in the kitchen table were big helpings of glazed cinnamon apple–topped pancakes, scrambled eggs, hash browns, and slices of savory ham. Nora enjoyed her cooking, but she liked Nadine's fluffy buttermilk pancakes and apples the best. Nora picked the apples first, swiping through her tablet to check for any messages from Hogan.

Nothing. Not even a word from Angeline.

After the hearty breakfast, she ran patrol on foot, something she did often in her early years of finding Mason. Nora got a good lay of the land that way, figuring out all the best hiding spots and forgotten crevices. It took twice as long but not as long as when she first started. She anticipated more time travelers or quakes, yet all was silent. Nothing was out of the ordinary. Once she was satisfied, she booked it home twenty minutes past eight o'clock.

The missing car from his driveway told Nora Mason left for work to begin his short shift. The note on her back door confirmed it.

It also said she would land herself in another ring of hell if he caught her near his job again.

She picked up the crumpled piece of paper, rereading his tiny cursive boyish writing. Nora found herself laughing instead of boiling with fury. In her other hand was her phone, an open text message to Hogan. A single word was typed, but not sent.

Report?

Nora deleted it quickly. She didn't want to bother him. If he was in danger, there was a risk he was compromised or worse dead. She didn't want to find out the answer to either. It was better to wait.

The minutes ticked by closer to eleven. Nora hopped out of bed with her pancake scraps. The soccer game was today at one. It was the tenth game of the season. Thankfully, it was a home match. The university housed a new stadium for the team. They were just as important or more so than the football team. It deserved the notoriety; each game was like an elegant performance.

She enjoyed watching all of Mason's hard work pay off on the field. When it was him and the ball, time didn't matter. All he cared about was getting the ball into the opposing net. Lately Nora sat through his games not only to share in his victories and losses but because it was the only ninety minutes he dropped his grudge.

Once it neared Mason's punch-out time, Nora got dressed, throwing on gray leggings and a faded lavender-and-white sweater. She decided to pull on a jacket in case the temperature kept dropping.

Nora inspected her reflection for a moment in front of the full-length mirror. The same rich brown hair, the precise hazel green eyes, and the structure of her slender body changed little over time. Unlike most days, she noticed the differences: the way her bangs had grown out, the flecks of brown surrounding the pupil, the squareness of her shoulders, and the lighter olive complexion. All past versions of her living in this body. She reached for the sundial around her neck for comfort. She felt the warm hum in her palm as it tracked Mason. He would be home at any moment to prepare for the game. She decided to finish getting ready in case he happened to stop by her room. Nora ran her fingers through her hair to tame it into place for the rest of the day.

Fifteen minutes later a knock on the door made Nora turn. Behind the curtains of the back door she saw Mason's silhouette standing outside. She walked over, slid the blinds over, and let him in.

Mason stepped inside gingerly, looking around in curiosity. This was his second time he visited Nora's bedroom in the past month—one too many for her liking. Within the four walls, she tried to keep the space a Mason-free zone. It was her sanctuary after the hassles he put her through. Alone she reminded herself he was someone she protected and nothing more. He must have had a similar train of thought because he didn't venture too far from the door

He shuffled his feet and shoved his hands into his soccer hoodie, doing his best to ignore the uncomfortable situation. "I figured I'd ask. Need a ride?"

"You say it like I'm a chore," Nora said, picking up her bag.

"Do you want the ride or not?" Mason asked.

She quickly rechecked her profile one last time, tugged on her shoes, and walked to the door. The chilly afternoon made them both shutter. Mason and Nora walked to his driveway to the idling car.

"The guys want to go out and celebrate after we win," Mason said, his voice changing to casual.

"Awfully confident," she noted.

He ignored her. "We'll be at Gio's if you want to come."

"Is this an invitation?" she asked.

"It is," he said curtly.

"We'll see," Nora replied, keeping her eyes on the road.

They arrived to campus. Mason pulled into the northern parking lot by the athletic building. It was packed with wildly obnoxious fans supporting both teams. Nora thought it sounded much like downtown New York City on a good day. Several concession stands popped up to serve drinks and snacks to the incoming spectators. With a shutter, she thought of how it reminded her of the fundraiser.

"Want anything?" Mason asked, nodding to the long lines.

"No, I'm fine, thanks."

They stood there for a few minutes, checking out the arrivals. Classmates stopped along their way to the stands to wish Mason good luck. He chatted with them briefly before sending them on their way. A large white coach bus pulled in close to the sports building. Some cheered and clapped at the sight. Others booed. Mason craned his neck to get a look at the competition.

"Nervous?" Nora asked him.

Mason looked down at her with a roguish grin. The familiar shine of defiance flashed in his eyes. "Hardly," he scoffed. "Are you doubting me?"

"Doubt is a strong word."

"You *are* doubting me."

"I'll be watching," she said, taking her first steps toward the soccer field. They walked over to the packed bleachers. He followed, walking her to a seat of her choosing between a line of rowdy soccer fans and the stairs, in case she needed to make a swift escape during the game.

The first half was slow. No team scored, yet the attempts were awfully close. Wedged alongside the loud fans, she couldn't understand the sports announcers' commentary. The opposing team came from a rival university four hours away. Mason's team played them the year before, and many of the players were the same. All except for one.

Nora's hand flew to cover her mouth to stifle a gasp when her eyes landed on number four, a defensive midfielder. It was the man who attempted to get her in his car. He had yet to recover from his injuries: a faint streak of a purple bruise was between his eyes, and another plum-size blotch below his eye. Nora shifted in her seat, feeling anxious all over. Something about him sent fear down her spine. He wasn't supposed to be here; he didn't belong.

She had to warn Mason.

Mason moved down the field with the ball. The roar of the crowd continued to drown out the excitement of the commentator yelling into the microphone. Everyone jumped to their feet, cheering and clapping in encouragement. They wanted him to score so badly. Nora hopped to her feet, too, in order to see Mason over the sea of fans. The time traveler kept his eyes on him as he moved closer.

Her heart raced in her chest, hoping Mason was quick enough to pass the time traveler. She'd even settle for one of his teammates to intervene. Mason neared the goalkeeper but came across a block, so he sent the ball over the heads of the players to reach the open right midfielder. The time traveler stopped advancing, and she relaxed. Mason's team juggled the ball around, trying to find a clear opportunity to get the ball to sail into the net. The crowd buzzing with anticipation bellowed their approval.

The buzzer blew to signal the end of the first forty-five minutes. Both teams lingered on the field their chests heaving at the sudden stillness. It was only a second later they retreated to the coaches to huddle in close for halftime instructions and a well-deserved break. Nora darted down the bleachers toward the approaching team. Mason saw her coming and moved away from the others. They shouted after him to return, but he ignored them rushing to meet Nora. He studied her concerned expression, looking for an answer.

"He's here!" Nora shouted over the loud crowd behind them.

"Who is?" Mason asked, nearing to hear better. He glanced over her shoulder to figure out who she was talking about.

"The creep from the other day," she told him. "The one who tried to get me in his car. He's here! He's on the opposing team, number four."

Mason looked over his shoulder to look at the visiting team across the field. Number four had his back turned to them, too, busy receiving orders with the rest of his teammates. He must've felt Mason's and Nora's gazes drilling into the back of his head because he looked around a second later. He spotted them, but he didn't show any signs of caring that they were there too. That was all Mason needed to turn around sharply, fist clenched.

"What do you think you're doing?" Nora demanded, darting around him to stand in his path.

Mason took another step forward, not caring that Nora was in his way. She kept him at bay the best she could.

"I can't just stand here!" he growled.

"You can't go over there!"

"Why not? He deserves—"

She shoved him back. "In the middle of a game? You'll get benched!" Nora hollered. "Besides, there's something not right about him. How did he all of a sudden get on their team when their roster is already full?

"You think he's a time traveler?" Mason asked, letting his eyes drop to her.

"No, well, yes, I'm pretty sure he is," Nora said flustered. "He *is* a time traveler. I've seen him before, in another time. I'm not sure what he wants, though."

"We can always ask him," he joked. "Or bulldoze him out of my way if I have to."

"No!" she hissed, hitting his chest. It was all she could do instead of strangling him. "Don't you dare look for a fight. That's the last thing we need when we don't know why he's here."

"I was kidding," Mason said, touching her arm. "I know how to lay low. I won't even kick the ball in his direction." He jogged back to his team.

After a good earful from the coaches and refreshments, the buzzer went off, declaring an end to the halftime. Both teams scattered onto the field ready for battle. Nora took a seat a few rows closer to the ground. From then on, the time traveler did his absolute best to avoid eye contact with Nora or Mason. He knew they recognized him. Whatever he planned to do out in the open had her on the edge of her seat more so than the game.

The first goal came minutes after the second half. The other team scored with a beautiful shot with the help of a corner kick and a spectacular kick into the net. Mason's team caught up not long after with a headshot from one of the forwards. The game progressed. Both teams were desperate to make one more goal to tip the scale, to claim victory. The players were exhausted, but the spirits of the crowd propelled them onward, exerting a final burst of effort.

A long-range kick sent the ball flying over to Mason. He jumped in the air to stop it with his chest. Two players swooped in to keep him in place. They didn't want him to score. Mason kicked the ball to a teammate closest to the goalpost. Once the heat was off him, he ran forward, trying to make himself available once more. Mason struggled to keep himself open, shoving his elbow into the sides of his guards.

Mason's teammate cautiously dribbled the ball, leaving himself unprotected. The poor guy didn't understand how grave his mistake was until he was ambushed by the other team. Out of panic, he kicked the ball back to Mason, who by now had a perfect shot for a goal.

No, Nora thought. *No, no, no.* She jumped to her feet, watching number four head straight for Mason. He picked up speed and barreled into him, knocking him clean off his feet. Mason landed on the grass hard. The rest of the crowd behind Nora shot to their feet, shouting their outrage.

The referee blew into his whistle and ran over to the time traveler, holding up a red card. He was escorted off the field, followed by a cry of disdain and disappointment from his team. Mason, still on the ground, looked shocked and a little disoriented as if an elephant rammed into him. One of his teammates helped him to his feet, then pointed out the player who assaulted him. Nora saw his fists clenched and took a few menacing steps after him. The referee quickly got in his face, yelling at him in warning. All Mason could do was watch him go.

Nora slowly walked down the bleachers just in case she needed to break up a physical fight. She tugged at her sundial, twisting rather than pulling. *Who was this guy?*

"Walk it off, Mason!" the coach yelled from the sidelines.

The referees gathered together to discuss the matter. Mason paced until they came to a decision. He was awarded a penalty kick and given the ball. The audience grew quiet, eager to witness the last minute of the game. If Mason made this shot, they would win.

Mason scored, and the crowd raved so loudly Nora winced. Although he made the winning goal, his heart wasn't in the triumph. His eyes searched for the time traveler sent off the field just a moment ago. The final buzzer sounded; the game was over. He broke away from the celebration to meet with Nora, who was jumping onto the grass.

"Where'd he go?" he asked at once.

"I don't know," Nora replied.

Mason looked over his shoulder, still searching. "Wait for me here. I'll change, and we can get out of here."

She nodded.

The stands cleared out fast. The early evening turned even cooler with the growing gaps in the stands. People trickled out to the exits to get out of the frigid autumn weather. Nora walked on to the empty field, looking around at the discarded junk food and paper cups cluttering the bleachers. She kicked a blade of grass, wondering why Mason was taking so long.

"Good. You're all alone."

Nora turned at the sound of the voice. The hostile time traveler posing as a soccer player crossed the field, already dressed in his day clothes. His hands were shoved deep in his pockets. She could feel his cold stare analyzing her as he walked closer. His blue eyes struck her as the most memorable thing about him. Those eyes had pried into her before.

"And that's what you wanted since the moment you saw me?" Nora guessed. "How do you know who I am?"

"Funny how you time guards are so oblivious to your own fame," he scoffed. "The only true travelers of time, thanks to that." He nodded toward the black sundial around Nora's neck. "It's why I'm here."

She clutched it self-consciously. "My time key and I are one in the same."

"I know," he went on. "No one else holds three original fragments of the key outside time. Not only do the keys open time but they have the ability to corrupt it as well."

Blood roared in her ears, dreadful recognition taking a spark. He was using his own words against her. "Copies of your own time key aren't authentic, but they get the job done." The man pulled out a black wristwatch from his pocket for her to see. The white Roman numerals glinted.

"Russell," Nora said with disdain. She remembered at last who he was, who she made that time key for. She regretted the promise she made not to hurt him all those years ago. "How long have you been time traveling?"

"Long enough to learn *all* of your story."

"You can't be here. You need to leave. If Mason—"

"You found him already? Now I must stick around and say hello," Russell said. "Give him my thanks."

"No," she said sharply, taking a step toward him. She wanted to have him gone before anyone spotted him. "Give me your time key. I'll fix it."

He eyed Nora distrustfully, then clasped the watch on his wrist.

Nora looked around. "If you want to leave this time, you have to trust me. I'll fix it."

Russell frowned. "I made the mistake of trusting you once, Nora. You and Mason."

"You betrayed us," Nora said, her voice full of fury. She willed herself to stay put. He twisted their history, throwing the baton of blame to her. He had no right to call out her past. "We gave you a time key to protect yourself, to use it for emergencies only, then you ratted us out. You got us killed!"

His cool exterior finally broke. His blue eyes took a darker shade. "You abandoned me to die!"

"We had no other choice! We had to run!"

Russell lunged at the black sundial. She jumped back just as his hand closed around nothing but air. He swooped in for another try as she backpedaled away from him. A hand gripped her elbow tightly and yanked her out of Russell's reach. She slammed into a body. It was Mason. His eyes were fixed on Russell. He shoved Nora aside. She stumbled back, unable to stop him when he rushed straight to the time traveler. He balled his fists into Russell's collar and landed a good punch to his gut. He doubled over to catch the breath Mason knocked out of him. He dropped to his knees.

"That one's for the foul," he snarled, flexing his knuckles.

Russell clutched his stomach before staggering to his feet, letting out a wheezy laugh. He looked at Mason in disgust as if he didn't approve of his new body. "I see you still have your temper," Russell noted. "But I bet you forgot mine." He made a move to hit Mason.

Nora let out a scared yelp and jerked Mason out of the way, not wanting them to continue. He staggered back, and with a definitive shove she pushed him behind her to put as much space between them as possible. Russell advanced, keeping his eyes on the sundial. Behind Nora, Mason did the same, his glare on Russell never wavering. She raised a hand to keep him where he was. It was hard to imagine they were friends a long time ago.

She needed to get Russell on his way fast. Mason didn't deserve to learn any of his past from him. He came from a time where Mason lived in a particular kind of hell, where his escape was at the cost of others.

"Enough!" Nora demanded. "Leave him out of this. Give it here. I said I'd fix it."

"And I said I don't trust you!" Russell shot back.

"Then it looks like you're not going anywhere."

Russell hesitated. His fingers curled around the wristwatch protectively. It was the only item he treasured above all else. She wondered if he carried it close to remind him of the friends he once had or because he got to keep the reward despite his betrayal. Finally, he unclasped his time key and handed it to her.

Nora moved toward him, reaching for the time key. As she neared, Russell made a grab for her neck. Mason shouted out in protest. His fingers circled around the chain. Her hand flew to his wrist, twisting it away. His bones cracked, and he cursed her name in between his teeth. She caught his other hand holding the time key, dragged his arm behind him, then elbowed him in the spine to thrust him to the ground. To keep him there, she planted her foot on the middle of his back.

She examined the black watch he held. It was entirely black except for the white Roman numerals marking the face and needle thin hands. The metal practically glowed despite the lack of sunlight. Nora noticed what Russell meant when he said his time key was broken. The hands were frozen at eleven on the dot. For a moment she thought time stopped ticking, but then she heard the usual rhythm of time ticking inside. It was in perfect condition; it was programmed to short circuit. She smiled in spite herself. Russell's time had run out. Nora pried it out of his hand, then tossed it to Mason.

Russell bucked under her foot like a bull. He half grunted, half laughed when he realized she wouldn't give in. He stayed limp for a long time, laying his cheek on the trampled grass. "Just kill me already," he muttered. "Kill me. It'll be a far better fate than going back home."

"I'm not going to kill you," she told him, hoping the pity in her voice didn't betray her. Nora's mind flashed to another Mason long ago who made her swear not to harm him, although he betrayed them. She forced herself to keep that promise. She shifted her knee onto his back, leaning in close to his ear. "I'm not going kill you, Russell," she repeated as he groaned under her weight. "I'm going to give you the one thing you fear more than death. I'm going to send you home. I'm going to send you back to your pathetic little life without a time key. You'll be trapped there with no way out. You'll live and grow old and die a poor squatter boy—the exact same way I met you. This is your punishment for not following our agreement." She let him go at last and moved back to stand in front of Mason.

Russell pushed himself off the ground and dusted himself off, his face twisted in humiliated defeat.

The sundial around Nora's neck hummed as if it knew it was about to be summoned into action. She pulled off her time key and willed it to open a time warp. It burst open, revealing the hollow darkness inside. The whooshing sound rattled the entrance.

"Walk."

Russell glared at Mason and Nora hard. She knew what awaited him when he returned: poverty and hunger. He had no hope of surviving unless he returned back to his life of a petty thief on the streets. Nora saw the dread in his eyes. He knew it too. He turned and disappeared inside. She turned away once the time warp shut itself behind him.

"Who was he?" Mason asked, offering her Russell's broken time key.

She shoved it into her bag. "He was a friend of yours. I thought he helped us escape when we were on the run," Nora said. "Turned out to be a sneaky piece of trash. He tricked you into talking me into giving him a time key. I should have stuck to my gut and stole it back the moment we decided to take off." She began to walk toward the parking lot. "I was so stupid."

Mason hurried after her. "We made a mistake," he said. "We put our trust in the wrong person. It wasn't your fault."

"Mason, I *made* him this time key." She shook her bag at him for emphasis.

He slipped his hand around her wrist, then took the bag from her. The empty weight in her hand made her shoulders relax. Her hands stopped shaking in anger. She looked up at him only to find his brown eyes staring at her. "We both screwed up," he said. "No one has my back like you do. If I asked you to make it for him, I didn't make the right call. We won't let that happen again." Mason offered back the raggedy old knapsack.

He threw her for a curve using the words *I* and *we*. Mason referring to his other lives was something he didn't often do. And to share in her blame. It struck a cord with her. Nora didn't know what to say.

Chapter 8
Foul Play

The sun was lowering on the horizon as Nora and Mason pulled into Gio's crowded parking lot. When they couldn't find parking, Mason moved to the adjacent street from the pizzeria.

The celebration of today's victory meant he would be welcomed in like a hero. The entire place erupted into applause and whistles as soon as they entered. Some of the fans held up jerseys with his number, and others hooted his name. The sudden attention made Nora want to disappear. She tried to slink behind Mason. Walking in together made a statement.

"Hey," Mason said, finding her hand behind him and pulled Nora to stand at his side. His arm brushed against her. The closeness of their bodies caused goose bumps to run up and down her spine. "Sit with me."

Her palms began to sweat. "Your friends are waiting," Nora replied.

"I'd rather sit with you."

Nora sucked in a breath. She wanted to cave. Every fiber in her was aware of the sensation of his touch, how her hand fit into his so easily. She drew her hand away.

"Go, celebrate," she urged. "I'll be okay on my own."

"Everyone saw us come in together," Mason insisted. "It'll look like I'm blowing you off."

Irritation flared, prickling every nerve in her. "Not like you haven't done it before," she muttered. Nora dashed over to the nearest lonely booth away from the packed center. Mason slid across from her, not letting her have the last word.

She didn't bother to meet hiss gaze. "You need to stop, Mason."

"I didn't mean it like that," he protested, leaning forward so their conversation wouldn't be overheard. "You know that's not what I meant."

She couldn't help it. Nora looked up, annoyance clear in her hazel green eyes. "Then what did you mean?" she demanded. The growing pit in her stomach plunged deeper. "Tell me you won't read too much into tonight. Tell me this isn't a ploy to change my mind—"

Mason glared at her. All he heard was her rejection once more. His brown eyes darkened in understanding. "I won't," he cut her off. His words lingered. "Stay here alone for all I care." He got to his feet and drifted over to the awaiting crowd, leaving Nora with self-inflicted agony.

She sighed, slumping in her seat.

It wasn't fair. Nora couldn't keep doing this to him. She hated herself for purposely running his heart right into the ground, smashing it into dangerous shards he flung back at her. It was cruel how she was always handed the short end of the stick. He kept putting himself on the line, despite her constant efforts to reinforce her boundaries. How did he muster enough courage to pursue her over and over again, when all she did was crush his hopes?

Throughout the night, Mason didn't even give Nora a second glance. She shredded napkins into pieces most of night wondering what was going on in his mind. He sat with his teammates having a good time. A complete fleet of fan girls arrived a little later. The team pulled up chairs to have them sit down. A pretty brunette took a seat beside Mason. He shifted in his seat, but didn't ask her to move. She leaned in to speak to him.

"Looks like you and Mason aren't on good terms again."

Nora looked up to see Diego sitting across from her. He studied Nora with narrowed eyes as if he could gather information by simply looking at her. It didn't take long for his gaze to flicker to pity. She didn't have the energy to tell him to buzz off, so she let him stay.

"I certainly know how to step on his toes," Nora agreed. "I'm under the impression we aren't friends. Why are you talking to me?"

"Because Mason likes you," Diego clarified. He spoke slowly as if she were a child. "Which means I have to dislike you a tiny bit less." He indicated with his pointer finger and thumb, making a small space in between them. Tiny. Nora tried not to roll her eyes. "I came over to only say this once: quit leading him on."

"I'm not—"

"Whatever," he cut in, waving a hand dismissively. "This thing you two got going on—it keeps hurting Mason. Drop him or talk to him."

She shifted in her seat. Nora wanted to remain angry. She liked her anger; it kept her in check from breaking any more rules. Smoothing things out right away never left her with a clear head; it only caused more doubts.

Nora looked around to search for Mason. His seat was empty. She kept shifting her gaze from table to table before coming to the conclusion that he left the restaurant. She rose from her seat, panic swelling into a new knot in her throat. Mason couldn't have gone far. She shouldered her bag and hurried out the building.

As Nora stepped outside, a chilly gust of wind blew her hair into her face. She reached for the sundial. It rose out of her palm and yanked toward her left. Nora tucked her hair behind her ears and let it lead her to Mason.

She let out a breath of relief when she found Mason sitting on the hood of his car. Nora hurried over. As she neared, she realized he wasn't alone. The pretty brunette had escorted him out. She sat next to him ankles crossed, listening. She nodded to his words and offered few words of advice. From the corner of his eye, he saw Nora crossing the street, but didn't make a move to acknowledge her.

The girl on the other hand noticed Nora coming. She must have sensed the sudden rise in tension because she hopped off Mason's car, heading toward Gio's. Mason stayed put for a second longer.

"Hi," Nora tried.

He slid off his car and shouldered past her. "Don't talk to me."

"Don't be so hard on me, Mason."

He didn't bother to look back or slow down. She watched him catch up with the brunette following her in. Mason was beyond angry if he didn't want to speak to her. Nora crossed her arms as the door shut behind them. If he thought she would run after him, he had another thing coming. She had enough anger to hold her out for days. He could play the role of a broken soul to a tee, she could play it far better.

Nora decided to walk home. She rushed away from the parking lot, not letting herself get a chance to regret it. Leaving him unprotected pulled at her gut. She ignored the nagging feeling. When the selfish parts of her surfaced, it was better Nora was left alone to regain her thoughts. He was a few blocks away, she reasoned. She trusted him enough to handle himself for two hours.

It seemed as though all of Torch Crossings was celebrating. Much of downtown was lit up and cars lined the streets. Restaurants with outdoor tables were at their limit despite the chill. Loud laughter and chatter outnumbered the cars parked along the street. It wasn't until Nora reached the gas station by the library that the noise began to thin out. The occasional car flew by as the streetlights blinked on.

As she walked, Nora watched her breath come out in wispy clouds. She walked fast counting ten more blocks to her street, almost home where she could find some peace of mind. The familiar sound of her phone vibrating in her bag made her scoff. She wasn't eager to reply to any of Mason's texts quite yet. If he had any dignity, he would speak to her in person.

Except her phone kept vibrating.

Nora stopped walking to rifle through her bag. An unknown number was coming through. She found it strange. No one had her number aside from Mason. She decided to answer.

"Hello?"

"It's me," came Hogan's voice. He sounded far away like a long distance call. "Is this a secure line?"

Nervously, she looked around. She already felt like she was being watched. "It is," she replied.

"Angeline is on the run too," he reported.

"My location hasn't been compromised. What should I do?"

"I suspect it won't be that way for long," Hogan pondered aloud. "Travelers will appear with more frequency soon enough. We're being hunted, Nora, more so than usual. You have to run. Fetch your time marker and flee to a new location." He paused. "Once we're secure, we'll sever ties."

"I understand. I'll be gone with my time marker in less than twenty-four hours."

"Stay low," he said, his voice growing fainter.

The line went dead. Nora kept her phone in her hand. Her mind was racing. Time travelers were coming, they'd find her and Mason. What she should have done was run back to Gio's and drag him home to pack and pick a new town far away to settle in, instead Nora kept heading home. They needed time apart to recover from their wounds. She would give him space; he could have this one night because time wouldn't allow him another.

The streetlight flickered over Nora's head. She sat on the curb, still coming to terms with Hogan's call. Her new reality was beginning to sink in. She was meant to run once more. To pick up and leave unexpectedly was nothing special. It was a craft she learned that helped her remain alive. It was easy for her. Nora never had anyone to miss or a permanent home. But that wasn't the problem—it was Mason.

She pressed her palms to her eyes until flashes of her past lives loomed on her eyelids like a flipbook of polaroid pictures. Nora didn't have ties here, but Mason did. He had a family, friends, an education, and a budding soccer career. How could she ask so much of him at once? Especially right after the series of arguments they've had. It wasn't a life she wanted for him. He shouldn't have to look over his shoulder wondering what eyes were on him.

Nora got to her feet and crossed the street leaving the library behind. The cold autumn night air gnawed at her cheeks and fingertips, but she hardly felt it. Nora was too busy making a mental list of everything they would need while on the run. She quickened her pace.

The sound of car caught her attention. It was coming from the way she came. Nora heard the moment the transmission shifted from second shift back into first. It was slowing down, yet she wasn't. When she saw it was the silver Nissan from the corner of her eye, she huffed and rolled her eyes.

The window rolled down as she moved to the center of the sidewalk hoping to hide her sudden flush of anger. The last thing Nora anticipated was Mason to come after her so quickly. And she was damn certain it wasn't to sort out their differences.

"Why am I not surprised you ran off?" Mason scolded.

Nora kept quiet. She could tell he was ready for another go. This time she refused to let him drive her to the ground with guilt. Flying off the handle wasn't just Mason's specialty. She was all fire that night too.

"What if something happened to you? Or me?"

She snorted.

"Talk to me, damn it!" Mason demanded.

"So I'm allowed to do that now?" Nora shot back, throwing him a dangerous look in his direction. Mason cruised along matching her stride. "You made it perfectly clear you don't want to speak to me."

"Quit it, Nora," he warned. "You wanted to talk first."

"That was before you brushed me off."

"I'm here now."

Nora didn't reply. Her sight was set on the next stop sign. She stopped under the streetlight, finally able to see her street corner six blocks away. Despite the dark, the hedges were visible under another pool of light.

"You're heading home," Mason noted. "I'll take you."

"No."

"Will you just get in the car!" he exploded, his patience growing thin.

"I don't want to go anywhere with you!" Nora shot back. She couldn't hide her displeasure in her voice either. Ironically, they would have plenty of time to get into a messy fight while they were on the run. Right now she wanted him far away from her.

Mason slammed his palms on the steering wheel in frustration. His anger only made Nora want to retaliate. And she did.

"Fine, let's talk," she said. "Let's start with how you treat me like the biggest bother in the world, how from the instant I met you all you've ever done is put me through hell. Even when you were nice to me you still made my life hell. And now you go out of your way every day to spite me!"

She hopped off the curb to cross the street. Half way across Mason swooped in with his car nearly running Nora over. She almost tripped over her own two feet stumbling out of the way. With surprising speed, Mason abandoned his car and gripped her arm sinking his nails into her skin. He yanked her to him hard.

Nora struggled against him, but his hold was strong. She wasn't going anywhere.

"Stop it!" Mason hissed. His brown eyes were like daggers pinning her down to the asphalt road.

"You don't know what it's like hurting you!" Nora said, her tone softening. "I told you we can't. That *this* can cost us our lives, your life! You made me think you understood, that you'd stop, but you lied. You're still trying. And I hate it because then you force me to do something I don't want to do. I *have* to hurt you … every time."

Nora felt tears sting her eyes, and Mason's grip on her slackened. She wrestled herself away from him, wanting to hit him, but settled for a sloppy shove, making him stagger back as though her words had already done most of the damage before her hands did. She dashed past him and his car to the other side of the street.

"Nora," Mason called out. He sounded defeated. Exhausted. "Nora."

She took off in a run. Behind her, she heard Mason get back in his car. He appeared at Nora's side a moment later. He drove in silence, not pressing the matter further. Nora caught him sneaking glances at her in an attempt to find an opening to speak to her again, she didn't let him. It only made her run faster.

All the pain she had blocked out from the day she had to end things with Mason came flooding back in. Her own heartbreak rose to her throat. How many more times did they have to go through this? Why couldn't he just let her go? If he wanted to live, Mason had to forget the idea that he and Nora could become anything more. She was his time guard, a job not suitable for the faint of heart. She was supposed to be strong enough and overcome all obstacles at any costs. Nora's soul was chosen to protect him. She didn't just protect him from time travelers or a gruesome death, she had the duty to shield him from the biggest threat of all.

Himself.

She didn't slow down when she rounded the corner to her street. Mason went on ahead without her to park in the driveway. Nora pushed herself to catch up. The engine to his car shut off just as she cut across the lawn.

Mason opened his door. "Nora, wait!"

Nora pushed past the back gate, letting it rattle loudly. She rushed to her door, let herself in, and shut herself inside. Instead of a wave of relief washing over her, Nora still felt agitated. She threw her things at her bed as hard as she could, then slumped to the floor sucking in air. Fresh tears gathered, but she wiped them away before they could drop.

Two steps forward, ten steps back. For the first time in centuries, Nora felt like she wasn't an adequate time guard. She was breaking all the rules. And for what? A time marker who only made her miserable.

A soft knock from the door interrupted Nora's thoughts. It came from the hallway.

"What?" Nora asked, sounding harsher than she intended.

"I heard you come in," came Nadine's voice. "I wanted to pop in and say hello before bed."

"I want to be alone right now," Nora replied, trying not to lose her patience with Nadine. She shouldn't let her anger spill out on the only person who showed her a shred of kindness; none of her current problems were Nadine's fault.

"Is everything okay?"

"Yeah, fine."

There was a pause. Nadine was most likely debating whether or not to respect her wishes. A moment later Nora heard Nadine shuffle away from the door. Another door closed somewhere further in the house.

Nora picked herself off the floor to throw herself onto the bed. She sank into the sheets letting it engulf her like a warm home. She blinked up at the ceiling closing her eyes. Just as she began to relax, Nora's phone vibrated. Sitting up with a sigh, she plucked her phone out of her pocket ready to chuck it if it was Mason.

It was Hogan checking up on her.

Update?

In the heat of the argument Nora forgot to tell Mason about leaving Torch Crossings. She was too fired up to even mention it. They wouldn't leave tonight or tomorrow morning like she hoped. She and Mason needed time to heal before asking him to drop everything and leave his home. Unfortunately, Nora didn't have time. Mason was in danger, and Hogan was expecting an answer.

Preparing exfil.

He responded back. *Move. Now.*

She pressed the phone to her lips. She had a handful of scattered safe houses to pick from. Finding a temporary place to hide wasn't an issue. She'd pick one and go from there. Nora decided she'd talk to Mason first thing in the morning. Even if they were still at each other's throats, she'd plead with him to see things rationally. His life was more important than any fight. They had to leave. It was their only way to survive.

The next day Nora woke up early. Fully dressed, she paced the length of the room, anxiously waiting for the sun to rise. Next door Mason was surely still asleep unaware that his time guard was attempting to find a way to deliver the news. She checked her phone to see it was five minutes til seven. Nora pulled on her shoes, she couldn't wait any longer.

There was a knock on the door and Nadine popped in.

"Mason's at the door asking for you," she told Nora, jerking her thumb over her shoulder. Nadine's eyes held a hint of suspicion. "Why is he here at this hour?"

Nora ignored her question. "Tell him I'll be right there," she replied. She waited for Nadine to have a head start before following. It wasn't like him to use the front door. If anything, he was cautious in approaching her this time. She hurried to the front of the house running a hand through her hair wondering what he had to say. The foyer door shut behind them to keep their conversation private.

Mason was on the other side of the half open door watching a pair of squirrels flying from tree to tree, chasing each other down the street. Nora fully opened the door, and he turned to look at her. He looked a little embarrassed, yet he tried to offer her a smile.

"Sleep well?" he greeted, shoving his hands in his jeans.

"Hardly," she said bluntly. "Listen, Mason, we need to talk."

"Yeah, I know. Let me go first," Mason cut in. "I was being a total jerk yesterday. My bad—"

Anger flared in Nora. "My bad doesn't quite cut it!"

His eyes flashed dangerously, annoyed that she didn't take his apology as he hoped. "Then what does?" he snapped. "That I'm an ungrateful idiot?"

"Keep going," Nora encouraged. "It sounds a hell of a lot better than my bad."

He turned away from her to mutter under his breath. Nora crossed her arms leaning on the door hinge to wait. She wasn't going to let him get away with thrashing her around like he had grown accustomed to. She was putting her foot down.

Mason turned to her. "You're really going to make me work for this apology, aren't you?" he asked.

"You can make it up to me later," she said. "Right now we have other things to worry about." Nora stepped aside to let him in. He followed her back to her room muttering an awkward hello to Nadine brewing coffee in the kitchen. Nora offered no explanation and shut the door behind her.

Mason sat on the arm of the recliner waiting for her to speak.

She kicked a pile of clothes in the middle of the floor out of the way toward a corner. "I've been in touch with another time guard," Nora began. "Things are getting shaky out there. They're being tailed and targeted. I expect more time travelers will come. It's only a matter of when Torch Crossings won't be safe for you anymore. We need to go."

"Go?" he asked.

"Like we need to leave here. Today."

He shook his head. "I can't leave."

"Look, I know this isn't what you want," she insisted, taking a step closer to him. "But we can't stay. Anachronisms will find us. We'll be putting everyone you know in danger. And I don't have enough resources to protect them too. We need to run far and fast, Mason."

"It's not that I don't want to," he clarified. "It's that I can't."

She gave a look to further explain his choice of words.

Mason shifted his seat on the recliner. "I can't physically leave Torch Crossings. I think I'm tied to this region. If I leave, I start seeing layers of places, things, like I'm being shown every version of it through time. I went down to New Mexico to visit my aunt when I was a kid, and everywhere I looked kept changing. It was impossible to tell what or when I was looking at. I was stuck in bed with a splitting headache. Why do you think I always find a way to squirm out of away games?"

She crouched down next to him. "Time reading," Nora muttered more to herself than him.

He nodded, as if he recognized the term. "It's because of it that I can't leave the state. I can't."

"Can you time read now?" she asked curiously. The last time the ability presented itself was in his life cycle in Iran. There was no visible pattern or reason when it manifested.

He shook his head. "No," Mason answered. "It only happens when I go someplace new."

"I can help. With some training the time readings effect will turn minimal."

"Great. Let's get started."

Nora bit her lip. "It'll take days to train you."

"So what are we going to do?" he asked.

"I'll figure something out," she promised, standing straight. Mason got to his feet as Nora went to unplug her phone from the charger. She nodded to the back door to indicate he was free to leave, then dialed the number she knew from memory.

He took the hint. "I guess I'll just go work on that apology, then," Mason teased. Nora followed him to the door hearing the phone ring. She shut the door after him and the blinds. On the fourth ring, the person on the other line picked up.

"Change of plans," Nora said at once not giving Hogan a chance to say a word. She reached for her tablet opening numerous windows to begin conducting various searches as she cradled the phone to her ear with her shoulder. "There will be no exfil, not right away. I'll have to move delicately."

"Understood. Changing course," she heard Hogan say. "Patrol within thirty-six hours?"

"Passage will be clear."

Hogan cut the call.

They were coming.

Chapter 9
A Place to Hide

It took Nora most of the morning to find a secure location. She sat cross-legged on the bed, rubbing her temples. There was no place else to look. A hotel was out of the question. Checking in with their names in the system would be like sending up a flare. There also wasn't time to find and purchase a house. Abruptly buying a home anywhere local would also be a waste. When the choices became limited, she began to search outside Torch Crossings to the neighboring towns. She was careful not to step beyond the boundaries of the time read's usual range, she didn't want to hurtle Mason into an awful time trip.

It was only when she rifled through the newspaper that she found what she was looking for. There was a picture under a historical piece of an abandoned boardinghouse an hour away from Torch Crossings heading toward Salem. In the photograph, she could see the property had a rusting water tower. According to the article, before its closure fifteen years ago it was a bed and breakfast. The lack of tourism caused the government to auction off the home, but it was never sold. Now it stood forgotten and unwanted. Curious, Nora took to the internet to dig deeper into the house's history. She discovered it was once a shelter for Chinese immigrants who scattered after the flare of the California Gold Rush. The two-hundred-year old structure looked worn and uncared for, but still in tact. Nora decided it would have to do.

She jotted down the address and directions on a scrap of paper. She would get a look at it in person once she finished patrol. Nora bounced out of bed, threw on her bag, and headed toward the door. There was still plenty to do in such a little time frame.

"Hey, where are you going?"

She spun around to see Mason in the backyard raking leaves. He walked over to meet her by the fence. She walked over too.

"Where are you going?" he repeated.

"Out," she replied. "I have a few things to take care of. Now that I think of it, Nadine isn't home. Let me borrow your car."

He raised an eyebrow in disbelief. "My car? Yeah, no. Not happening."

"Fine, I'll walk, then." Nora headed toward the front yard.

Mason followed. "Wait," he huffed. "Tell me where you're going first at least."

"You do realize I'm the time guard here, right?" she reminded him, stepping onto the empty driveway. Nora didn't mind doing patrol on foot, but over the past year she had grown dependent on Nadine's car.

"Why can't you just tell me what the hell you're planning?" he called after her. "I'm a part of this too! I can help!"

"You aren't and you can't."

He caught up and whirled her around to look at him. Nora narrowed her eyes at him expecting him to lash out at her again. But he didn't. His eyes bore into hers, a trace of desperation apparent. "Nora, come on," he protested. There was an urgency in his voice. "Let me in."

She pinched the bridge of her nose, squeezing her eyes shut. Nora hated it when he looked at her like that. The look always made her cave. Although she would never say it aloud to a soul, she found comfort in Mason's anger long ago. His anger kept her angry too. It was much easier to pick a fight than admit his rare moments of determination affected her. "There's this house I want to check out," Nora began, letting her hand drop to her side.

A rush of terror swept over his face. "We can't leave—"

"I know. It's only an hour away," she said quickly. "I'll take you to it when I come back."

"Why don't I just come along now?" he asked. "Save you a trip?"

"Because I haven't run patrol or scouted the area. It's not safe for you yet."

"And leaving me here alone is?"

Nora also hated it when he was right. She wasn't sure how long she'd be away from Torch Crossings. "No games. You follow my rules."

Mason tossed her his keys. "Your rules," he agreed.

She caught them midair, then moved to Mason's car before he could change his mind. They hopped in and tore out of their street. Nora gripped and reaffirmed her grip on the wheel, feeling a little uncomfortable that he had joined her on patrol. It was always an assignment she carried out on her own. It was also the best time to come across trouble. She prayed no time travelers were out there waiting for them.

Mason looked out the window, staring at his hometown with new eyes—through Nora's eyes. Luckily, he didn't ask many questions as she checked all the misbegotten corners of Torch Crossings. Every crack he ever overlooked was every place she turned to for answers. Once she deemed the town safe, she headed south in the direction of the boardinghouse. She eased onto the interstate. The silence ended after she mulled over his words. He was eager to be a part of it all. She wasn't sure how much of it would inevitably kill him in the end.

"The initial plan was to get you far away from here as quick as possible," Nora told him. "That's still the plan … eventually. In the meantime, we'll go into hiding. The time markers and time guards are on their way over to provide support. I can't exactly house them with me, and you can't house them with you, so I found this boardinghouse out by Lys Gate that could shelter us for a few days while we come up with a plan."

"Wait, so the future and past time markers are coming here?" Mason asked.

The hint of excitement in his voice made Nora glance over to him. "Their stay will be short," she said. "It'll only be for a few days. Coming together like this is forbidden."

"Why?"

Nora weaved through the lanes following the directions she had written. "Time marker souls are like beacons, the 'you are here' dot in the ongoing stream of time. Apart and scattered is the only way to keep you hidden. It weakens the signal, but when the three of you come together it'll be like a light show. Any time traveler will be able to find you."

Mason's eyes looked to her, then downward in sudden comprehension, the danger all of a sudden real.

She veered to the left heading toward an exit ramp. The gravel road she was looking for wasn't very far. It was two miles out just outside a town smaller than Torch Crossings. Most of the small residential streets and shops revolved around the main road. The staggering small size was a risky move. It wouldn't be easy to blend in or find back roads for escape routes. Nora decided to take a chance. *No risk, no reward,* she thought, pulling into the long driveway.

The boardinghouse was much bigger than she expected. The two-story structure was capable to fit well over two dozen people. The house was sculpted in a perfect right angle, offering a right and left wing. When they came to a stop at the house, Nora could see the rusting water tower in the back by the property line.

Nora parked. She and Mason got out of the car to get a closer look. Although the chipping, deep, emerald-green paint revealed a murky brown coat underneath and strings of shingles no longer clung to the roof, it held promise.

"What do you think?" she asked, turning to look at Mason.

He fell behind still standing by his car door. He studied the boardinghouse. Nora noted that his mind was racing by the way his demeanor changed. He was still and rigid, his gaze somewhere beyond the building. She rushed to his side anxious that she may have sent him into a time read. She touched his wrist wondering if he needed her to pull him back in. His skin was cool to the touch.

"Mason?" she asked. "Are you time reading?"

He blinked and looked down at her. He wasn't time reading. "Sorry, it's just, this place—It feels familiar."

"You and I used to live in a boardinghouse in the 1820s, if I remember correctly," she told him, leading him to the door. "It was you and your father then. I moved in when I turned sixteen. It was pity to see it burn down two years later." Nora squatted to get a look at the lock on the door.

It was a brass number sequence padlock. A thick layer of dust made it hard to tell which number was pressed last. The lock was old and too hard to break. She gave it a few tries, but no luck. It remained shut.

"Did we get along?" he asked.

She laughed at his question, fumbling through her bag for her lock opener. "More or less," Nora replied. "We didn't speak much. We shared the same tutor for a number of years."

Her fingers found the jagged tip of slim pen like device. She fished it out with a huff. The lock opener was a tool that came in handy to pick door locks and some padlocks. Now would be the moment to discover what else it could open when there wasn't a key hole involved.

Nora poised the jagged tip of the opener over the numbers wondering if it would react to the lock in front of it on its own. She clicked the opener once. Her hand suddenly felt a magnetic pull leading her to the four-digit code: 6, 0, 1, 3. With a snap, the lock opened and dropped into her palm.

She twisted the knob and pushed the door open. They entered the boardinghouse to take a look around. Amazingly, the whole place was still fully furnished. All the furniture that remained from the days as a bed and breakfast were covered in drapes to keep the mounds of dust off. The living room was more of a lounge area with five large sets of outdated deep burgundy corduroy couches and love seats. The off-white walls were lightly decorated with paintings, the side tables were crowded with empty candleholders, and the coffee tables were crudely punctured in the middle. Above it was the spacious kitchen with one long wooden table and benches to fit half of the tenants. Grime and rust plagued the bath tub-size sink.

"I'm going to look upstairs," she said, letting the drape drop over a lamp. "Check the basement."

Nora wandered off to the bedrooms first. The left and right wings of the house were identical: twelve rooms up top and bottom. The rooms were of generous size. Each was equipped with a full and twin bed, a dresser, a wardrobe and a tiny bathroom. Some even had the luxury to have a fireplace of their own or a television. She went from room to room making sure all was as it should be.

She headed back to the first floor just as Mason emerged from the stairs. "Just a library, a laundry room, and a rec room," he reported.

"We should check the well and water tower too."

"Let's go."

They exited through the back door. The dry grass folded under their feet. The well felt like a bit of history, untouched by time with its huge bucket and thick chain still geared up ready to be lowered. The concrete bricks were five feet high. Nora had to dance on tiptoes to peer inside. Mason helped her sit on the well before jumping up to join her. They used their phones to have a look. The surface of the murky water shimmered up to them, making it impossible to determine how much deeper it really was.

The water tower beside it was wider than it was tall. The wooden base under it was decaying. Regardless of its sketchy condition, Mason climbed the ladder. Nora followed. He sat on the ledge cautiously with his legs dangling as she peered inside.

"How will you teach me how to control my time reading?" he asked.

There was nothing more than a pool of brown water. "A little bit of exposure therapy should do the trick," Nora replied, shutting the heavy rusted door.

He groaned. "That sounds painful."

She took a seat beside him. "It might be."

"When can we start?"

"We can sneak in a lesson or two before we leave," she told him. "It won't be easy at first." Nora stared out into the stark three acres of land. Most of it was overgrown dry grass except for the scattered trees.

There was no place for anyone to hide for miles. From their spot on the water tower, she could see the slope of the Oregon mountains in the distance. The postcard image was all but perfect, except for one peak. The peculiar point was overturned like a witch's hat: flat top with an upside-down peak.

Nora checked her sundial. It was half past noon. Instead of moving on to the next task on her list, she was sitting on an old water tower with Mason. She needed to move.

She handed him back his keys. "I have one more thing to take care of, and I can't take you with me this time."

Mason looked at her. "You're just going to send me home?" he asked.

"Yes," Nora said. "I need you to trust me, to listen to me. I can only explain things to you after I come back."

He hesitated. "All right."

Nora willed a time warp to open. Its black nothingness whooshed and rattled beneath her feet, waiting to whisk her out of time. She let her legs dangle, and her feet disappeared into the gaping hole.

"Hold on!"

"What, Mason? I need to go."

"I wanted to apologize again," he said quickly. "I'm an ungrateful, self-absorbed, rude, unfair, sorry-ass jerk. You have every right to be upset with me. I was putting you in a tough spot. And I shouldn't have done that to you." Even though his words were rushed, Nora could tell he was being honest. The set look in his eye made her want to close the time warp and stay.

Nora reached out to him, caressing his cheek gently. Mason closed his eyes, feeling the warmth of her fingertips on his skin. Lately, it felt as though they were magnets. Every time they repelled, they would come closer again to produce friction. The spark. The jolt raced up her arm.

"I wish you'd stop questioning where you stand with me," she told him.

She pulled away from him and jumped into the time warp. The pull of gravity stopped when she plunged into the darkness. She was kept afloat like a puppet on strings. A bright flash of white made the time warp pulse. The light was coming from Nora. She emitted uncontrollable rays of light stretching into the infinite depths of the time warp. In a blink of an eye, the burst of light evaporated into a dull silver aura. Nora's joints twitched, shaking off the grip time had in an attempt to restrain her. It took a brief moment for her to feel like she was back in control of her own movements.

She squinted into the darkness, looking beyond the layer of protection to the thousands of images beneath it. All of them were of places in real time, close or half a planet away. Nora saw her latest visits the clearest: A playground in Hastings, Nebraska. A castle in Romania. A zoo in Kuwait. Finally, the image she searched for bubbled to the surface.

Nora reached for it, letting herself be guided to it. Her hand seeped through, then the rest of her was sucked in like a vacuum. She tumbled onto a patch of trimmed green grass. The odd sensation of leaving a time warp left her legs uncoordinated. It felt as though she jumped off a spinning merry-go-round after a hundred spins. By the time Nora regained her balance, the time warp behind her closed.

The sun above warned it was almost four o'clock. Within a time warp, there was no such thing as time distinction. It simply didn't exist. Once trapped inside, it was hard to tell how much time had passed until time spit the trespasser out. By then a minute, an hour, ten days, or six months may have passed, yet in a time warp it all felt the same.

She landed in front of a willow tree in the middle of a research nature preserve in Austin, Texas. The preserve was enormous, full of trees and wildlife. And most importantly off limits to the public. Nora found it six years ago, her meticulous search to hide her most valued possession was impressive for a middle school student. It was also a grand success. She checked on it yearly to make sure it stayed in place and no one accidentally found it.

The limp dangling branches were like curtains shielding most of the trunk and roots from view. Nora parted the leaves and weaved her way to the clearing under the tree. It wasn't very big. It was large enough to fit a midsize pool. Most of the space was taken up by a shrub full of light yellow marigolds. She shuffled toward it, remembering the entrance to the hiding spot was behind the threshold of flowers. The marigolds were in full bloom, puffing out like cotton balls to greet the sky. Nora cupped one thankful that these beautiful bright pieces of nature provided the cover she needed. She readjusted her bag around her, got to her knees, and crawled into the bush.

Beyond the leaves, there was a section of the ground and tree trunk carved out as though someone decided to scoop out a portion of the earth and trunk. She shoved the branches behind her to get a view of the crawl space. The shallow dugout was wide enough to hide a large suitcase. She knelt and with two hands reached inside until her hands closed around a handle. Nora tugged once, twice, then the box inside began to move upward. As it neared the surface, she shifted her weight onto her feet, tugging harder.

Nora pulled with all her might. It moved a few more inches before all of it broke free of the dugout, cracking the tree bark on the way out. She tumbled through the shrub back into the clearing. The old wooden trunk flew out of her hands, crashing into the willow's branches.

Feet away, wheels screeched to a halt.

"Garcia, did you hear that?" came a man's voice.

Park officials, Nora thought immediately. She didn't even hear the rumble of their pickup. "Crap," she muttered, crawling to the trunk she just recovered.

"It came from the willow tree. Wait here." A door opened and closed.

She crouched beside her trunk and grabbed her sundial, willing a time warp to open. A seam of darkness began to open in front of her.

"Come on," Nora hissed, hearing the footsteps get closer.

The curtain of branches opened and with an arm wrapped securely around her trunk Nora threw herself into the time warp. She coasted into the darkness, her feet no longer feeling gravity's pull.

"What the hell!" the park official shouted, watching her escape.

The time warp closed behind her, not caring that the man caught a glimpse of her. His mouth fell open, not believing what he saw. It didn't put her in any imminent danger if word spread. Nora left feeling reassured that no one would believe in his wild story.

She scanned the moving images behind their black veil, searching for Torch Crossings. Her eyes landed on Nadine's backyard. From within the time warp, Nora could make out the fence that separated their lawn from Mason's. She could even see the faint glow of a bedroom light. She drew herself closer to it and let herself get sucked in.

Nora landed with effort on her feet, making her knees rattle. The weight of the trunk hit. She dropped the trunk with a loud thud, then took a seat on it to catch her breath.

It was night time. The crescent moon was high overhead, offering little light. Nora pulled out her phone to check the time. It was fifteen minutes until eleven o'clock. She hoped Mason was awake at this hour. She dialed his number.

"Hey, where the hell are you? You've been gone for hours!" he scolded. Mason sounded more relieved than mad.

"I need your help," she said breathlessly. Her fingertips felt the trunk she was sitting on. She watched Mason's bedroom light turn on in his window. "Do you mind coming out here for a minute?"

Chapter 10
Disappearing

"**Y**ou're going to do what?" Mason asked Nora after she watched him jump the fence and cross the patio. He eyed the trunk she was sitting on with crossed arms and skepticism. Despite the hour, he was still fully dressed. She guessed he stayed up waiting for her to return.

"I need to wipe Nadine and Isaac's memory before we leave," Nora repeated, closing the lid to the empty film canister that was once full of amnesia capsules. He paced the length of the patio, scratching his head. "They can't remember I ever lived with them. Their lives could be in danger if I let them remember who I am. This is my way of protecting them, Mason. Time travelers will come and they can't know I found you."

He stopped pacing to run a hand through his hair. "I dunno, Nora, wiping their memories—" He sounded uncertain. "You lived with them for years. You'll be altering their lives."

It was the only choice Nora had. Ignoring Isaac's reluctance toward her and Nadine's constant effort to involve her in their lives, Nora felt a strong sense of responsibility toward them. They were her cover after all, they fell under the umbrella of her protection. All the years she spent in their home, she grew to appreciate them. She didn't want to be the cause of any trouble down the road if time travelers arrived in

Torch Crossings. Nora knew guilt would find her if she didn't leave them somewhat protected.

"Don't you think I know that?" she replied earnestly, jumping to her feet. "This isn't easy for me. I've never erased years of someone's life. The amnesia capsules I use on time travelers erase hours maybe days. I'm going to have to do this manually."

"What if it goes wrong?"

"It shouldn't, I mean I hope it doesn't."

"That's reassuring," Mason scoffed.

"Look, I just need you to look after this while I go in there. Will you help me or not?"

He looked over to the house she learned to call home for the last several years. There was a hint of doubt written all over his face. For a split second, Nora was afraid he would refuse, but then Mason sighed and nodded her to the door.

"Go."

Nora handed him the tablet she carried. On it was an automated shell program she planted in the university computer system months ago. Once active, the program was also to target Torch Crossings security cameras. Any footage of them would be wiped.

"Here, take this," she said, tapping at the screen. "Run the app 'Bubble Shooter.' It's disguised as a game. It'll wipe everything." Nora didn't give him a chance to say no. She shoved it in his hand.

She dashed to the back door and disappeared inside. Nora ran to her bed sliding her hand under it to pull out the briefcase. She dug her nail into her palm, then pressed the droplets of blood onto the silver plate. It snapped open. Instead of going for the jar full of lavender amnesia capsules, she grabbed the orange sedative vials neatly stored in a pouch.

She knew first hand what kind of kick even a trickle of the liquid could cause. She stole the sedatives from a future time traveler who foolishly thought it would completely take her down. His second mistake was letting her live. Although her mind was groggy and her movements were sloppy, Nora escaped with his arsenal of the mixture. She guessed Nadine and Isaac could share a vial.

She walked to the door trying to listen where they were in the house. The light shuffles of feet on the other side told her Isaac was in their bedroom and Nadine was in the kitchen. Nora took a breath and opened the door.

Nora hurried down the hall to the bathroom only slowing down when she passed Isaac in his bedroom. She hoped her less than brisk walk displayed that she had been home all night rather than just arriving. The door slammed behind her.

"Nora?" Nadine called out. "Is that you?"

"Yeah," she shot back, opening the medicine cabinet to rifle through old boxes and plastic baggies of left over prescribed medications. "I'm going to bed soon." Behind cough medicine boxes, Nora found an unused syringe in a clear zip lock bag.

"Please don't go to bed on an empty stomach," Nadine called again. "You've been looking thin lately."

She didn't reply. She was too busy washing the syringe in hot water. Nora uncorked the vial, then carefully added water to the solution. It shimmered against the fluorescent lighting, meaning it was activated. She dipped the needle into the mixture to let the orange liquid fill the syringe.

"Nora?"

"Be right out."

Slowly, Nora opened the door avoiding the dreadful squeak. She tiptoed over to the doorway to look inside the bedroom. Isaac was shuffling through the last few papers of the night. His back was turned, she had a perfect window of opportunity. She sucked in a breath, hoisted the syringe close to her body as if it were a firearm, and sneaked into the room.

Isaac didn't hear her soft footsteps as she neared. Nora gripped him firmly by the shoulder and plunged the needle into his neck. He grunted in surprise the papers in his hands falling to the floor. Half of the liquid poured into his bloodstream. The sedative worked fast, Isaac went limp a second later. Nora eased him onto his bed pulling the syringe out.

A scream from behind made Nora spin around. It was Nadine. She was standing in the doorway watching in horror. Her blue eyes were on her husband, collapsed on their bed. Nadine tried to make a run for it; however, Nora was quicker. She slammed the poor woman to the wall.

Nadine gulped. She looked at Nora with wide eyes, the fear in them never wavering. Her eyes darted to the syringe in Nora's hand. She wanted an explanation.

"I'm so sorry," was all Nora could say before the syringe found its way to Nadine's neck.

The last of the sedative drained into her bloodstream. Nadine's eyes became glassy, then fluttered shut. Nora caught her and dragged the unconscious woman into the bedroom. With some difficulty, she heaved her onto the mattress. The two of them would be out for at least half an hour. Nora had to be quick.

She knelt at their bedside, watching them sleep. A bundle of nerves settled in the pit of her stomach. Nora didn't have much practice in manipulating memories. The mind had a strange way of interpreting time. It was stored into memories: people, images, sounds, events. It was also unreliable. Memories were based on each's perception of the world. It focused and held on tightly to events with great meaning. To negotiate with someone's time stream, the sequence of time as they knew it by aging, was like correcting a teacher when they made a mistake. Because they held authority, they could never be wrong. It was absolutely possible to change a time stream, but it was impossible to predict if the changes she caused would cement themselves in their brain.

Nora closed her eyes, listening for time's peculiar rhythm. She ignored the ticking clock out in the hall. It was there to mark seconds and minutes, a man made instrument that only measured a fraction of time's infinite course. She was searching for the very fabric that propelled time forward. Unlike her previous attempts to stop time, Nora right away felt time's pulse vibrating all the matter in the house. Each beat felt like a tug of war: the past stubbornly refused to be swayed any further, and the future itched to race onward. The present was the force that stabilized the two conflicting notions of time, providing an equal give and take.

She didn't find it hard to grasp the delicate mechanism and stop time. It stopped on her command. The pulse of time slowed, growing fainter and fainter until all was quiet. The vicious cycle of the past, present, and future suspended at a stand still. Nora felt time poking at the block she put in place. It sent painful surges of power up her arms, trying to get her to release the hold.

The discomfort was bearable, but the pressure would eventually kick away Nora's block. She rolled up her sleeves and laid her fingertips on the base of Nadine's skull. Her memories came to Nora in a hot flash causing her to shutter. An overwhelming heap of memories flooded in.

It came to Nora in broken pieces. She saw a spunky blond-haired little girl swinging on a tire swing with her barefoot brothers, then the same girl in a school uniform scribbling on a chalkboard. Before Nora's eyes, the girl grew to be a teenager sneaking into the drive-in with her friends, and the next moment she was opening a mailbox to send a stack of college applications.

The memories started to come in faster after Nora saw the instant Nadine met Isaac her first year of college in a biology lecture. She saw their first date to the museum, a series of conversations in a coffee shop, a trip to visit her parents in Portland for Easter, the ceremony of their wedding, and the moment they bought their first home. The pace quickened yet again when her children were born. Birthday parties, first days of school, episodes of teenage angst, family dinners, and countless hours of raising her children blurred together. It became hard to tell the order of the memories.

Eventually, Nora found herself in Nadine's memories. She flinched watching the memories Nadine stored of her: the moment she opened the door to find an orphan girl with nothing more than a backpack slung over her shoulder, the awkward withdrawals when she was invited to participate in daily family conversation, the unwanted calls from the middle school Nora attended reporting too many truancies, the sound of a fence opening and closing in the late hours of the night, and her premature graduation from high school and early acceptance to college.

The last memory Nadine had was of Nora sneaking into the bedroom, the syringe clasped in her hand.

Nora's eyes flickered open to study Nadine's relaxed features. *I'm so sorry*, she thought. She brushed her hair out of her kind face, then shut her eyes again as she willed Nadine's memories to erase Nora from her mind. While every trace of her was being deleted, the gaping holes in her memory didn't remain vacant for long. It crafted new memories to fill in the missing blanks. It came up with stories for Nadine to later find. The girl on her doorstep soon became a neighbor coming to ask for a ride to school, wistful glances at the spare empty room in the back, the calls from a middle school turned into calls from telemarketers. The last thing she remembered was reading a book in bed after a long day at work.

She withdrew her hands and reached over to Isaac. His time stream shot into Nora's brain like a strike of lightning. It was easier to wipe his mind. He held less memorable moments of Nora. She was in and out of Isaac's head before she knew it.

The time block lifted. The pressure gnawing at Nota stopped. Time fell back into its natural state: the past and future in a constant competition over the control in which direction time ought to go. The present was right in the middle keeping the two at peace. The clock outside the bedroom was ticking, time had resumed.

Nora straightened, backed away to the door, turned off the light, and slipped out of their room. She left their door ajar just as they left it every night.

She rushed back to her room and let Mason in. He jumped to his feet and barreled inside with her trunk. It landed with a thud on the carpet. Nora hurried to her bed pulling out a duffel bag and backpack from underneath. She tossed the backpack to Mason. Together they began to clean out her room. He dumped all the contents of her desk while she scooped clothes into the duffel. They worked fast careful not leaving anything behind.

"Need help?" Mason asked as Nora wrestled with closing her bag.

"I wouldn't say no," she said. She watched him zip all her belongings away in one swift movement.

"That everything?" he asked, slinging the duffel over his shoulder.

"Almost." Nora looked under her bed again to pull out a messenger bag. She stuffed it with her briefcase, tablet, and other important items. She knelt at her bedside for a moment, looking around her soon to be former bedroom. Its purpose, just like Nadine and Isaac, was over. "Let's go."

Mason picked up her trunk as she swung the remaining bags over her shoulder. They slid out of her room and hurried to his car. He opened the door to the back seat to shovel his mess around to make room for her things. He shoved in her trunk and duffel, then reached for the bags she was holding.

"You can pack a bag, too, you know," she told him, letting him take the backpack first. "Clothes or something?"

He took her messenger bag last. "Can't we just get things along the way?" he asked.

"We could, but it'll only slow us down."

"And would that be such a terrible idea?" Mason asked, closing the door. "Slowing down."

It wasn't the first time Mason asked such a question before. The answer was always the same. "For us it is. Time isn't an ally we can turn to when things get rough. And it sucks. You don't deserve being ripped away from your home like this. No one does," she told him.

"I'd rather just go."

Her eyebrows drew together in confusion. "And leave it all behind? What about your parents?"

"I have everything I need. I've kept a spare duffel in the car in case we need to run," he told her.

"Your parents …" Nora insisted again, but stopped.

Mason was lost in thought as he looked at his childhood home. He studied the details of the house, soaking in the memories he wanted to take with him. His gaze turned wistful as though he missed it already.

"I don't know how to say bye to them yet," he finally said. "I'll find a way to tell them on my own."

She nodded in understanding.

Nora watched him look up and down his deserted street. His gaze lingered on the patio behind Nadine's house. At once she knew what Mason was remembering. It was the first time she broke his heart, the exact moment she failed as a time guard.

"Does your offer still stand?" she asked, cutting the silence. "You're still playing by my rules tonight?"

"Yeah, why?" Mason asked, giving her a sideways glance, then shoved his hands in his pockets.

"Because I need you to get to the boardinghouse on your own."

Nora gave him explicit instructions. No pit stops, no detours, no slowing down. The only valid reason he had to be late was if he were being followed. Even then she told him to shake them at any cost and find a way to the boardinghouse. She waited until his car pulled out of the driveway. Nora walked down the driveway as the taillights turned the corner.

A time warp unraveled itself above the sidewalk. The darkness inside beckoned to her. It let out a shrill gust of wind as if it wanted to Nora to cross in quickly. She stepped through it deciding it was best not to look back.

Chapter 11
Today's Tomorrow

Nora skid out of a time warp. Her shoes scraped the wood floor as the shard of hollow darkness behind her weaved itself back together. She landed in the middle of the boardinghouse's vacant living room. The weight of the crate in her hands returned making her stagger forward. Boxes and bottles clattered to the floor.

"Don't go any further!"

A hand pulled Nora back a few steps. Mason took the crate from her hands to set it on the end table beside the broken lamp. She looked around to see the light in the room was coming from the fireplace. The burning logs crackled, sending a burst of embers into the air. Their things were stacked just feet from where Nora landed. If it wasn't for Mason, she would have crashed right into it.

"This everything?" he asked, picking up the items that fell.

She set the tank of gasoline on the floor. "Yeah," Nora said, wiping her hands. "The backup generator is busted, and I don't think I can fix it, so I brought a few things to get us through the night." She rummaged through the crate, pulling out two battery-powered lanterns and two flashlights. Nora handed him one.

"You forgot something," Mason pointed out.

She checked her crate wondering what he was talking about. She had gathered all the essentials: water, matches, extra blankets, batteries, tools to fix the busted generator, toilet paper, over the counter medications, and rope.

"Food," he told her when she failed to realize what he meant. "Unless you want to eat dust bunnies. I think I saw a gas station open on my way over."

Her stomach ached at the thought of food. In the process of gathering last minute materials, Nora forgot about her own hunger. She wanted to get to the boardinghouse and find Mason there safe.

"Don't take long," Nora said, waving him off.

In his absence, Nora wandered out of the house to plant the marble-size motion sensors around the property to have a better lay of the land in case they were found. The sensors emitted signals projecting a picture directly into her tablet. Any new heat signature would send an alert. She set the last sensor out by the water tower as it began to drizzle. The cold rain sent her back to the boardinghouse.

She trotted to the back door just as Mason shut the door to his car. He held a carry out bag and darted to the house. She rushed after him. They crossed the threshold before closing the door behind them. Nora shook the water out of her hair, then followed Mason to the fireplace, where he dragged her trunk over to use it as a table to eat. She sat Indian style across from him watching him spread out the food. She pulled the chicken biscuit sandwich, hash browns, and an apple toward her.

"So what's in this thing?" Mason asked, gesturing to trunk between them and took a bite of the sandwich in his hands.

Nora lay a hand on the wooden surface protectively. "Things from my past and what once was my future," she replied. "Or as you like to remind me, pointless souvenirs."

"You don't have anything from the present?"

"Every time at one point is part of my present."

"And all the stuff you carry around, it's important to you," he guessed, taking a hash brown.

She nodded, holding the cup of hot chocolate in her hands. "The other two time guards wouldn't agree, though. I keep it to remember things that should never be forgotten."

"Like a photo album."

"Kind of. This is a little more personal."

Mason tried to look uninterested. He focused on the food in front of him. Nora's vague answers were her way of avoiding the details. She wasn't eager to share with him the contents of her trunk yet. All the things inside were items she collected to represent her different lives with Mason, relics that dated over one thousand years. It mattered to her to keep bits and pieces of previous lives in case she needed to remember who she had once been, who she needed to be for Mason. It was more of a diary than a trunk full of keepsakes.

Nora finished eating first. She got to her feet and tossed another log into the fire. Amid the flames, she saw the reflection of another time. Long ago she sat by a fire like the one in front of her, except she was in the kitchen of a cottage. A boy had handed her a sketch pad; inside was an image he had captured earlier that day.

She blinked. One piece of the trunk was with her. Nora went back to get it ever since Mason began to show a romantic interest in her. It kept her from doing anything too foolish. She got to her feet, grabbed her bag, then went to sit in front of him.

"What's that?" Mason asked, watching her pull out a flat parcel.

She handed it to him. He eyed her for a second before taking it. Nora watched him carefully slide the parchment paper out of its envelope. The corners were yellowing with age, and the sides were tattered. The dark lines were sharp, but the once vibrant colors were fading and smearing together.

The present time marker and his time guard sat on the branches of an oak tree on a late summer evening. They sat on separate branches talking. He wore his father's dirty linen shirt, rolling the sleeves to his elbows, and his breeches bore gray patches. His blond curls hid under the shade of the leaves. The girl opposite him sat an arm around the trunk while her other hand played with the strings of her apron on her lap. Her brown hair was pulled back away from her face. The sun behind them was dipping into the horizon. To date, it was the only lifetime Mason ever climbed trees with her for pure sport.

"When was this?" he asked.

"Portugal, 1504," Nora told him. "I was your family's nursemaid when your mother got ill. After she passed away, it all went straight to hell. You suffered a lot at your father's side. He was less than kind on most occasions, and his heavy hand was the best way to keep you in line." She touched her own cheek, remembering how her skin tingled the night Mason's father struck her too.

Mason looked up at her in shock. "He hit you?"

"Once. He was a very cruel man; he wasn't ever remorseful for treating you the way he did. You were so unhappy. It was one of your roughest lives."

He looked down at the photograph again. "I'd never be able to tell from this picture."

She leaned in to get a glimpse of the pair sitting on the tree. "One night you had enough and decided to run. You took me with you. We crossed over to Morocco. You built a good life for yourself there."

Mason relaxed, studied it a moment longer. "Did we stay together?"

"We ended up leading different lives, I was never far, though. I think you had enough of me for one lifetime."

"I don't think so," he chuckled. "I think he loved you."

Nora shrugged, not wanting to give too much away.

"That doesn't mean there wasn't anything there," Mason said, not taking his eyes off the photograph. "And her, the girl in the picture, she knew it too."

The tablet in her bag blinked on flooding new light into the living room. Relieved at the distraction, Nora fished it out swiping in the password as she pulled it toward her. An outline of the property quickly etched itself onto the screen. Two blinking dots were approaching the boardinghouse.

"Two heat signatures, and they're coming in fast," Nora muttered. "Coming in from the west." She scrambled to her feet and ran to the nearest window. She parted the blinds just as the car turned onto the driveway.

Mason followed. "Time travelers?"

She elbowed him hard away from the window. "Possibly. Stay here," Nora replied as she raised the hood of her sweatshirt.

Nora bolted out the door. In a matter of seconds, she found herself drenched in rain. The storm was coming down hard. A harsh spray poured down on her, blurring her vision. She wiped the rain from her eyes and headed to the driveway to meet the vehicle.

Immediately, she knew something was wrong. The driver was struggling to keep the car straight. The headlights swerved left and right. No time traveler in their right mind would risk a full frontal assault. Someone else was arriving. And whoever was behind the wheel was injured. As the blue pickup truck came closer, she saw how damaged it was: a crack split the windshield into thirds, a missing rearview mirror, and a scorched hood. Heart racing, Nora realized who had arrived.

She waved them to the back of the boardinghouse. The truck rushed by, and she followed. It came to a stop behind Mason's car. The driver's door was kicked open letting a man collapse to the ground as he clutched his side. He attempted to get to his feet, but he grunted and stumbled back into the mud. She ran over just as the passenger climbed over the driver's seat to them. Mason hurried over too.

"Hogan!" Nora shouted over the rain. She dropped to his side. He was covered in blood, there was a bullet wound right below his ribs. "Why aren't you healing? Hogan!"

The time marker hopped down helping Nora raise Hogan. "He got shot passing Idaho a couple hours ago," he explained quickly. "But the bullet never came out. It's lodged somewhere in his body. He's been keeping his wound from closing so you can get it out."

"Find towels and grab the gallon of water inside the crate," Nora told Mason, draping Hogan's arm around her shoulders to heave him up.

"First aid kit," Hogan rasped at his time marker. "In the truck. Find it."

"Meet us inside," she added.

He nodded.

Nora half dragged Hogan into the boardinghouse. She tried to move fast without hurting him. She steered him in the direction of the closest couch. Hogan eased onto the cushions wincing. Nora knelt next to him, ripped the rest of his shirt open, and with the scraps tried to clean the wound. He sucked in his breath, trying to withstand the pain.

"Shit," he gasped.

She moved his wet blond hair away from his forehead. "You'll be fine soon," she promised. "I'll get started as soon as the boys get back. I need them to hold you down while I get the bullet."

"Were we followed?"

"I don't think so," Nora answered. "Don't move."

He grimaced. "What's taking them? I can feel myself healing."

Mason got to them first handing her the towels, then set down the water. Nora splashed some on her hands when Hogan's time marker approached with the kit. She rifled through it taking the peroxide, bandages, and gauze. With the peroxide, Nora poured it around the wound to clear away the blood. She saw him healing rapidly. The skin around the wound was regenerating and closing; his insides were pooling with fresh blood.

"Hurry up!" Hogan hissed with gritted teeth.

"I'm not going to lie," she warned, rolling up her sleeves. "This is going to hurt, a lot."

"I can take it. Just do it."

Nora threw him a towel for him to use as a mouth guard. "Hold him down."

The two time markers stood on either side of Hogan one holding down his legs while the other gripped his arms. He nodded at her to go on. She took a deep breath and plunged her hand into his abdomen. His whole body arched in pain. Her fingers felt the warm, wet surface of digestive organs, the courser texture of his muscles, and the slippery substance that was surely blood in between her fingers. Nora swallowed her disgust, Hogan needed her to be all in.

Her hand searched gingerly trying not to damage his organs. Any wrong move could cause him to bleed out. She found his liver first. Hogan thrashed, doing all he could to push her arm away. Her hand still in him slipped knocking into his rib cage. With her free hand, Nora gripped his shoulder and continued to search for the bullet.

"We won't be able to keep him down long!" Mason said over Hogan's groans.

She stroked his liver with her thumb to double-check. No bullet.

"Give me twenty seconds," she told them.

Next she felt his stomach feeling for anything out of the ordinary. Hogan didn't appreciate that gesture either. He twisted, but stayed put letting her probe him further. Nora let it be and moved on.

Her fingers landed on his colon. Nora winced when she automatically felt the rough puncture wound. The bullet was lodged inside. She pinched it in between her fingers and removed it. Hogan groaned into the rag. It sounded like a mixture of relief and pain. Nora held him down a little harder.

She looked Hogan in the eye. "I'll make this quick."

He nodded.

Nora wrenched her hand out of his innards in one quick movement. Hogan spit out the rag and cursed. His words bounced off the ceiling. The bullet glistened in her bloody palm. Mason and the other time marker let Hogan go. She set it on one of the towels before cleaning his wound one more time. His skin closed itself meaning he was healing within as well.

The four of them were out of breath.

"That was murder," Hogan panted, readjusting on the couch.

"You look like death," Nora agreed as she wiped her bloody hand clean. "Stay put for a few hours."

He checked his stomach under the towel, then up at her. "Does it look like I'm going anywhere?" he teased. His marvelous brown eyes were like warm maple syrup, just as she remembered.

"No, I suppose not," she said with a smile.

Hogan looked up to the time marker who came stand next to him. They shared a smile, they were safe. "Nora, this is Charlie—"

"The future time marker," she finished, reaching up to shake his hand.

Charlie took hers.

A serious jolt shot up her arm. The sudden rush told Nora her suspicions were right. The lanky man with coppery brown hair and light brown eyes was the soul she cared for when she was too late in finding Mason. She had known it when he caught her eye in the flurry of his arrival. His eyes met hers in the rain when the truck sped past her. Charlie had the familiar spark that called out to her, the bit of his soul burning like a flare for her to find.

"I'd know your soul anywhere," Nora told him.

Chapter 12
Where the Future Lies

Charlie and Mason claimed two bedrooms in the east wing for the night after they helped Nora haul in the suitcases from the pickup truck and burn the bloody towels. Although Hogan opposed, Nora firmly kept him stationed on the couch. She didn't see him fit to move yet. She would stay the night on the opposite couch. The flames in the fireplace were dwindling as Nora lit a candle. She strolled over to Hogan, and draped the extra blanket over him, yawning into her blood stained sleeve.

Hogan flinched when the blanket hit his shoulders. His gaze left the arches on the ceiling to look in Nora's direction. A dark shadow crossed his brown eyes. She knew that look. He was lost in deep thought.

"Sorry," she apologized, sitting next to him to fold her hands on her lap. "I didn't mean to distract you. You okay?"

"Angeline isn't here yet."

"Haven't you spoken to her?"

He shifted in his spot trying to sit. "Very little. I rushed here hoping to find her. I'm worried, Nora. She agreed to be here by now."

"Easy," she warned. "You aren't completely healed yet." Nora rested a hand on his shoulder. "She's probably on her way now. Give it till morning."

Hogan let out a breath of defeat, then sank back into the couch. "Yeah, okay."

She got to her feet to let him rest. Nora took the candle into the bathroom to swap clothes. She threw the blood stained clothes in a pile to hand wash them first thing in the morning. She was too tired to do it now. When she returned to the living room, Nora noted Hogan was still awake. Every couple minutes he tossed and turned in place. The weight of Angeline's impending arrival would keep him up all night. Wordlessly, she strode over to the couch, blew out the candle, and lay down to stare up at the ceiling until her eyelids became too heavy to keep open.

Despite the revolving problems, Nora slept at ease. With Hogan's arrival she felt secure. Two time guards were better than one. He was also a skilled warrior and an even deadlier strategist. Out of the three time guards, he was classified as the most dangerous. Most time travelers knew of his ruthless nature when it came to protecting his time marker. The risks he took were to keep them all alive longer.

"Nora?"

She stirred awake to find Hogan struggling to sit up right. The blanket she had draped over him the previous night pooled onto the floor. He squeezed his eyes shut in pain. Nora jumped to her feet to help him.

"Does it still hurt?" she asked.

Hogan eased up slowly. "It's manageable," he replied, clutching his side. "Check my phone. It should be in that red backpack over there." He nodded to the cluster of bags on the floor.

Nora went in search for it. She rifled through his things. Much of his belongings closely resembled her own backpack: extra burner phones, a stack of phony passports, cash, water, light snacks, matches, and a change of clothes. Charlie and Mason walked into the living room when she spotted Hogan's phone jutting out of a side pocket.

Her heart sank as she stared at the screen. It was passed noon, and Angeline hadn't arrived. There wasn't even a missed call or a message.

"Well?" Hogan asked.

"Nothing," she replied, shoving it back in its pocket.

Hogan made an effort to stand. "I need to find her."

Charlie rested a hand on his shoulder to keep him from rising. "You can't go anywhere," he harped. "Look at you."

Mason ran a hand through his hair and leaned on the couch closest to Nora. "Sorry, but who are we talking about?" he asked.

"Angeline, she's the third time guard," she answered.

Hogan shook Charlie off roughly and struggled to his feet regardless. He looked over to the back door wishing it would open, that it would be Angeline walking through it. Nora knew what she meant to Hogan. Angeline was his girl. Nora could never form the right words to describe their unique relationship. There wasn't a point in time they became something more, they just were. It made sense somehow, even though Nora didn't understand why. Hogan and Angeline found a way to make it seem so natural, like time and space didn't matter.

"She could be in danger," Hogan said, locking eyes with Nora. His eyes were heavy with worry. Nothing hurt him more than not knowing where Angeline was. "It's not like her to keep me waiting."

"I'll find her."

Mason shifted in his spot to discreetly throw her a look of disagreement, but she ignored him. Angeline and her time marker were out there. Both could be injured, or even worse dead. They needed to be found and brought in.

"Besides you won't be of any use to her in the condition you're in," Nora went on. "If things get shaky here I can count on you to run. Take Charlie and Mason as far away as possible."

Hogan thought about it for a long moment. It visibly crippled him to have Nora tell him to stay. He wanted to be the one out there looking for Angeline. "I'll need a new set of wheels," he said at last. "Can't cruise out of here in a car with bullet holes without being noticed."

Nora nodded in agreement. "Leave that to me. I can dump it and get you a new one. Easy."

He tossed her the keys to the truck parked outside. "Don't get me a crap car."

She caught them and grabbed her bag from the floor. "You," she pointed to Charlie who stood behind Hogan. "You're coming with me."

After Hogan gave him the okay, Charlie followed Nora to the back door. They waved and walked out into the cool day. It took two tries to get the banged up truck to start. It rumbled in protest, but it halfheartedly sprang to life. Nora reversed and lurched the miserable thing in a circle back to the driveway.

"Did Hogan ever tell you about me?" Nora asked, easing onto the interstate. "I mean, you must've known about Angeline all this time."

Charlie half shrugged. "Only bits and pieces. He didn't want to give away too much."

"That sure as hell doesn't sound like Hogan."

The only rule Hogan broke was opening his fat mouth as soon as he found a time marker. Unlike Nora, he didn't believe in stealth. He refused to watch from a distance and keep the time markers in the dark. He made it clear from the get go what his purpose was and the delicate nature of his existence.

"I suppose not," Charlie chuckled. "There was a lot of time to kill on our way here."

"Australia?"

"New Zealand."

"You always were an island hopper," Nora said, ignoring the car in the next lane. The woman in the yellow car eyed the truck in mistrust. She stepped on the gas and out stepped the car with ease. "You and I were family once in Saint Lucia, long before it was a colony to the French."

"Siblings?" he guessed.

She nodded. "Half. You were older by six years."

The sign to Santa Luz appeared fast. In ten miles they would reach the industrial city nestled amid the hilly Oregon landscape. It was the place Nora lived in for two years before barreling into Mason's life in Torch Crossings. Although the town housed many factories, it also served as a home to former convicts and felons. She shifted lanes anticipating the exit.

Santa Luz was the only place she could take in a beat up truck with minimal questions. The torn down town would pay no attention to her when it had a connection to the bustling crime circuit. Nora infiltrated it years ago to get items she couldn't pick up at the local hardware store. She knew someone on the inside who could help her get rid of Hogan's truck.

She weaved her way through the town only making a stop for some coffee at a 7-Eleven. They ended up in a neighborhood across Santa Luz where a majority of the low level punks lived in, those that grew up into the trade or settled in the bleak borough when no one else would have them. The broken houses looked dark and soulless. Some of the houses had shingles, siding, or both missing. Others had entire windows blown out. If it wasn't for the occasional movement of curtains, Nora would have guessed that all the houses were unoccupied.

Nora turned into a dead end street. She drove slow as though she were afraid to scare away the remaining life still there. In the distance, a train's whistle blew into the cold early afternoon.

"Sketchy area, isn't it?" Charlie asked as she came to a stop in front of a two-story yellow house. "What are we doing here?"

"Negotiating," she said, looking toward the door.

The porch light flickered on.

Nora cut the engine, then hopped out of the car. A man in his late twenties shuffled down the driveway. His hands were shoved deep in his pockets. His blue-gray eyes sparked in recognition as he neared. He looked over at the truck suspiciously.

"You in some sort of trouble?" Lenny asked, jutting out his chin to the distance before returning to study the truck.

"No, but I do need your help," she replied.

"What d'ya need?"

She waved Charlie out of the car. "I need this gone. All of it. No traces found."

"The most I can get you is fifteen hundred," Lenny said.

"Five grand," she retaliated.

He raised an eye brow. "Two."

"Five."

"You're kidding me?" Lenny laughed in disbelief. With his hands behind his back, he circled the car once inspecting all the damage. "There's no way anyone would buy this from you at such a high price."

"Then take it apart and sell the pieces," Nora pressed on. "Sell every scrap of it."

Lenny circled it two more times. His eyes darted from one bullet hole to the next, then to Nora. He looked like he wanted to ask her a million questions, but he never did. Instead, his lips moved as he did calculations in his head. On his third round of the inspection, he asked her to take a look under the hood, to which she complied.

"I don't got all day, Len," she said impatiently. "Can you get it off my hands or not?"

He let the hood drop with a slight thump. "Three. That's the most I can get you."

"Done. Can you get me the money today?"

"Almost all of it, yeah."

Nora shook her head. "I need it all now."

He gave her a side ways glance crossings his arms. Nora was asking for a lot, and she could tell he was doing his best not to pry. "What did you do?" Lenny asked. The slight concern in his voice almost made Nora regret asking for his help.

"It isn't me," she replied. "It's for a friend who's just passing through."

Lenny gave her a hard stare like he hoped she was telling the truth. "Wait here." He shuffled back up the driveway and disappeared into the house. As the door closed behind him, Nora grabbed her lock opener from her bag. She crouched down to fiddle with the screws on the license plate.

"How exactly do you know this guy?" Charlie asked, watching the door to the house.

"I used to run with a tough crowd before Mason and I met," she told him. The plate clattered to the ground. She moved over to the plate in the rear. Charlie followed. "It was mostly runaways and homeless kids down by this park. Lenny looked out for the younger kids, kept them warm, fed, and out of trouble. A lot of those kids wouldn't have survived without him."

"Including you? You're trained to survive anything."

"For a time I let him. I was under cover, laying low."

Lenny walked out of the house holding a thick white envelope. He handed it to Nora. She didn't bother checking if all the money was there, he wouldn't give her a penny more or less than what she asked for. "I know a guy out by the junk yard who sells old clunkers," he said.

"We'll need a lift," Nora said.

He dropped off Charlie and Nora at the junk yard ten minutes later. They wandered in looking for the keeper. He showed them the small selection of vehicles parked behind the heaping piles of trash. The purchase was quick. Charlie picked out an overpriced, horrendous, outdated, blue-and-white two-door pickup. It easily had to be fifty years old or older. Hogan wasn't going to be pleased. He liked newer models, but everything else was utter garbage.

On their way back to the boardinghouse, they stopped at a gas station to fill up the truck's tank and another round of coffee along with breakfast. She handed Charlie the food, then hopped in.

"I hope you still like your coffee half and half," Nora said, starting the engine, then pulled out of the parking lot.

"Yeah, how'd you know?" Charlie asked, sounding impressed.

"Because you told me. Well, not you *you*, but another version of you. I was on my way to Mason. I bumped into you in a coffee shop outside D.C."

"So you found me first?"

Nora drummed her fingers on the wheel. "I wouldn't say that," she replied, slowing down as they caught up to the steady flock of traffic. "We exchanged a few words, and I recognized you. I didn't leave right away, even though I should have. I stayed to make sure you were in the care of a time guard. You met up with Hogan later that day, so I jumped on the next flight to Europe."

Charlie fiddled with the radio as the car came to a standstill. "When you talk about it I feel it, like some part of me wants to remember."

She understood the meaning behind his words. Mason expressed the same feeling to her countless times. He was always excited to learn who he was; it was something he waited to hear all his life. He hated not remembering, but he grew weary of it as time passed. Nora knew Charlie went through the same experience. It was the only thing that marked them as equals. Because of their nature, they couldn't trespass into a realm that didn't belong to them. The past was out of their reach.

The traffic inched forward. "It doesn't make it any less real," Nora said, following the sign that pointed in the direction of Lys Gate.

To pass the time, Charlie told her about their rough journey to America. Time travelers seemed to have been one step ahead, beating them to certain locations before they got there. By the time they got to Mexico, Hogan was desperate. He sent Charlie off without him and caught up in Torch Crossings by time warp the night they arrived to the boardinghouse. It was a miracle they made it to her in one piece. She shifted lanes noticing the upcoming exit was the one she was looking for. She stole a glance at Charlie, wondering why he had gone quiet midsentence.

He was staring out the windshield. His eyes were clouded over, fixed on something in the distance. Charlie's posture was unnaturally stiff. It was the same way Mason looked when he was time reading. Panic washed over her, and she slammed on the brakes.

"Charlie!"

The cars behind them honked their horns angrily and went around.

"Charlie, you okay?" she asked, grabbing his arm.

He snapped out of it the instant he felt her touch. He blinked and sucked in a breath of air. Whatever it was, the moment passed. He was back with her.

"Drive. I'm fine," Charlie urged. "Come on. Go."

She continued to drive, but periodically looked over to Charlie to make sure he was okay. "What was that? I thought I was losing you to something for a minute there."

Charlie shook his head, readjusting in his seat. "I was having a vision."

Nora held her breath in interest. She heard of his ability to see glimpses of the future, but never witnessed the time marker receive a vision. He never manifested any psychic sight while she guarded him. She didn't exactly know the terms of his condition, like how accurate the images were or what to do with the information. Hogan took the information as it came. From what she understood, Charlie's sight foretold many years ahead—nothing too immediate.

"What'd you see?"

He closed his eyes trying to recall the images he had seen. "I saw you," he said slowly. "You're at an airport terminal. Flight 0106, heading to San Francisco."

"Can you see a date? Place of departure?"

Charlie opened his eyes. "No, sorry."

These fragments of information meant nothing to Nora. She had no intention of flying while on the run. Thousands of feet suspended above sea level and no way out was just an invitation for time travelers to cause a terrible accident. They would be helpless up in the air. Nora would never risk it. She wondered what force would eventually drive her to set foot on a plane.

Chapter 13
Two Lost Souls

The boardinghouse was no different from the moment they left. There was no new car parked behind Mason's. Even with the delay to run a quick patrol of Lys Gate, Angeline failed to arrive. As soon as Nora stepped through the door, she felt the tense atmosphere Hogan created with his limping pace back and forth across the living room floor. Mason slumped in an arm chair looking exasperated. He jumped to his feet when they barreled through the door.

Nora tossed Hogan the keys to the truck. "You can't be on your feet yet. Why is he up?" she demanded, looking to the both of them for answers.

"Does it look like I could have kept him down?" Mason asked, then gestured to Hogan, who had hobbled over to the window. Charlie dashed after him to help him back to the couch. "He's been going nuts."

Hogan sank into his seat roughly. He reached for his phone checking for a message. When he saw there was still no reply, he threw it on the floor. It skidded away knocking into Nora's shoe.

She bent down to pick it up. "You need to calm down," Nora told him. "You won't heal properly if you don't keep still."

"She's out there, Nora—"

"We have to believe she's okay," Nora told him. "Angeline can take care of herself. I'll head straight out that door once I know you can stay put, but you gotta trust her."

He glared at her hard. His light brown eyes held so much frustration. Nora knew he wasn't angry at her. Hogan was furious that he was vulnerable and powerless to go find the girl he loved. Instead of talking him down, Nora decided to let him be. She'd give him space to relax and settle before taking off.

She gave Charlie the okay to make a quick run to the store to bring extra essentials for the day.

"Fifteen minutes. No more, no less," Nora said to Charlie leading him to the door.

"Or you come get me," Charlie finished with a chuckle. "Yeah, I know the drill."

After she saw him turn out of the driveway, Nora gathered her bloody clothes from last night and decided to get them washed. She was willing to bet she wouldn't have a chance to clean up or replace the garments later. They could pick up and go at any moment when she returned. Nora also couldn't go around leaving clothes behind either. She already had so little to carry.

She borrowed a few supplies from Hogan's pack. He was more prepared for a bloody clean up than she was. He had bottles of different solutions specifically manufactured to wipe away all traces of a brutal fight. She took a flask labeled blood stain remover and headed outside to scrub the clothes on the stone basin.

The smell of the yellow brew was pungent. She recoiled from the awful smell. Her eyes watered, and the stench burned her nose. Nora sucked in a breath, then poured it over the clothes. Halfway through the cleanse, Mason stepped out of the boardinghouse. He sat on the old picnic table, holding a coffee.

Nora could feel his side way glances drilling into the back of her head. She ignored him for an entire minute. She knew why he was here; she wasn't off the hook for volunteering to leave. His displeasure radiated like heat.

He broke the silence first.

"Is this safe? You leaving," Mason said at last.

Nora stopped scrubbing her sweater to look at him over her shoulder, then turned on the hose to rinse the blood off the fabric. Cold water sloshed in the basin as she moved the sweater around. It looked better, the color popping out rather than the crimson red of Hogan's blood.

She opened the flask once more, poured it over the jeans, and kept washing. "It's not," Nora admitted. "But we can't leave them out there. Angeline would do the same thing for us if the roles were reversed."

"And you have to be the one to go?"

"Hogan's been dodging anachronisms left and right for days. Look at him, he's in no condition to be out looking for anyone. It has to be me."

From behind Mason hopped off the table. "Come on, Nora. You don't have to go. If she's as capable as you say, Angeline will find her way here."

"What is with you?" Nora snapped, whipping around just in time to see him approach. "I'm going, Mason. Don't argue with me because this isn't up for debate."

"Why can't it be?" Mason challenged. A flash of defiance crossed his dark eyes. "You want to run off straight into the heart of danger and I don't have a say? What if I don't want you to go?"

"What *you* want? What about what needs to be done?" she asked in disbelief. The water swirled down the drain. She snatched the damp clothes to hang them on the clothes line she hung up earlier near the fireplace inside. "How can you be so selfish? They're risking their lives coming here to meet us!"

Mason followed and grabbed her by the elbow. "Me, selfish?" he practically shouted.

Still in his grasp, she shouldered him away from the door. "Will you be quiet?" Nora hissed. Hogan was still inside. She didn't want him to hear that she and Mason were fighting. "Yes, you! Don't you get it? It's not just you and me anymore. We're a part of something with Charlie and the others. You out of all people should know what it means to be a part of a team."

"That's not what this is about," Mason growled in outrage. He tried to keep his voice down, but it wouldn't last long. He was angry, more than Nora had ever seen him before. "In a blink of an eye, you can be hundreds of miles away without any backup. And that isn't suppose to worry me?" He shook her arm roughly. "You matter to me. Everything we've been through matters. How can you keep insisting there's something more important than you and me?"

"Because there is!"

"Forget about that right now," he said at once. "Forget about the others—"

"Don't," she muttered, her voice faltering. "Don't ask me to do that. I—I can't be selfish right now."

Mason softened, his grip loosening. "Sometimes I think I love you more than you love me."

Her hand flew across his face, delivering an all too harsh slap.

Abruptly, Nora withdrew her tingling hand in fear. Her eyes widened in shock at what she had done. It wasn't her intention to slap him, but Mason brought out the worst in her. The more he pushed the topic, the harsher she had to be.

Mason shoved past her to storm into the boardinghouse.

A car door slammed causing Nora to jump. She blinked to retract the tears that threatened to fall. Charlie stood by the truck door with a look of plain curiosity. He was trying to piece together what happened seconds ago.

Nora pulled at her sleeve wondering if he overheard Mason.

"Everything cool?" Charlie asked, nodding over to the spot Mason disappeared beyond the door. He eyed her suspiciously. "You landed a pretty good wallop on him."

Her shoulders relaxed. He didn't manage to hear a thing. By now Hogan must have taught him the three most important rules of a time guard. Would he have ratted her out to Hogan if he discovered what she and Mason were arguing about?

"We've been fighting lately," she replied, fiddling with the damp clothes on her arm.

His expression changed to confusion as he neared. "Mason's been causing you trouble?"

"Nothing I can't handle."

"He'll come around," Charlie said thoughtfully. "I just met him, but he doesn't seem like the kind of guy to hold a grudge, especially against you." He wasn't in the receiving end of Mason's cold shoulder. "You two seem close."

"More or less."

Charlie nodded to the door, lugging the bag of food. "See," he said with a slight smile. "No worries, then."

As they entered the boardinghouse, a door slammed shut upstairs. It was followed by a muffled thud. Nora flinched. Charlie noticed her discomfort and nudged her in the direction of the fireplace. He led the way, offering another encouraging smile. She hung her clothes while he went on telling her stories about his childhood—in particular, a week stay in a small dusty Texas town. His lame attempt at a southern drawl almost cheered her up.

He was distracting her, and she appreciated him for it. Time had a funny way of putting the future time marker in her path. Under the pressure of her never-ending job, other versions of Charlie renewed confidence and clarity to her purpose in the universe. His open, transparent disposition made Nora seek him out at least once every lifetime. Every encounter he offered her words of encouragement she didn't know she needed to hear.

"Finally," Hogan called from his impatient perch on the couch when he saw Nora begin to shift her things around to free up a backpack.

Charlie and Hogan watched her cram in all the necessities. She decided to carry light: a flashlight, a small blanket, matches, a few rolls of money, a fake passport, and a thermos with a plastic baggie of multivitamins courtesy of her briefcase instructed for extreme circumstances. She shoved an extra set of clothes inside as well.

"When was the last time you spoke to Angeline?" she asked, clasping her bag to a close, then straightened.

"Two days ago."

"Do you know her location?"

Hogan shrugged.

"Am I really supposed to believe you haven't traced her last call?" Nora asked, raising an eyebrow. "I need some sort of lead if you want me to find her by sun down."

Hogan flushed in embarrassment. "She was somewhere in Quebec."

Canada. That was odd, since she usually veered away from cold places. "That's some heavy distance away," she replied, handing Hogan the tablet. "Everything you need to know is on this. Follow basic protocol until I get back. Don't bother sticking around if trouble comes your way."

He got to his feet. "Bring her back to me."

Nora nodded, slung the bag over her shoulder, and walked to the back door. She hesitated at the bottom of the stairs stopping only to stare at the second floor. She couldn't sort out her thoughts with Mason around to cause another whirlwind in her head when he came running after her to apologize. The vicious cycle was the cause of all her problems.

The door shut behind her as she stepped out. The afternoon sun was obscured behind a cloud, and the breeze picked up. Nora started toward the water tower. She wanted to be a safe distance before disappearing.

Along the way, Nora touched the black sundial. She felt the gentle tug of the dark chain against the back of her neck as it tried to lead the way. It was pulling her northwest. Nora willed it to open a time warp, trusting it to guide her toward Angeline. It unraveled itself slowly. The unnatural vacant darkness beckoned. Nora stepped inside, leaving Lys Gate in her wake.

Chapter 14
The Diner in the Middle of Nowhere

The time warp wove to a close behind Nora, her feet adjusting to the lack of gravity. She soared into the nothingness as though she sprouted wings on her way in. Her aura of light stretched beyond her reach, then pulled back around her. Nora squinted into the darkness searching for a moment in time that could lead her to Angeline. The dark barrier held thousands of images. Every fleeting moment captured blinked in and out of the time warp replaced by a fresh updated version.

Nora didn't want to linger too long in the time warp. It was primarily the last line of defense time offered, which meant that any time traveler trapped in there could find her. Being in there was like yelling, "Olly olly oxen free," into open time.

A flash of light caught her attention.

"Oh no," she muttered, her heart sinking.

She whirled around to see a pair of silvery lights pulsing against the dark. The lights came in weak; it needed one more jolt of energy to shine at full capacity. She recognized what those lights meant. It was Charlie and Mason's souls burning through the dark shield. It was a dead giveaway to their location.

It was no use in dwelling on the matter. She and Hogan knew this was the risk of gathering. Their souls would only burn brighter once the past time marker joined them. Nora took comfort in the fact that time travelers didn't have the skills to look for their souls. But that could all change if the time markers together shined past the darkness. She hoped that wasn't the case.

Nora turned away and looked down at her sundial. It jittered left and right scoping out the unfamiliar place. It was there and nowhere all at the same time. She tried to follow its guidance, but once it swerved backward with such a force Nora threw herself around to keep up. The sundial came to a quivering stop. She looked up and caught sight of a two lane road.

The sundial pulsed like a heartbeat tugging her forward. The image reacted; it zoomed in to the abandoned street. Nora willed it to stay put as she drew near. Her hand phased through first, and the rest of her followed.

She stumbled out, landing on the side of the road. The cold drop in temperature stung her skin. From a distance, Nora heard the sound of waves crashing into the cliff as well as the occasional call of seagulls. The salty sea air tickled her nose. She was standing in the middle of a coastal highway. She was so close to the water that the crashing waves sent a cold spray over her head.

Suddenly, the phone she carried in her pocket exploded with new messages. Nora scrolled through the incoming texts from Hogan and Mason. When the messages came to a stop, a little red x appeared over the signal bar. No signal. She was too far out of the service area to respond back.

Beside the signal bar, the digital clock on her phone read it to be four in the morning. *Damn*, she thought. Nora wasted too much time traveling. She looked around. There wasn't much of anything except the meandering road and ocean for miles. Her time key was never wrong. Angeline couldn't be far.

She rechecked her sundial. It was still pointing northwest, then it settled on her chest again. Nora decided to continue on foot.

After a mile or so, Nora felt discouraged. There were no signs of life. She could count on one hand how many cars passed her in the last fifteen minutes. Four, only four. There wasn't even a sign declaring a nearby town. She stopped walking to look at the sky, anticipating a sunrise, but the forecast was gray and dull. Rolling clouds lined the horizon as a thick sheet of fog clung to the ground. She squinted wondering still where she landed.

She found a soft glow coming weakly behind the haze. The light looked to be floating and stationary. A spark of hope granted her energy to keep going. It had to be a gas station or a rest stop. She would gather her bearings, find her location, and decide on what to do next.

Two miles later the glow turned to a beacon of light, then to a streetlight outside a diner. A fainter neon purple sign hung over a restaurant called Three Star Dine In. It was decorated with a moon like orb and twinkling lights meaning to portray the stars. Pickups and semitrucks lined the side of the highway, almost blocking the building from view.

Nora dashed over in relief. She crossed the road, darted through the maze of vehicles, and climbed up the wooden stairs to the diner. Inside the diner smelled of burnt toast, coffee, and cigarettes. She shook the water out of her hair like a mutt after a heavy storm, then walked to an open seat.

As she weaved through the tables, Nora looked around at the array of characters settled in for an early morning breakfast. They sat grumbling to one another, sipping coffee from chipped mugs and scarfing down their hearty meals. The drivers stole glances at her, but said nothing. By the way they looked at her, hitch hikers were a common occurrence in these parts. She made a note to lay low and found an old torn booth near a window.

The only other woman in the joint, a middle aged waitress, hovered over to hand her a menu. "Hi, there. Coffee?" she greeted with an easy smile.

"Please."

"Anything else I can get you right away?"

"No, that'll be all."

She nodded and made her round to the other tables.

Nora watched the woman go before she pretended to contemplate the menu. She peered at the laminated card, her eyes fell on the address: Port Union, Alaska a small fishing town miles away from the Aleutian Islands. That explained the salty air and the abrupt change in temperature.

The waitress returned with a coffee only to leave again and give her time to order.

A persistent shake near her thigh caused Nora to jump. The useless phone in her pocket shook until she fished it out. The cell phone's reception returned. It was an incoming call from Mason. Nora ignored the call sending him straight to voicemail. Seconds later he sent a string of angry text messages. Annoyed, she finally sent him a reply.

Quit calling me. I'm fine. Tell Hogan I've landed and still looking.

He responded at once, but she set her phone on silent. She would not be answering anymore messages.

"Excuse me, do you do take out?"

Nora looked up. Something about the voice caught her attention. She didn't have to search hard to match the voice to the speaker. A young man hovered over by the podium beside the cash register. His back was turned to her so all Nora saw was a black mop of hair and broad shoulders. The answer must have been a yes because he shifted and fumbled for his wallet as he placed an order.

"Are you ready to order, dear?" The waitress had returned. Her pen was poised over a note pad.

Nora's eyes flickered to her, then back to the man. She didn't want to lose sight of the new customer. Something in her wanted to meet him. He took a seat on the nearest barstool and checked the time on a wristwatch.

"Another coffee," she said in a rush.

She slid to the edge of her booth to get a better look at him. He was built like a lumbar jack: tall, muscular, and tan. His raven black hair was shaggy, clearly he had missed one too many trips to the hair dresser. Nora was too far away to see his whole face. He sat with his head tipped forward, gazing at the countertop in front of him. She squirmed in her seat. She yearned for him to cast a glance in her direction, even if by accident. Nora needed to see his soul shining in his eyes.

It struck her that he was alone. She checked the window for a get away car with a driver, but saw none. He arrived to the diner alone without Angeline. What kind of situation were they in that she let him wander on his own? Something was wrong.

A bag was brought to him. He got to his feet. Nora threw a ten on the table deciding to tail him. She first had to determine if he was a time marker before moving on. He grabbed the bag and scurried out the door. She let him have a ten-second head start, then followed.

Nora trotted after him quietly. She did her best to keep up and remain hidden at the same time. He weaved his way around the disarray of large vehicles. He reached a black car nestled between two semitrucks. He set the bag on the hood to find his keys. She leaped back and crouched behind a tire, afraid he might see her. She peeked around the corner to see he hadn't opened his car door. He wasn't moving.

"I know you're there," he called out to her. "Come out."

She hesitated, straightened, and came out of her hiding spot.

"You've been watching me," he scowled. He advanced, squaring his shoulders to appear intimidating. Nora wasn't phased. "What do you want?"

"I was on my way out," Nora lied.

"Are you a traveler?" he asked sharply. "Did you know I was going to be here?"

"Traveler? What? No," she protested. Now Nora knew she was right, he was the past time marker. His eyes were intense and prying for information. In one quick move, he slammed her to the closest semi, which made her yelp out in surprise. With both hands, he restrained Nora by the wrists and pressed them to the base of her own neck making it difficult to breath.

"Tell me who you are!"

She wiggled from her restraint, but he held her down. When he tried to press down on her esophagus, Nora fought back. She threw him off her, and he hit another semitruck. He grunted, but that didn't stop him.

"No, wait!" Nora shouted. He aimed a left hook, then right, and finally landed a punch to her stomach. He knocked the wind out of her. She doubled over, gasping for breath. Nora heard him coming. She sidestepped him, grabbed his arm, twisted it behind his back, and shoved him against an old beaten truck.

"Stop!" she ordered. He struggled in her grasp, but she kept him still. "I'm a time guard. I'm a friend of Angeline. Don't you remember me? I'm Nora."

The past time marker elbowed her in the ribs to propel her off him. Nora stumbled back, and he whipped out a blade. He slashed it at her, ripping her sleeve. She felt the tip of the metal scratch her wrist. A few dots of blood appeared on her skin.

"The next one will be straight through your throat," he warned. "Or your heart."

Nora raised her hands in surrender, she was willing to be at his mercy to gain his trust.

"How do I know you're not lying to me?" he asked.

"My time key, it's around my neck. It marks me as a time guard." His eyes narrowed trying to decide if she was telling the truth or not. He stepped forward cautiously, moved her hair aside, and pulled the sundial from under her jacket. He studied it in his hand turning it over. It gleamed when it caught the light of the neon sign.

"You could have stolen this."

He made a valid point. Time travelers often stole and created their own time keys. Nora didn't know how but they did. Also nothing in her backpack could reveal her identity. The fake passport held her picture, but another name. She had to make him remember her. Unlike his counterparts, he was able to unlock his past lives. Nora protected him dozens of times all over the globe. Their history wasn't a mystery to him.

"I know Angeline. And Hogan too. They're my friends. *You're* my friend," Nora began. "We always have been. I've met you more times than I can count. We crossed paths during the French and Indian War. You were a naval officer coming from Europe. You turned a blind eye when I told you I was on my way back to Mason, you did it because you remembered me. You knew it was important for me to return to him.

"And I met you once outside Paris when I stopped by to visit Angeline. I was on my way to the Ivory Coast from Denmark. You were her groundskeeper, her friend. You talked us into riding horses."

His eyes flickered, something in him was stirring. "And Angeline fell off her horse."

"Her dress got caught on the saddle," she corrected.

"She was so pissed. She wanted the horse executed—"

"But you gave him to me so I could continue my journey," Nora finished.

Finally, he withdrew his blade. He tucked it back in his belt. Recognition filled his eyes with her words. Nora waited for him to say something else, but he didn't. Instead, he headed back to his car door and fumbled with his keys.

"Are you coming or not?" he asked.

Nora hurried over to the passenger door and waited for him to unlock the car. She scrambled in as he set the breakfast in the back seat. He got in and started the car. It hummed to life, pulled out to the main road, and headed south.

Chapter 15
Found at Last

Nora and the past time marker rode in silence for the next several miles. He lowered his window to let the whistle of the wind sing in their ears. Her hair whipped around her until she pulled it back into place. As they drove, the fog cleared, allowing them to have a better view of the rolling bluffs. The sun broke through the clouds finally able to cross the horizon. Down below the water shimmered in its reflection, sparkling like an endless perfect crystal. Half an hour into the drive, he turned left heading inland to another two lane road. Nora blinked and crossed her ankles in her seat.

"Why isn't Angeline with you?" she asked. "Is she—"

"No, no," he said, checking on her. "She broke her leg two days ago in Thunder Bay. It slowed us down quite a bit. We decided to lay low until she recovered. We would have called in sooner, but our phone got smashed. I'm Wesley, by the way, thanks for coming." He offered her his hand.

She took it in a brisk shake. "And this is as far as you got?"

Wesley nodded. "We left most of our supplies when we ran. You caught me stocking up." He jerked a thumb to the back seat. She turned to see giant totes full of clothes, snacks, disposable phones, and an array of item she collected while on the careful route to safety.

"I still don't like that you were all alone," she said thoughtfully. "It's dangerous for you, especially now."

"Angeline was hesitant too," he agreed. "But we were already wasting too much time. Besides, I know how to be out on my own."

"I'd say," Nora said, remembering his remarkable precision with the dagger. Self-consciously, she touched the torn fabric of her sleeve. He had hundreds of years of training under his belt; he was just as dangerous as any time guard.

Wesley chuckled. "Sorry about your wrist."

She raised it at him. "All healed."

He took her arm to have a proper look at the new smooth layer of skin. "I forget how quickly you time guards heal," Wesley muttered.

The drive continued without a motel in sight. The road only held dirt and tall withering grass. There were no signs or streetlights. Her patience eventually paid off when at last she saw a cul de sac with a few sturdy buildings. She counted three total. The biggest of them all was a low two-story motel heavily covered in graffiti on its back wall. Across was an equally run down gas station with one available functional pump. In the far end of the dead end street was a pathetic convenience store. Less than a dozen cars were parked in the little lot between the gas station and motel. The dusty car they rode in would fit right in.

He slowed and pulled in to the motel parking lot. Nora stepped out of the car to look at the desolate place.

"This way," Wesley said, nodding to a back of the building. He led her alongside the motel avoiding the security cameras. They reached a rusting fire escape ladder. A good portion of the bottom half was missing. The grime and rust threatened to snap the entire thing in two. Nora was surprised it still hung in place.

"Can't go through the front," he explained. "More cameras."

Wesley climbed onto a trash can, grabbed hold of the fire escape, and pulled himself up. It groaned at his weight, but it didn't collapse. Once he was securely aboard, he reached down to Nora and hoisted her up as well.

He pulled her up with ease, then led the way to the second floor. Nora noted how Wesley was tactful and resourceful. She was impressed. She lost hope of teaching Mason any particular set of skills ages ago. He and Charlie were blank slates each time they were reborn; they couldn't retain anything they were taught. Instead, Nora taught him to survive on his own in case time ever took her before he passed on.

They entered the motel through an emergency exit. A bent soda can lodged at the foot of the door to prevent it from closing entirely yet closed off enough to keep the siren from blaring. The hallway was dim; the lights above cast a yellow hue. The rumble of the heater and creeks of the floor board sounded when the door shut behind them. Wesley stopped at room twenty-nine and knocked twice. He waited a complete ten seconds before opening the door.

Nora followed.

The room was almost as badly lit as the hallway. A flood of pale light from the other side of the room revealed two tidy beds and two backpacks resting against a night stand.

"Hey, I'm back," he called out. "I got everything on your list. And I picked up Nora along the way."

"Nora?" she heard Angeline call incredulously from the bathroom. "What on earth are you talking about?"

"Nora," he replied as if it were the most obvious thing in the world. Wesley set the to go bag on the night stand. "Come look."

Angeline waddled out casting shadows on the wall. She looked a mess: the braid over her shoulder was coming undone, a once deep cut on her forehead was in the process of healing, and her delicate neck was bruised purple meaning someone tried to crush her windpipe. Under her baggy jeans Nora noticed the brace Angeline was trying to hide.

She lost her balance at the sight of Nora. Wesley jumped to his feet to catch her, then helped her over to the bed. Nora sat next to Angeline taking her by the forearms. Her warm fingers grasped Nora in return, unable to find the right words.

"What are you doing here?" Angeline asked after she snapped out of her astonishment.

"For you and Wesley, of course," Nora replied, letting her go with a smile. "I couldn't let you and Hogan have all the fun."

Angeline closed her eyes as if she just remembered the man who longed for her hundreds of miles away. "Hogan. He's worried?"

"I'm here, aren't I?"

"Right," she agreed. "I'm ready to leave when you are."

"Hold on," Wesley chimed in. He crossed his arms at Angeline. "You can't go anywhere. You can hardly walk. We won't get far, not like this."

"None sense," Angeline replied, waving him off, then got to her feet again. She peered into the bag of food. "With Nora here to escort, we can keep moving. Have you scouted a truck stop like I asked?"

"I did, but—"

"Good. We'll pack up and go."

Wesley bit his lip down wanting to argue more, then gave a nod in defeat. He finished his breakfast before leaving the room to bring up the items he gathered. Angeline and Nora sat on the bed emptying the bags and dividing the essentials into their backpacks. As they sorted through it all, Angeline told her their journey from the other side of the country, some fishing town in between Canada and Maine where Wesley grew up. They wove through the two countries going as low as Minneapolis and as high as Calgary in hopes for better coverage against time travelers.

"So, tell me, have you had much trouble with any travelers?" Angeline asked, handing Nora a burner phone and charger for her to pack in Wesley's blue backpack.

"Russell found me," Nora told her. "He wanted his time key fixed."

Angeline shoved a flashlight into her bag, her jaw hanging for a second. "And did you?"

"No. I took it from him and sent him home without it."

"Let me take a look at it."

Nora stopped packing to shrug off her own backpack. She rifled through it to pull out the black wristwatch she kept with her at all times. Angeline took it to examine it thoroughly. Her own time key hung around her left wrist in the form of a thin black bracelet with a pendant the size of a quarter. Inscribed in it was a delicate hourglass. The tiny white sand on the inside sparkled marking time. She always wondered how Angeline could tell time on such a small hourglass.

"It's broken," Angeline noted, handing it back to her.

Nora shook her head. "Not exactly. I programmed it to stop opening time warps once he drained it."

"Clever. You want it fixed?"

Nora opened her mouth to tell her no, but a knock at the door stopped her. Wesley came in. "Everything's all set out there. We should go, Hogan's waiting," he said. He shouldered his now heavy backpack.

"We're ready too," Nora said, shouldering her own and jumped to her feet.

"Go on. I'll catch up," Angeline said still sitting on the bed.

Wesley and Nora exited the building the way they came in. They hopped down the fire escape, scoped out the parking lot, and crossed to the idling car. They set their things in the trunk. From a hidden compartment inside, he pulled out a dark zip lock bag with an extra pair of license plates and a screw driver. Nora stood look out as he swapped the plates. He knelt down to unscrew the back plate first.

"Who are you guarding now?" Wesley asked. "Mason?"

"To my misfortune, yeah."

He glanced up at her in an amused smile. "How is he this time around? You two always get along well."

"Different," Nora replied with a shrug. "He's a hell of a hand full."

"We time markers tend to be." He straightened and handed her the screw driver. "I'll go help Angeline down."

She took it from him to finish the job. Wesley half jogged back to the motel sweeping his eyes over the lot one more time as he went. Nora worked fast the plate clattering to the ground. She installed the front plate with ease.

A knot of uneasiness formed at the pit of Nora's stomach. She knew from here on out would be dangerous journey home. With Angeline injured, Nora would have to carry the weight of protecting her and Wesley. She hoped to arrive at the boardinghouse sometime before dusk tomorrow—that is, if it all went well.

Wesley returned a second later with Angeline in his arms.

Even in the total distress they found themselves in, Angeline managed to clean herself up. Her long honey-blond hair was tied into a perfect waterfall braid, clearing her neatly touched-up face. Hey eyes were like sapphires, blue, sharp, and intense. The brace on her leg was gone and a scarf was wrapped loosely around her neck.

"So which way are we going now?" Nora asked as Wesley set Angeline down. "Time travelers will be prowling border checkpoints and the larger highways."

Angeline limped over to lean on the passenger side door. "I know," she replied. "I have a strategy in play. We've been using alternative methods of transportation, less conspicuous."

"Boat, train, bus, car," Wesley cut in.

"So what's next?" Nora asked.

"Hitch hiking."

Chapter 16
All In

Angeline, Nora, and Wesley scattered on foot at the rest stop beside the interstate highway. They went about their separate ways looking for the perfect lift to the U.S.-Canada border. The plan was to get to Vancouver hidden in a cargo truck. From there, the three of them would cross the border by boat, sailing all the way to Seattle, then they'd find an extra set of wheels to get to Salem, and lastly they planned to cross the Oregon mountains on foot until they reached the boardinghouse.

The rest stop was a never ending loop of incoming and outgoing truck drivers. Many lined up at gas stations to fill their tanks and bum a cigarette before continuing on the road. Others pulled aside to the designated rest area where the drivers disappeared into the cabins to catch up on the sleep they had been putting off. Only a select few truckers flocked to the restaurants to eat a quick meal.

Nora hovered just outside a gas station to have a look around. She sat on the curb eating a cold sandwich and tapped at her phone screen researching the logos she saw on the parked trucks. Most were heading east, toward Chicago or New York.

In the middle of tracking a soda company, Nora's phone vibrated. Mason's name flashed on the screen. Her heart skipped a beat with agitation. She clicked his name putting him on speaker.

"What do you want?" Nora greeted.

"You really have to ask?" Mason seethed. There was a loud thud, meaning either his foot or fist hit something. "What the hell, Nora, you haven't answered any of my texts or calls! You just left without telling me, without saying goodbye."

She stopped her research to argue. "You thought I was going to stick around until you came to your senses? Listen, I don't have time for this. I'll be home in a few days and—"

"Wait, wait," he said hastily. He took a moment to sooth his tone. "Where are you? Are you okay?"

"Mason, I'm in the middle of something. I have to go."

"Just tell me if we're okay."

His words caught Nora off guard. She had little time to mull over their last fight, all her attention and energy was dedicated to Wesley and Angeline. Her mind was there with them and not at all back home.

The silence lasted longer than a minute.

"I don't know, Mason," she finally replied.

He muttered some kind of farewell, then the line went dead. Nora's throat went dry like she should have said more, but it was the only truth she could offer him. It was also the most she could say without hurting him. The phone still in her hand lit up again showing a new message from Angeline.

Found a lead. By the pancake house.

Nora got to her feet and headed to the cluster of restaurants across the rest stop. The pancake house was easy to spot with its blue roof. Wesley arrived the same time she did. They met Angeline under the shade of a pine tree in the parking lot.

"Which one?" Wesley asked.

Angeline nodded over to a furniture-hauling truck on the other side of the lot. "It's heading to a furniture store based in Vancouver. We better move fast, though. I'm not sure who the driver is."

Wesley led the way giving them signals to follow when the coast was clear. Angeline and Nora followed behind wading through the cars in a crouch. The girls watched him reach the trailer before waving them over. Nora crept passed him to the passenger door with the lock opener in hand. She gently pried the door open and climbed aboard the tall truck. In a mad flurry she checked the glove compartment and sun visor looking for a spare key into the trailer.

She climbed back out. "Nothing."

"That doesn't matter," Angeline said. "We found a latch just get us in."

They shuffled to the back and sure enough there was a metal latch just like Angeline said. Nora clicked her pen, the lock snapped open, and it dropped to her waiting palm. Wesley stepped forward to shove the large door a quarter of the way open. With difficulty, Angeline rolled in, then held it for him to come inside.

"See you in a bit," Wesley said with a wave.

He ducked in after her as the door slid to a close. Nora fit the lock back into place. She looked around crouching when she saw a trucker stroll over to a nearby trailer. She waited a few moments until she heard the rumble of an engine. Still close to the ground, Nora clasped her time key to open a time warp. She threw herself in sinking into the darkness.

Nora landed on something smooth and flat. She turned her head to see she had landed on a mahogany dinner table. The slight rumble below told her the semi was moving. She strained to hear voices in the distance as well as music. The drivers and the radio. Nora blinked up at the metal wall inches from her face. Carefully, she rolled onto her stomach and army crawled her way out. She jumped down landing on a love seat. The plastic wrap deflated like a balloon under her feet.

"Shh!" Angeline squeezed in between two arm chairs. "We found a nook to hide in. Follow me."

Angeline and Nora caught up to Wesley. They had made a nest for themselves in a navy-blue suede sofa and a brown recliner. Their backpacks were stacked on the floor. Angeline threw herself onto the couch looking very much at home. Nora settled herself in the recliner dropping her own bag beside it.

"How long have we been moving?" Nora asked.

"I'd say twenty minutes or so," Wesley replied. "The driver picked up speed a few minutes ago, we must be on the highway."

"Good."

"We have a long way to go," Angeline said. "We should all get some sleep."

Nora nodded. Now that she was in a comfortable seat she felt exhausted. She opened her mouth, another thought occurring to her.

"I'll keep first watch," Wesley offered, kicking his feet up on a chair. "Between the three of us I think I got the most sleep in last twenty-four hours."

"Then I'll keep watch, and you can finish up the ride," Angeline agreed and looked over at Nora to confirm.

"Sounds good to me."

The three of them settled in. Angeline was the first to fall asleep amongst the cushions. Nora was a bit more restless in her sleep. She shifted around and around until she curled to a tight ball. Even when she managed to sleep a few minutes, she remembered waking briefly to hear the silence in the trailer.

Sometime later in the day a faint buzzing sound woke her. Nora opened her eyes to see Wesley rifling through her bag.

"Sorry," he apologized, noticing she was awake. He found her phone at last. "It just wouldn't quit vibrating. Here. It's Mason." He handed it to her.

Nora uncurled herself to take it. She stared at Mason's name on the screen and waited until his call came to a stop. He called twice, sent a voicemail, and wrote four text messages and six emails in a span of a few hours.

Where are you?
Can we talk?
Say something.
Talk to me.

Her thumb hovered over the keyboard hesitating her reply. They were *not* okay that much she was sure of. And Mason's relentless attempts to catch the fragile pieces before there was nothing to grasp made it difficult. It made Nora uneasy. He wanted a sign of hope, and she didn't want to give him that. A part of her knew there was no fixing what was happening between them. The current rift, Nora hoped, would keep them apart. If he wanted to repair a fraction of it, Mason would have to wait in silence while she found her way back to him and figured out what to say.

She eventually typed two short sentences:

Not now. On our way.

"What'd he say?" Wesley asked, snapping her out of her thoughts.

"He wants to know if we're okay." she half lied. Nora shoved the phone back into her bag as her phone lit up again with a new message.

He nodded thoughtfully. Wesley folded his jacket into fourths to use as a pillow. "Go back to sleep, then. I think we still have some ways to go."

Nora agreed. She stripped off her own jacket, at last feeling the heat that turned the trailer a little stuffy. Wesley and Angeline must have had the same idea because they already peeled off their coats. She draped it over a cushion.

She settled back in her seat throwing her legs over the armrest. Nora blinked a few times, heaved a heavy sigh, and closed her eyes. Sleep was out of the question; she was still too wired thinking about Mason. Although she would never admit it, she missed him. Since she found him, they had never been this long apart. He was always less than thirty feet away from her most of her life. She wanted to be at his side again fighting or not. It was simpler to say it was the time guard in her, but it was more than duty.

When she least expected it, Nora dozed off. She fell in a light sleep filled with nightmares she couldn't quite remember. She stirred awake when the movement of the trailer began to slow. Nora straightened in her seat. By looks of it, they fell asleep forgetting the previous agreement they made hours ago.

Wesley and Angeline were already awake listening to what was going on outside. A few minutes later, it came to a complete stop, and the three of them sat very still. They heard the drivers clamber out of the cab, slam the doors, and shuffle away complaining about their aches and the long drive. Once the voices faded away, Nora darted into a time warp to let Wesley and Angeline out.

As Nora locked up, Wesley jerked her away from the door pulling her behind the enormous tire where he and Angeline were crouched. He pressed a finger to his lips signaling Nora to keep quiet. Angeline was keeping watch. Nora didn't protest, looking around she noticed they were parked at a truck stop. They had reached the parking lot of a retail store, out in the public for all to see.

"Meet back here in ten," Angeline muttered.

They separated. Nora ducked behind a row of cars, then trotted ahead into the store to purchase cold meals for the final stretch of their journey. She collected sandwiches, salads, cheap snacks, and bottles of soda into her basket. Standing in line, she took this opportunity to call Hogan.

"Is this a secure line?" she greeted after the fourth ring.

"It is," Hogan said. "You have them?"

"I do. To my knowledge we're moving undetected. I expect another forty-eight hours or less." She paused. "How is he?"

"Agitated. Come back soon."

Hogan hung up.

She exited the store and found Wesley standing outside the sliding doors waiting for her, a bag of his own slung over his shoulder. He caught up to her leading her toward the semitruck they disembarked earlier.

They crossed the lot together.

"You didn't have to wait for me," she told him.

"I wasn't," Wesley said flatly, a tinge of cold in his voice. He stopped walking to look at her. His dark eyes stared at her with accusation. "I was tailing you the whole time in there and you didn't even notice me. Where is your head right now, Nora?"

Her heart sank to her stomach, then rose to her ears, pounding. "What do you mean? Why'd you tail me? I'm on your side."

"You're not here with us," he shot at her. His eyebrows were drawn together, serious, bordering on suspicion. "You've been off your game since Mason contacted you. Is something going on between you two?"

"Don't be silly," Nora said, mustering haughtiness in her voice to sound offended. He seemed unconvinced so she went on. "He's been making things difficult, but nothing is going on. He knows his place and I know mine."

"Angeline isn't fully healed, and I can't survive without you right now. I need you to get to the safe house. I need to know you're here with us, one hundred percent," he said seriously. "You and Mason are a dangerous pair. It wouldn't be the first time your reckless choices get us all killed."

Nora winced at the painful reminder. She was well aware of her mistakes. It was a great deal different to hear it coming from Wesley. He knew the fatal flaw that Mason could be for her when he set his sights on her beyond that of a time guard. His life as well as the others was drastically cut short the moment he decided to pursue her.

"I'm with you," she said at last and followed him to the trailer.

Chapter 17
Time at Sea

The clock tower struck two o'clock in the morning a few blocks away from where Wesley, Angeline, and Nora kept quiet inside the trailer for the last twenty minutes. They stood huddled in a cramped space in the back listening. Angeline closest to the door finally gave Nora the sign to check the outside. Nora nodded, opened a time warp, and disappeared.

She landed beside the trailer. A brisk cold air greeted her making her shiver. Nora looked around to see they had indeed arrived to their destination. The furniture store was dark. The dumpster behind it carried pieces of broken chair legs, terribly scratched headboards, crushed card board boxes, and soggy cushions. To their luck, the store was closed off by a high wooden fence. The semitruck was parked right outside a loading dock. She squeezed into the narrow space to let them out at last.

The door rattled open and Wesley jumped down first. A fully healed Angeline hopped down next. She was consulting her phone pondering it with narrowed eyes. Nora wanted to suggest they keep moving, but the lonely lot gave the impression it would remain deserted until first light. She leaned on a lamp post with crossed arms as Wesley sat on the dock.

"Well?" Wesley asked, rubbing his hands on his jeans for warmth. "Where do we go from here?"

Angeline didn't reply right away. Her eyes were still glued to the screen, which cast a white-blue hue over her elegant features.

"The harbor," she finally said, looking at the both of them. "We'll be taking the channel to Seattle."

"As in, a boat?" Nora asked. "You arranged to have one waiting for us?"

"Well, no—"

Wesley caught on, jumping to his feet to argue with his time guard. "Are you insinuating we *steal* a boat across international waters? The moment we set foot in Seattle, everyone'll be searching for the culprits. We'll have two countries looking for us, Ang. If that isn't a giant flare for time travelers, I don't know what is."

Nora straightened to defend her. "We can't exactly wait for a ferry in the morning, can we? We'd be wasting hours," she rounded on him. "I know a thing or two about sailing. We can easily throw anyone off while at sea. I can get us there."

"And the *three* of us know a thing or two about stealing," Angeline added. She walked toward the fence, calling over her shoulder as she went. "We know what we're doing, Wes. We'll cover our tracks."

They followed.

A loose board beside the dumpster allowed them to slip into a narrow alley. In a single-file line, they shuffled in the direction of the way out. When they reached the still boulevard, Nora understood why Angeline chose the particular trailer parked on the other side of the fence. The store was right on a sloped corner overlooking the harbor. From the curb and on tip toe, she could make out the tops of the tallest boats poking at the horizon. Angeline calculated the whole thing way before Nora came along.

With the last of moonlight shining through the trees, the three of them walked the eight blocks. They made it to the pier where most of the private owned boats were docked in three neat lines. Boats of every shape, size, and color waded in the water. It was closed off by a ten-foot gate. There was a reasonable-size tollbooth that surely opened the doors.

"No cameras," Wesley noted. "This feels too easy."

"That's because there isn't a need for them," Nora replied.

One by one they hopped the tall gate. The sound of the waves lulled their landing. Wesley sneaked off to the booth, whispering something about more information, which left Nora and Angeline to walk the docks to look for the perfect vessel to stealthy take. They walked passed a few old fishing boats, none of which were up to snuff for Angeline.

The girls stopped in front a patched-up fishing boat named *Neptune's Tide*.

"Think you can handle it?" Angeline asked. "I know you're used to bigger ships with a crew."

It was true. Nora had a vast experience with sailing. She was a part of ship that taught her to master the ocean; however, her knowledge was rather outdated. Nora dealt with ships the size of a house and not at all equipped with radars or motors.

"It can't be that much different," Nora reasoned.

They kept walking, stopping every now and then to inspect another boat. They were practically at the end when Angeline lingered on an eggshell-white cuddy cabin boat fashioned as a fishing boat. She shined the light of her phone toward the bow to find its name *West End Current*. Nora thought it was too big and attention drawing. It would certainly cause a stir when the owner noticed its absence.

"This one," Angeline said as Wesley jogged over.

"There's an overnight net that seals the harbor in, a rather crude safety precaution if you ask me," he told them breathlessly. "We can move it manually or cut through the rope."

"Jump in the water and slash the net," Nora ordered. "And untie a boat or two. Make it look like an amateur heist—that we tried to take more than one. Ransack the inside of another boat if you have to. The more confusion we can cause the better."

"I'll even take the money hidden under the floorboard," Wesley replied with a halfhearted salute.

"I'll help you," Angeline said, sounding excited. "Nora, get ready to set sail in a few minutes."

Angeline and Wesley hurried away as Nora jumped aboard. The boat creaked and shifted at her arrival. Right away she noticed how untidy the fishermen kept the deck with a mass of tangled nets, fish scented crates and dirty half open foul-smelling cooler. Gagging a little, she held her nose and edged alongside the boat toward the cockpit. Her hands felt for a spare key to start the boat, but gave up and fumbled for her bag. She jammed the lock opener into the ignition. With one click, the boat roared to life, making Nora flinch. It might as well have been an air horn cutting through the silence of the morning. Instantly, the radio spewed loud static, and the navigational system blinked on, pinpointing their precise location. She switched on the lights illuminating the dark water ahead.

To her relief, there was a wheel to steer. It was much smaller than what she was used to. The rest of the board consisted of knobs and levers leaving Nora doubtful. All of a sudden piloting the boat seemed daunting. How could she possibly man a vessel with only a push of a button? She didn't have time to learn the proper mechanics so she opted for trial and error. Nora pressed a sequence of buttons matching each reaction to its manual counterpart. Near the end, Angeline and a drenched Wesley clambered on to join her.

"Do either of you carry a knife?" Nora asked.

Wesley reached into his wet boot and handed her a Swiss army knife.

Nora took it, flipped out the blade, and plunged it straight into the navigation screen. Sparks flew making them all jump back. It flickered, fighting to remain on, then after a moment it turned blank.

"What the hell!" Wesley exclaimed.

"It'll buy us a few days when we leave it behind," Nora explained, reaching for her back pocket. Her phone would serve as the new map.

"Are we ready to go?" Angeline asked.

The boat glided away from the dock with ease. It sailed over the water at a steady pace toward the opening Wesley pointed her to. They passed the line of wading boats and out of the silent harbor.

"How long will it take to get to Seattle?" Wesley asked as he emerged from the cabin below, now in a new dry set of clothes. He ran a hand through his wet hair.

"If there's no fog and we go undetected? Three hours—just enough time to stay clear of any cargo ships taking their daily routes," Angeline answered.

The boat picked up speed once they were surrounded by darkness and water. Wesley and Angeline took a seat, gazing into the morning. Nora's hair whipping behind her and the salty air sent a chill down her spine. It was so familiar to her, she could picture her past life aboard another ship. She fought to keep the memories from coming, but they only came in faster and in flashes. The large house by the beach, the masts of the biggest ship she had ever seen, a damp prison cell, and Mason jumping off a cliff. All the images made her heart sink at the reminder at how it all ended.

A sudden heaviness in her bones made Nora release the wheel, causing the boat to slow down. Angeline sprang to her feet staring up at the sky in concern. Wesley caught on to their strange behavior.

"What is it?" he asked.

"Don't move!" Angeline and Nora said together.

The boat came to a stop. It waded in place for ten long seconds before the waves around the ship grew stronger. They crashed against the boat harder and harsher sending water onto the deck. It spun the boat furiously as though they were caught amid a whirlpool. The three of them stumbled. Nora grabbed the wheel, afraid of what was happening. Angeline knocked into her. Wesley was thrown back to his seat looking around in amazement at the absence of a storm. Eventually, it all came to a stop.

"It's a time quake!" Angeline shouted.

Nora pulled away from her. "Go!" she ordered to Wesley and helped him to his feet. She shoved him in the direction of the cabin. "Inside there now!"

"Here they come!"

Nora whipped around and squinted up at the sky. It took her a moment to find them. She scanned the skies until a spec coming from the north grew bigger. A squadron of five time travelers were plummeting to earth at an alarming rate. Their long black robes whipped behind them. They were heading straight for the boat. As they soared closer, Nora distinguished two men and three women.

"Grab a net!" Nora said, running to the disorderly bundle on the floor.

Angeline followed. The two girls picked up one of the nets and hurried to the stern of the boat. They stood waiting until the time travelers swooped in close. Nora and Angeline threw it as hard as they could. It smacked two out of the incoming five. The pair yelped in surprise and fell in the water. The other three knocked the time guards back onto the deck.

Nora rolled onto her feet.

All three girls managed to land on their feet aboard the boat. They couldn't have been much older than sixteen. Two of them hurtled themselves at Nora full speed. Nora grabbed the blond ponytailed time traveler by the scruff of her robe and sent her headfirst to the port of the boat. The girl collided and slumped to the floor. With one down, the fight became much easier. The second girl took her turn aiming a swift set of punches and kicks in Nora's direction. She blocked her hits with ease, the girl was clearly an amateur because she left herself at times defenseless.

The two time travelers that had fallen into the water climbed on board. Angeline tossed her own time traveler into a waiting time warp and went to fight the new arrivals. Momentarily distracted by the emerging men, the girl slammed Nora to the wall of the cabin, and her small hands found a neck.

Nora was surprised at how strong the girl was. She could have crushed her windpipe with the right pressure. She didn't let the time traveler play on with the farce of a fight much longer. Nora gripped the girl's forearms, hoisted herself off the ground, and kicked her in the chest. The girl tumbled right into the time warp. She ran over to join Angeline and the remaining time travelers.

Unlike the girls, the two men were armed with glistening pitch black blades the size of a small pocket book. Nora leaped over the coolers to trip the time traveler who had his back turned. He hit the floor, but jumped to his feet when he noticed Nora had entered the fray. He made vicious swipes at her missing her by inches. The time travelers advanced, then made a deadly target of her neck. He plunged his blade in her direction. She caught him mere centimeters from her skin. With two hands, he added more pressure.

"Nora!"

Nora stole a glance in Angeline's direction. She had gained a new opponent: the blond time traveler who Nora thought to have knocked out by the stern of the boat. She was back on her feet and holding a dark blade as well. With all Nora's might, she struggled to push away the blade.

"Hold on, I'm coming," Nora grunted.

"Not me," Angeline shouted, sending a good kick to the time traveler's jaw. "Her!"

Somehow the girl blasted the cabin door open. Splintered wood flew everywhere. Little by little, Nora began to divert the direction of the dagger. With force, the blade sank into the wood right above her shoulder. It cut into her skin, but only barely. Nora's hands flew to the dagger, withdrew it from the wall, and in one blunt shove the blade sank into his chest. Nora let it linger before flinging it at the girl standing on the deck. The entire blade disappeared into her back. She collapsed wordlessly.

Angeline took the man at Nora's feet by the ankles dragging to the time warp where she had been sending her victims. Nora did the same to the girl.

"Don't move," Angeline warned Wesley still inside the cabin. "Nora, keep going. We aren't in the clear just yet."

Nora rushed back to the wheel. She restarted the boat, plotted the course, and took off. They sailed in silence checking the purpling sky to make sure no other time traveler dropped into their time. It wasn't until an hour later that Angeline let Wesley come out again. By then they sailed a majority of the way to Seattle. The journey lagged only when they crossed international waters. Nora steered clear of the coast guard. She felt a jolt of delight when the Space Needle came into view.

"Nowhere to park?" Angeline asked as they passed the harbor.

She shook her head. "Look for a cove."

They let themselves into a small bay. Angeline quickly wiped the boat clean as Wesley disheveled it for show and Nora dropped anchor. They lowered the flimsy orange life raft, disembarked, and rowed to the muddy bank. The three of them crossed the brush toward a lonesome road. Nora calculated to be ten miles out the city. If they were lucky, they could score a car and hit the road before the morning rush.

"What now? We walk all the way?" Wesley asked.

"Don't be silly," Angeline said, wiping the mud off her shoes on the grass. "There's a coach bus that should pass here in five minutes. Let's get some distance from the bay and hitch a ride."

They began to walk.

"I hate to say it because I don't want to jinx it—this trip has been a little too easy," Nora thought aloud. "Should I be worried?"

"Not much work to do is Angeline's MO," Wesley replied.

Angeline shot them a reproachful look. "I'm not much for excitement like you or Hogan," she said. "The less work, the better."

"I think Hogan called it solving the problem."

"Whatever," Angeline replied, her lips twitching into a smile.

"Bus," Wesley chimed in.

"Let me do the talking."

"Pull up your hood," Nora muttered urgently to Wesley.

Nora and Wesley shuffled to the side of the road shoving their hands in their pockets as Angeline waved an arm at the incoming bus. The ominous lights of the black-and-white bus came to a halt. The doors opened. Angeline climbed aboard to speak with the driver. They chatted, and she tossed him a dazzling smile, followed by a swift flick of her hair. A moment later she trotted back down to wave them over.

"There aren't any seats available, but we can stand in the back for the twenty-minute trip," she told them as they neared.

They followed her in. The driver looked at them with doubt, as though he was close to retracting his decision on allowing them in. They hurried along before he could change his mind. The bus was full of sleeping passengers. Angeline led them to the back near the emergency exit. She looked over her shoulder to Nora nodding behind them. Nora understood, she wanted to keep a tabs on the bus for any suspicious travelers. They stood cramped together, Nora wedged in front of Wesley. The bus took off again and Nora grabbed a hold of the railing.

To not draw attention to themselves, they kept quiet all the way to the bus station.

Fifteen minutes later the bus doors opened. Being already on their feet gave Angeline, Nora, and Wesley the opportunity to hop off right away and take off into the morning. The sun had reached the horizon turning the sky pink and orange. They followed Angeline through the streets. Nora was eager to be on her feet, to put in actual effort in the last stretch of the journey. They had traveled incredibly fast, left no trace of themselves, and played it safe all the way. It was a four-hour drive to Salem, Oregon and a nine-hour hike to the boardinghouse. All three time markers would be together in the same room by nightfall.

Chapter 18
The Summit

For the most part, the drive to Salem was uneventful. The cloudless blue sky showed no signs of more time quakes. The beautiful morning held little traffic to set them back. They arrived at the Emerald Crest Campsite fifteen minutes passed noon. The dull orange Mini Cooper Wesley stole from a cramped little neighborhood a mile away from the bus station was parked at the entrance. Nora shouldered her reorganized backpack as she walked toward the dirt path up ahead. The previous stop allowed them to pack last minute things for a day long hike: rope, harnesses, an extra pair of shoes, and water. Angeline stayed behind to swap the car's license plates.

Nora squinted beyond the campsite. The hilly landscape eventually gave way to bigger, steeper slopes and peaks several stories high. Those who weren't aware of the area were none the wiser to the cluster of towns hidden among the mountains. She searched for the peak that looked like the tip toppled over or as Nora liked to think of it a witch's hat. It was the mountain closest to Lys Gate. She reached for the sundial around her neck. It was still in her palm, then it rose to lead her home.

"Your time key is a compass," Wesley noted, looking over her shoulder. "How are you doing that?"

"I'm not doing anything," she told him. "When I turned it into a time key, it started to go haywire. It took me ages to figure out it points me in the direction of whatever I'm looking for. It comes in handy when I have a hard time finding Mason."

"And now it's leading you back to him."

The sundial pointed south east.

Angeline trotted over to them, tossing the unwanted plates in a bush. "Which way are we heading?" she asked.

"See that peak—the one with a bent point?" Nora pointed to the mountain she just spotted. "The boardinghouse is just beyond it."

"We have a long way to go."

The three of them began to walk.

Nora ducked under a wispy branch and took the lead up the dirt path. It was a perfect day for a hike. The day was quite warm without the sting of the sun. The transitioning lush campgrounds looked like something straight out of a seasonal calendar. Leaves clung to the trees in various colors of red and brown, occasionally they fluttered down to meet the yellowing grass. Her fingers brushed the rough patch of bark in longing. The tall, thick trees called to her in temptation.

She didn't mind the long silence. It left Nora with her thoughts, the ones she had been neglecting for days. The moment to face Mason drew closer. It sent a mixture of relief and dread in the pit of her stomach. What was she supposed to say to him? There was nothing more she could add on to what she already told him. His heart was set on her despite her constant aversion. It was an act of suicide, and he didn't care. *He doesn't know what he's risking*, she thought. And after what he said to her several days ago, she was certain they could never work. They were too different.

Within the hour, the three of them left behind the picturesque woodland. They slid down the first valley to the plateau below. The tall, brittle grass billowed below their knees. Wesley touched firm ground first followed by Nora.

It was well in the late afternoon when they were crossing a stream that Wesley called them to a stop. He dropped onto a small boulder as his backpack slid off his shoulders. His chest rose and fell rapidly, catching each new breath with difficulty. Nora rechecked her sundial. It was still leading them southeast. By looks, there were two more enormous mountains to cross. They had made a lot of progress in a short time.

"What is it?" Angeline asked, stopping to wipe the sweat from her forehead with the back of her sleeve. "You okay?"

He took a long swig from his water bottle. "Just give me a minute."

"Why didn't you say something earlier?" Nora asked. "We can slow down."

"No," Wesley said, a little too sharply. "I don't want to slow down."

Nora stole a glance at Angeline in question. The past time marker's hostility was a surprise to her. He was usually pleasant and upbeat. Angeline gave her a knowing sympathetic look. It was clear she had dealt with his attitude before. Instead of arguing, Nora walked ahead to consult the sky. The sun ducked behind the incoming gray clouds. She really hoped it wouldn't rain.

Angeline joined her.

"He isn't like us," Nora remarked. "We'll slow down."

Angeline nodded. "Being around me and able to talk freely of his knowledge about time makes him forget of his limitations, that he's only human. It's what kills him in the end, thinking he can conquer that part of himself."

"How do you keep him from—you know …"

"I can't stop him, no matter how hard I try."

Nora looked over to Wesley. He finished his half eaten tuna sandwich in four bites. She never pondered his demons, the ones that put him in danger.

"How much longer will it take to get there?" Wesley asked when he noticed Nora watching him.

"Probably another five hours," Angeline replied.

He jumped back on his feet. "Let's keep moving."

This time Wesley took the lead.

Nora walked behind him; her thoughts now revolving around Wesley. She stared at the back of his head wondering all sorts of things about the past time marker. She thought she had him figured out, yet it was no surprise at all how little she knew about him. Nora spent a handful of lives accompanying Wesley. All she gathered were the important aspects of him. He was serious, determined, and self-aware. He understood things Nora couldn't quite find the right words for and also didn't have to supply answers regarding their future. It never occurred to Nora that Angeline had to battle Wesley's issues concerning his mortality. She had to keep him alive in ways that Nora didn't understand.

She wondered what bothered Wesley about being mortal. Capable to remember his past and purpose, Nora thought he would come to terms with his mortality faster than the other two. In her opinion, death was the best thing about reincarnation. When the universe didn't deal them with the most favorable circumstances, it was comforting to know that she could return to earth and try again. The six of them were at least granted them this small mercy. It was easy to imagine what kind of trouble they could get into if they were truly immortal.

The early hours of the evening were well under threat of rain. The gray clouds grew thicker. To cut time, Angeline unzipped her bag to reveal zip lining equipment. She hoisted the large grappling hook gun onto her shoulder, took aim, and shot. With a loud bang, it flew to the other mountain hundreds of feet across. Wesley gave the cord a hearty tug, then fastened their end.

One by one they soared across the valley to the neighboring ledge. Nora glided over the abyss below watching the sinking sun dip further into the horizon. From this height, she spotted the faint glow of Torch Crossings.

Angeline lead the way after she found a narrow passage through the mountain. It was so narrow they had shrug off their backpacks and shuffle by on their side.

"Do you remember the life you had in Venezuela?" Nora asked Wesley aloud. Her voice carried above bouncing off the stone walls. "You were ten years old and starting to remember your past lives. Your dad sent word that you were allowed to join him in Texas. I caught up to you in Costa Rica. You were in such a hurry to get to him."

He stalled for a moment. "We spent the whole summer crossing Mexico."

"We almost *died* up in the sierra," she corrected. Thunder rattled over their heads. "We ran out of food and water. It was so hot."

"And I got sick."

Angeline let out a snort from the front. She knew this part of the story.

He was on the brink of death to be a matter of fact. Nora knew they should have stopped the night before when they ran out of supplies, but in Wesley's desperation he wanted to be reunited with his father. His tan little face was draining of color fast, and his temperature kept rising. She was alone and unable to call for help fearful that he would die in her absence. For a split second, Nora considered time hopping to Angeline or Hogan for help.

"We were lucky a healer found us a little after midnight," Nora went on. "You slipped in and out of conscious before you were okay. You spoke in your sleep, like you always do."

"Don't let me die," he muttered, repeating the words he said in his delirium.

The words caused a shiver to run down her spine that had nothing to do with the autumn chill. It made her heart ache all over again. It made no difference if it was the small Venezuelan boy or the man ahead of her begging to be rescued. It was unfair on her part if Nora didn't do all she could to ensure he survived under her watch. She wouldn't fail him.

"And you lived," she finished.

They fell silent again. Eventually, the path widened and they were free to strap their backpacks on. By the time they reached the end it was dark out. A little drizzle sprayed over them. Nora checked her sundial as she headed down to ground level, they didn't need the altitude any more. Angeline and Wesley followed. She decided to send word to Hogan to let him know they were finally close. If they kept the pace they had now, they could reach the boardinghouse around ten or eleven o'clock.

A dozen text messages made Nora's phone vibrate for a solid twenty seconds the instant they reached the base of the mountain. Behind her, Angeline's phone repeated the same short jingle three times. Nora checked her phone. It was Mason checking in. The three of them stopped once more to empty out their bags of remaining snacks to share. While Wesley made a small fire, Nora took a seat on a molding log to type a quick message to Hogan.

Make sure it's safe for us to arrive. Three hours. —N

He responded a second later. *Got it.*

"It'll be raining soon," Angeline said apprehensively as a clap of thunder rumbled. She touched the top of her head, feeling for droplets. "I hope we don't get drenched." To her dismay, the drizzle picked up, and the fire began to fizzle. Angeline scrambled for her beige coat.

"Doubtful," Wesley said, raising the hood of his jacket.

Nora paid no attention to the light rain. "Forget the rain. I hope we don't find any trouble this close to the safe house," she told them. "I've kept this place well hidden for years. If we somehow happen to lure any time travelers, none of us will be safe at this point. All of this will be for nothing."

"We'll be extra careful," Angeline promised.

Once the fire fizzled out for good, they gathered their things and headed toward the alluring glow in the distance. Despite the heavy rain and slick mud, the three of them kept a steady pace. Thunder and lightning orchestrated a thrashing spectacle. Each sudden crack of thunder made the ground vibrate under their feet, which in turn caused Angeline and Nora to shoot anxious glances up at the night sky. The bright flashes of light illuminated their way in erratic intervals.

The night dragged. It was impossible to see, and the temperature kept dropping at a fast rate. Nora abandoned her hold on the sundial around her neck to hide her hands in her pockets. She wiped the water from her eyes on her drenched shoulder. The other two weren't faring the nasty weather any better. Angeline's face was barely visible in her big coat. Her nose was pink with cold. Wesley's lips were pressed together in a thin line and his shaggy hair made him look like a wet dog.

An hour later, Nora began to suspect they were near when they crossed familiar roads. The grass also became less wild and their feet stopped sinking into the sloshes of mud puddles. They dashed across the pavement unseen.

The rain came down harder feeling more solid as the minutes went on. It pelleted Angeline, Nora, and Wesley on their heads. They had to keep their heads bowed to avoid being hit in the face. Nora only dared to steal glances every fifty paces to check her surroundings.

A brilliant flash of lightning parted the sky in two quickly followed by a tremendous clap of thunder that produced an earth trembling shake. Nora stopped walking. Before it all went dark again, she caught a glimpse of an array of trees and an outline of something low, large and cylindrical. She squinted into the night seeing a pillar of smoke somewhere beyond. Her heart started to race in excitement.

Angeline and Wesley were waiting on her to move.

"There!" Nora shouted over the rain. "I think I see it!"

They broke into a run toward the water tower. They huddled underneath it for a few minutes to catch their breath and take a break from the icy, cold rain. The water clattered on the sheet metal making the rain fall louder.

"Do the others know we're here?" Angeline panted.

"They should," Nora replied, hoping that the security sounded to alert the boys inside. She looked over in the direction of the smoke, she could have sworn that she saw the faintest light flicker.

"All right, let's go."

The three of them broke into a run. Angeline was the fastest. She took off into the night her arms and legs pumping so hard her hood slipped off. Wesley was close behind her looking relieved to have arrived. Nora jogged behind them slowing when her feet hit the patio.

The back door swung open. Charlie, Hogan, and Mason poured out to greet them. Hogan ran over holding an umbrella and Angeline threw herself into his waiting arms. She pressed her lips to his letting slip a delightful laugh. He whisked her away inside without so much as waiting for the others. Charlie ushered Wesley inside. Mason rushed past them to meet Nora.

He stopped in front of her, standing so close that their foreheads touched. Nora closed her eyes, a rush of relief flooded through her. She didn't have to open her eyes to notice Mason's touch. His fingers lightly traced her hand. It brought a fleeting spark that spread warmth down to her cold feet. His warm breath hit her lips. Her eyes fluttered open to find Mason's searching gaze. His expression was a mixture of relief and joy. There was also something else, a distinct flicker of hope. Recognizing the glint, Nora blinked, looked away, and clutched the umbrella he held. She was careful to avoid his touch again. No longer feeling the heavy rain and free of the burden of the journey, she let Mason guide her to the back door of the boardinghouse.

Chapter 19
Out of Darkness

Three hot baths waited for Angeline, Nora, and Wesley. It was a wonderful thing to come home to. Nora never felt so grateful to take a bath in her life. The girls shut the door to one bathroom while Wesley crossed the hall to another. The porcelain freestanding bathtubs were full of hot water. In the candlelight, steam unfurled gracefully into the air fogging the mirrors. Angeline stripped down in three quick motions and stepped into the water. She took the quickest bath Nora had ever seen, then swept out of the room, shutting the door behind her. The mud-crusted shoes on Nora's feet hadn't even landed on the floor yet.

Nora climbed into the tub clothes and all. The hot water stung like an iron, but then soothed the terrible cold away. She adjusted to the hot temperature before sinking in. Her clothes automatically turned from icy to warm. Eventually, she decided to peel off all her layers to scrub the dirt from her skin. As she washed her hair, Nora heard the muffled voices of Angeline and Wesley. They were no doubt retelling the events of the troublesome voyage to Lys Gate.

She waited until the water ran cold to scramble out of the tub. Nora tugged on a pair of black leggings and a white tunic. She ran a hand through her damp hair as she walked down the hall. Everyone had gathered in the living room near a roaring fire. Angeline was wrapped in one of Hogan's sweaters clutching a steaming paper cup in between her hands. Hogan knelt next to her talking to the three time markers. Charlie and Mason listened attentively. The moment he saw Nora approach Mason jumped to his feet.

He let her take his spot on the couch, and he moved to stand behind it. Charlie draped a blanket over her shoulders while Hogan handed her a cup of hot chocolate. Feeling warm and snug, Nora took a hearty sip.

"You all did well," Hogan said now that they were all together. "We should be safe for now."

"So what now?" Wesley asked, voicing what everyone was thinking. "Where are we running to?" He directed the question to Angeline.

Hogan answered for her. "Nowhere. We will talk strategy in the morning. Tonight we'll rest. We readied the bedrooms on the first floor, particularly those with fireplaces."

"What about patrol?" Nora asked.

"Already taken care of."

As soon as Angeline finished her tea, she and Wesley got to their feet. They bid everyone good night and hurried off to the right wing of the boardinghouse, their heads together in hushed conversation. Charlie trailed after them. Hogan lingered behind to take a step closer to Nora.

"You kept your word," he said, leaning forward to grasp her hand. "Thank you."

"I know how much you needed her," she replied with smile.

He gave her hand a gentle squeeze, bid her a good night, and followed after Angeline.

Nora watched them go. She was genuinely pleased to have them reunited. Over the centuries, carefully scheduled brief rendezvous and scattered tokens throughout history kept them together. They made it work despite all the obstacles in place. She hoped this illicit meeting brought them an ounce of joy rather than guilt or all consuming worry.

She finished her hot chocolate and got to her feet. She was surprised to see Mason still standing behind her. He had apparently been watching Hogan go too.

"I'm going to bed," Nora said awkwardly.

"I want to talk to you," Mason said.

"No," she said in a rush. Nora's eyes darted to the left and right halls hoping no lingering ears could hear them. "This isn't the moment or place."

"This is a good time as any," he argued.

"No, it's not!"

Mason's dark eyes studied her noticing the fear in hers. A wave of understanding crossed his face, but didn't say a word.

Nora set off down the left hallway. Three doors were ajar, alit a dull orange thanks the burning fireplaces. She slipped into the closest one. Her trunk and duffel bag were already inside at the foot of the bed. A moment later she heard another door close further in the hall.

She closed hers too. A newfound wave of panic coursed through Nora's veins. Mason brought out the worst parts of her: deceitful, haughty, rebellious, and short tempered. All those terrible qualities caused her to see red. She couldn't afford to be hung up in all his drama while the others were around.

A rasping knock snapped Nora out of her thoughts. She stared at the ugly mustard-yellow drapes, wondering if she was hearing things. Just as she was deciding to brush it off as nothing, a second knock sounded. She gripped her sundial. Slowly, Nora strode across the room and poked the curtains an inch to glimpse out into the night. She let the sundial go and rolled her eyes. With a huff, she drew the drapes to one side, then opened the window.

Mason stood outside. It had stopped raining, but drops from the gutter landed on his forehead.

"What?" Nora asked, crossing her arms. Hadn't she been clear with him? She didn't want to talk. What would the others think if they found him sneaking around in her room?

"Let me in, we have to talk," Mason insisted.

"No!" she said in a rush. "I don't have anything more to say to you."

"Great because I do. Move!"

"No!"

"If I can't come in through the window, I'm forcing my way through the door," Mason demanded, sounding annoyed.

Nora stepped aside to let him in. "You're unbearable."

"And you're stubborn," he snapped, climbing in. "Listen to me, okay?"

Nora glared at him shrewdly finding it hard to keep her mouth shut.

Mason didn't wait to gather his thoughts. He seemed to be prepared. "What I said the other day," he started. "It was unfair. I was being unreasonably selfish. I know you had to go, but some part of me thought you would stay. I get so angry because I have this stupid idea you'd pick us over everything, because I would have."

"It wasn't a matter of what you asked of me," Nora told him. "It has nothing to do with me or you."

"I know," he said quickly. "And because I'm such a screw up, I never say the right thing. Ever. I screw up all the time. You're all I think about, Nora, you and me."

She stepped away from him, real panic rising in her chest. "Stop, Mason!"

He stayed put very aware how afraid she was. "Come on, Nora," he pleaded. "Are you really going to make me work this hard?"

"You shouldn't have to."

He took a dangerous step closer to her. He moved slow as if afraid she'd scamper away. She felt herself caving. The heart inside her chest pounded wanting to force its way out to Mason. With gentle ease, he found her lips at last and pulled her to him. A wonderful hot jolt set the awful dread trapped in her heart free.

Mason's lips were no stranger to Nora. She had, after all, kissed him on a separate occasion. But to her it felt no different. It had been weeks ago, but at that moment she could have sworn it had been seconds ago. Their lips moved from where they left off.

He kissed her with the same soft intensity as though if he stopped she would melt right through his arms. When he kissed her the way he did, Nora understood why it was easy to fall in love with him. She wouldn't change a thing about him. He was every despicable thing she thought him to be: self-centered, stubborn, brash, impulsive yet equally gentle, thoughtful, witty, and alluring. It made protecting him nearly impossible, but loving him was all too easy.

⧗

The next morning Nora awoke curled in a tight ball in a pale pink blanket. She tightened her nest feeling far too comfortable to leave. Last night's events came rushing back to her. Mason, his arms around her, the rush of coolness against her skin during the night, the parting of her lips against his. Her stomach flip-flopped in delight, then anguish with the realization that it had been no dream. The reality of it would never keep Mason away. It would draw him closer. The night cemented where they stood.

Nora wrestled her way out of the blanket.

Mason sat on the edge of the bed reaching for his discarded shirt on the floor. His lean body was well toned thanks to the many years of soccer practice. She watched him pull it over his head, then grab his phone on the nightstand.

"I thought you left without telling me," she muttered.

Mason turned to her, chuckling. "What kind of guy do you take me for?" He leaned in for a good morning kiss.

They kissed for a long moment, her hands in his hair. Smiling, he pulled away.

"Leaving already?" Nora asked.

"I have to," he replied. "I hear the others, they're up. They shouldn't find me here."

Nora rolled onto her stomach and propped herself onto her elbows. "Right," she agreed. "They can't know. I'm already under suspicion."

"I know," Mason muttered. He leaned in for another kiss. "Wesley looks like he wants to punch me in the face every time I talk to you."

This time she pulled away from him, reaching for her bag under the bed. "I want to give you something," she told him. She gathered the black watch in her palm and showed it to him.

He took it by the armband. "This is Russell's time key," Mason noted.

Nora nodded. "I knew we couldn't trust him so I set a limit on how many times he could jump around in time before it burned out."

"So it's useless," he concluded.

"I plan on resetting it someday," Nora explained, sitting beside him. She helped him fasten it around his wrist. He got to his feet and walked over to the window. She followed. "It was your decision to have him keep it. You can have this one until you find someone worthy to wear it, someone you'll want to keep safe."

She opened the window.

"I think I've proven to be a lousy judge of character." Mason held up his arm. "You should choose."

Nora smiled a little in embarrassment. "Trust me, my judgment isn't any better."

Regardless, he kissed her hard, not wanting to leave.

There was a sudden knock at the door. Nora rushed him out the window, tugged on her tunic from last night, and opened the door.

It was Wesley.

"Time guards are to report to the library," he informed her.

"Okay," she replied. "I'll be right out." Several doors down Mason stepped out of his room fully clothed. He walked passed stealing a weary glance at them. Wesley followed him with a stern look in his eye.

Nora shut the door. She stood with her back against it trying to sooth her racing pulse.

Chapter 20
Practice

Anxiously, Nora headed to the library in the basement. She wondered why Hogan summoned her without the time markers. All decisions were in the end final, but she was willing to hear out what Charlie, Mason, and Wesley had to say if the circumstances were changing. They deserved a chance for input. It was their lives they were turning upside down. Another thought crept into her head: Had they noticed her odd behavior toward Mason? She clasped the sundial around her neck in worry. She forced herself to dismiss the idea. It didn't feel like she was walking into an interrogation.

She lit a candle to illuminate the staircase. The carpeted stairs creaked under her weight as she trotted down. The landing at the bottom gave way to a humid narrow hallway. Immediately to her right was the shadowy rec room. It served as a second smaller living room suitable for one family at a time with its plaid couches, ancient television set, and the forgotten mismatched board games sprawled on the coffee table. To her left were two doors. One was firmly shut, but the second door was open pouring light into the hallway.

Her fellow time guards were already scouring the shabby library. It was three times the size of the bedrooms upstairs. Along the walls were bookcases. Books and odd knick knacks lined the shelves in clusters and in no particular order. Water damage and the heaping piles of dust gave the room a foul, dank smell. Angeline still in her coat from patrol that morning knelt by a short filing cabinet trying to pry it open. Hogan stood by a pile of books thumbing the titles. Nora tapped the door.

"Come in, we have a few things to say to you," Hogan said. "Shut the door."

Nora crossed the threshold.

"Hogan and I have been talking," Angeline said, straightening. She moved over to the desk. "We don't want to take advantage of your hospitality. You've kept this area very well hidden, and we don't want it compromised in case you return in the future."

"We won't come back," Nora said. "That's already been decided."

"Doesn't matter," Hogan said. "We won't be lucky for so long, we'll have to come out of hiding. Not counting today, I think three whole days should be enough to discover possible locations, plot routes, and scout ahead."

"I don't have any loose ends," Nora told them. "We can leave in two days."

Hogan raised an eyebrow. "Is two days enough for your time marker to gain control over his time reading?" he asked.

"No, I suppose not," she admitted.

He could have granted her a week to work with Mason, and she wasn't sure how much progress he would make. Time reading was not a skill to be easily mastered. There was no cure or a will to stop it. All she could do was train him to minimalize the effects he endured.

"Three days. No more, no less. We'll organize a proper exit as soon as he's able to leave."

The girls nodded.

Angeline unfurled an old map on the desk. From afar Nora saw the tiny handwriting that covered the parchment globe. Nora recognized it right away: it was the tool that helped them coordinate their dates scattered across history. Hogan joined with crossed arms looking over her shoulder. Muttering, she pointed to a few places. He shook his head a few times in disagreement. It looked like the meeting was adjourned.

"I'll begin training," Nora told them.

She left them to strategize. Nora rushed back up the stairs and found Charlie and Wesley in the living space, sharing a box of doughnuts in dreadful silence. They talked very little, evidently struggling with general conversation.

Now that she had a chance to really see them together, Nora thought of how bizarre it was. The air was thick with an uncertain heaviness similar to the sensation right before an intense rain fall. The conflicting energies of the time markers struggled to be in the same room at once, as if they were incapable. There was an allure about it too. The way they radiated power called to Nora. Her feet drew her forward before her brain sent the signal to move.

"Sleep well?" she asked aloud.

"Better than most nights," Charlie said with a grin.

She sat on an armrest to take a plump, powdered chocolate doughnut. "I'm glad. I'm sorry this is all I could offer you on such short notice." Nora waved to the high ceiling of the boardinghouse.

"I wasn't expecting anything too grand," Charlie replied, kicking his feet onto the coffee table. "Very retro for my taste, though. I hear the seventies were a rough era." He patted the hideous love seat for emphasis.

"It wasn't that bad," Wesley said, holding back an eye roll.

She grinned at Charlie's remark. "That's a decade I definitely won't miss," she agreed. Nora cringed at the thought of bell bottoms. "Anyone see Mason?"

Charlie thumbed the back door. "I think he went outside."

Finishing her doughnut, Nora got to her feet. She wandered outside into the cold morning. Mason was on a clean patch of grass beyond the patio dribbling a soccer ball on his knee. She watched him for a moment, a slight pang of guilt rattled in her chest. Since he went into hiding, Mason stopped playing. Nora knew he missed the thrill of the game, the tactic. He'd been playing the sport his whole life, for him to just put a stop to that structure in his life must have been a new adjustment.

"Do you miss it?" she called to him.

The ball dropped to the ground, and he turned to face her. With a swift kick, Mason passed her the ball. "Soccer?" he asked.

Nora kicked it back to him. "Yeah."

He shrugged. "I do, but it's not like I won't be able to play it again."

"Once we get settled you can join a new team."

They kicked the ball back and forth in silence. He kicked the ball high in the air, bounced it on his chest, and used his head to let the ball soar over to her. Nora managed to catch it using the tips of her fingers.

"When are we going to start training for my whole time reading thing?" he asked.

"That's actually what I came to talk to you about," she replied, nodding behind her. "I don't know how much progress we can make in three days, but any bit of it can help. I'm not sure what I can do for you, time reading doesn't happen a lot."

Mason jogged over and they began their walk to the property line. "When was the last life I time read?" he asked.

"Modern day eastern Iran. Though that was well over three hundred years ago."

He looked over to the empty field ahead. "Are you sure this will work?"

"Not entirely."

Nora slowed as they approached the water tower. She lingered behind watching him wander over. The property line was easy to spot. A shallow ditch and the length of the grass made it clear where Lys Gate ended and where the next county started. From memory, she knew the neighboring town was called Lumina. In every aspect it was similar in size and population as Lys Gate.

She watched him closely. Mason encountered the new region with caution. He hesitated at the border, before stepping over it. He walked further in testing the waters.

"Anything?" Nora asked.

"Not yet," Mason replied.

His body went rigid. He staggered left, tripped over his feet, and fell over. Mason did his best to stand, but only came down just as fast. Nora rushed over and pulled him back into Lys Gate. She knelt in front of him waiting for his eyes to come into focus.

"Try easing into it," Nora said, although unsure. "Don't rush in."

Mason blinked and nodded. "Right."

It was the first of many trial and errors, no matter how he went about it. Each attempt brought him down hard and fast. Having him time read over and over made Nora realize how debilitating the ordeal was for him. Mason wasn't able to function. Out in the open would have made them targets, they wouldn't be able to move. The fact that Angeline and Hogan allotted them any days at all was a huge help. She really hoped it wouldn't go to waste.

She paced back and forth after every failure wondering why it affected him so roughly. In the past, he coped better. His nausea wasn't so extreme, and the vertigo was manageable. Several tries got him into the swing of his time reading. At it's worst, within hours the present time marker gained some control. But today there was no sign of improvement. No amount of practice seemed to be of any use. The best she could offer was halfhearted advice that would keep him grounded.

Nora winced as Mason stumbled and fell flat on his back once more. He sat up to dry heave over the grass. The more he time read, the worse the nausea became. He spat, muttering a few choice words that made Nora want to scold him. She pulled him back across the property line to let him gather his bearings.

When the color flushed back into his face, he looked up at her. "I'm not getting any better at this, am I?"

"It takes a lot of practice," Nora said, trying to sound upbeat. "Days usually. Focus on something here to bring you back." She gave him an encouraging smile. "Try again."

Mason huffed, held out his hand, she took it, and pulled him to his feet. He stepped away from her, looking to the grounds behind her. His eyes lingered on the boardinghouse and the water tower for a long moment, absorbing every visible detail as if it all mattered. Mason looked over to her for reassurance, and she urged him to go on.

He backed out of Lys Gate slowly. Past the property line, Mason's gaze swept over the boardinghouse again, anticipating the time read to whisk him away. Under her breath, Nora counted the seconds it took for his symptoms to manifest. *Twenty-one seconds*, she noted. He was maybe ten paces in when she recognized Mason giving in to the time read. His eyes darted back and forth with such a speed it made Nora nervous, thinking that he may start convulsing.

She moved closer. "Mason?"

He blinked furiously struggling to focus on her voice. Mason staggered, but forced himself to remain upright. The effort made him pale as beads of sweat raced down his neck.

"Come on," Nora called to him. "You can do this. Pull yourself out. Find your way back."

"I can't," Mason grunted with effort.

Delight and surprise burst in her. Finally, something was kicking in at last. She neared until he was less than three steps away. "Bullshit," Nora replied. "You may be hundreds of years away, but you can still hear me. Come back."

Mason fumbled as he shut his eyes. Under his eyelids, the rapid eye movement slowed. They gained their momentum forcing him to see whatever his mind was taking him. Suddenly, it all stopped. His features relaxed and and his body gave way. Nora swooped in to catch him. She brought him back to Lys Gate to recover. Mason's head lolled, unable to raise it passed his shoulder.

Nora knelt. "You okay?" she asked, brushing his cheek with her hand. The last try really took a toll on him. "Can you hear me?"

His eyes flickered up to her, then closed. "Yeah. Dizzy."

"We should take a break," she told him. "Try again tomorrow."

He nodded letting his cheek rest in her hand. Mason relaxed as if her touch brought comfort. He kissed her palm.

The gesture eased her concern. She sat next to him and patted his back. "You made progress. I'm impressed."

That made him smile. "I'm glad, it's not easy impressing you."

Nora smiled too.

They sat in silence avoiding their return to the boardinghouse. Inside their time together would be limited, and Wesley would be keeping a watchful eye for any slips. The few minutes alone in the cold delayed their time apart. Mason didn't move either. He stared out at Lumina with a passive expression, less fear in his eyes. She even dared to guess a hint of confidence. The dread of loosing himself to a time read was almost over.

Chapter 21
Places

By the time they entered the boardinghouse, Angeline and Hogan were setting up dinner near the fireplace. The wonderful smell of fried chicken, cheesy mashed potatoes, and buttery biscuits made Nora's mouth water. Pizza boxes and liters of soda joined the mass collection of food. Standing out in the cold for hours built her an appetite. Also, pulling Mason's dead weight around left her arms sore. She filled her plate to the brim with food. Who knew when she would eat a decent meal like this again in the next several days.

Nora sat on the floor beside Charlie. It was the safest spot in the room. Hogan lured Mason over for a word. She shifted in her seat tucking strands of hair behind her ear, straining to listen. Wesley padded away giving Nora a side glance.

Charlie nudged her with his elbow. "How'd it go?"

Nora blinked. "What?" She poked at the mound of mashed potatoes on her plate, and set her plastic fork down to pick up a slice of pizza instead.

"Outside. The training," Charlie prompted as she ate. "Hogan told us Mason's time reading ability keeps him grounded here. It's the reason we came to you to give you time. No pun intended."

"It's a work in progress. I think he'll have a handle on it soon."

"He always does, or so I'm told."

She took a long thoughtful sip of her drink.

They ate with casual chatter. Angeline wandered over to share the multitude of places she and Wesley had lived in, most of which were former French colonies. It was there where she picked up her impeccable sense of fashion and refined her cooking skills. Nora remembered the few visits she took to New Orleans, French Brazil, or present day Morocco to see her.

Mason questioned if he ever fell under her care. The short answer was yes. Angeline met previous version of him in the past. Time guards weren't assigned time markers, but there was an unspoken rule of luck of the draw. When Nora failed to find Mason first, it was usually Angeline who protected him.

After their meal, Hogan gathered the time markers using a deck of cards. He shuffled them over the coffee table like a professional dealer. The boys played a few hands of poker into the night betting loose change. It was unfair on his behalf; he was an excellent player. His face never revealed what kind of hand he held.

Nora sat forward in her seat quietly coaching Mason into a few victories. She pointed over his shoulders when he ought to stay or make a move. Annoyed at her interference, Hogan shooed her away.

She curled into the couch with her tablet and various copies of a world map balanced on her knees. While the others played, Nora began her assignment to find a new safe city for her and Mason. The first map, an extremely written over image of Europe, was color coded with symbols reminding her where she had been as well as the corresponding time marker. Asia, Africa and South America were marked similarly.

Anyone else reading the maps would say she lived everywhere at least once; however, Nora saw a lot of blank spaces. There were hundreds of towns and cities to choose from. Kyoto. Dubai. Saint Petersburg. Cape Town. Buenos Aires. All options were busy, vibrant cities, easy to hide in plain sight. They also provided the best advantages for escaping capture.

In the past, Mason thrived among the hustle and bustle. He liked being in the thick of things. The fast-paced lifestyle suited him fine, and he coped well. It was the rural areas he struggled with. He often told her he felt stuck in place that hardly ever changed.

Nora drew an X over the larger cities, changing her mind. Large cities held richer histories. It was sure to send Mason in a spiral of time reads. Instead, she circled lesser known cities around the globe. The tranquil atmosphere would make it easier to ground him.

Further into the night, a pair of hands raised her outstretched legs to sit beneath them. Her maps fluttered to the floor. Nora looked up to see Mason.

"How much did you loose?" she asked, picking up the papers.

He shrugged. "Few dollars maybe."

"I should have warned you," she replied with an apologetic smile.

Mason chuckled. "Yeah, you should have," he told her, patting her leg. "What are you working on?"

She shuffled through the pages to show him. "Looking for new places to go. Any ideas?"

"Let's hear what you have."

She showed him a map of Central and South America. Blue-and-black ink was scratched all over. "Mexico City. I hear they have an excellent soccer academy."

"I'm more of a Manchester United kind of guy."

Nora rolled her eyes and rifled through her maps before handing him a European map. It was just as heavily marked. She pointed to the upper peninsula in the direction of the Arctic Circle.

"Norway," she suggested. "You've never been there. It has a breathtaking landscape. We could see the northern lights in January and in the summer there's a day the sun is visible for practically twenty-four hours."

Mason didn't look wildly impressed.

Nora gave him a playful shove. "Pick something. Anything."

He took a moment to think about it. A minute later Mason gestured for her tablet, and she handed it to him. He opened a digital map, much like the one on his phone, swiped through the globe, and handed it back to her. It was partially zoomed on a province in Canada.

"What about somewhere near Toronto?" he asked.

"What's in Toronto?" she shot back.

"There's bound to be *something* there," he said with a shrug and a mischievous grin. "Otherwise we can stir up trouble."

She smiled too and took a closer look at the city. The grid pattern enlarged, naming a handful of streets and the tiny squares representing homes and stores lined the streets. She knew very little of Toronto, only that it was large, densely populated, and north of Lake Ontario. Nora drew a broad circle around the Canadian city to include the neighboring towns in case she had a change of mind later.

"No matter what I chose, you'll be okay with it?" she asked him, drawing the tablet to her chest like a book.

"I suppose I'll have to."

Nora looked around. Wesley wandered back into the living room to grab a water bottle. He shifted a glance at them making her flush. She swung her legs off the couch and got to her feet.

"I'll see you in the morning," she told him.

She caught Hogan over by the back door, most likely returning from running perimeter on foot. Unlike Nora, he personally wanted to make sure the boardinghouse was secure. He let her slip past outside to pick up extra logs for the fireplace in her room before he locked the door. She took a lit lantern and headed down the hall.

A dying flame greeted her when she opened the door. It crackled once, yearning to stay alit. She tossed in a log with a new match, and the fire grew. The dim orange light was enough to let her change into her pajamas and settle into bed.

As soon as the room turned cozy, Nora began to feel sleepy. A quiet knock stirred her awake. It was coming from the window. Draping the blanket around her shoulders, she slinked out of bed in annoyance. She pushed aside the curtains just as the window slid open. Mason pulled himself in careful not to make a sound.

Once he was safely inside, he moved to the fireplace first throwing in a new log into the fire. It disrupted the ongoing flames for a moment. Pops and crackling came from the fireplace, burning brighter and hotter than before.

As the wood ruptured and noisily burned, he gathered her in his arms blanket and all engulfing her in a deep kiss. Her heart fluttered as he lifted her off the ground. Although she spent most of the day with him, Nora missed him. It took a reasonable amount of energy to keep him at arms length and pretend all was the same.

"You got rid of me way too fast," he teased, swooping in for another kiss.

"Wesley was watching," Nora replied. "I couldn't ..."

Mason rolled his eyes. "An innocent conversation will always make his hair stand on end," he replied, pulling her in close and they kissed again. His cool delicate touch on her neck made her squirm, wanting to be closer. Nora maneuvered him out of the nightshirt he came in. He hoisted her off the floor, and the blanket fell to the floor. Her fingers traced the outline of his jaw, then disappeared into his dark hair as they landed on the bed.

The growing roar of the fire muted the sound of each lengthy kiss. It gave them a brief pocket of time to discard the remaining articles of clothing before the fire settled and silence fell over the room.

Further in the night well after Mason began to snore, Nora twitched in her sleep. Her legs involuntarily punted at the air while her arms tightened around her pillow, much like the way she slept as a prisoner. The memory was disguised as a nightmare tonight. She had no option but to live through the trauma. Midsleep, Nora let out a cry into her pillow as the dream started off the same.

She was back in the ship, trapped in the dark cabin pounding on the door. She threw all her weight at it hoping it would give way. The thunderstorm above grew rougher. It sent crashing waves stirring the boat like the indecisive compass needle. A sheet of water seeped through the floorboards soaking her feet. She had to grip the handle to keep herself from flying backward. After a series of rumbling cracks of thunder, harsh shouts from unknown voices made Nora's heart clench in dread.

"Mason!" Nora screamed desperately, yanking at the door handles. "Let me out! Mason!"

It was no use; the doors wouldn't move. He locked her in from the outside. Everyone was up above in the chaos; no one could hear her. Mason rushed up to the deck minutes ago to defend his ship from the unwanted guests. Nora couldn't be shut away while they were under attack. She needed to be in the fight.

Nora made a blind grab for the umbrella stand where Mason kept a spare sword and wedged the blade in the crease between the double doors. In one forceful move, she drew the sword upward. The ropes Mason used to lock her in dropped to the floor in a heap. She tumbled out of the room, darted along the hall, and ran up the stairs taking two at a time.

She was frantic to reach the madness ahead. The time quake Nora felt earlier that morning made her feel uneasy all day. She anticipated something awful to happen and this was it. This sudden assault on the ship was no accident, the people up above were bound to be time travelers.

As soon as she reached the deck, Nora was drenched with sea water and rain. She pushed her wet hair out of her face blinking rapidly to look for Mason. A flash of metal caught her eye. Nora raised her sword over her head in time to stop the man from slicing her shoulder. He shouted out in surprise that the girl half his size wielded the sword with such grace. With a brilliant flourish, she knocked his sword clean out of his hands and used the hilt to hit him in the chest. He stumbled back stepping into an open time warp. It closed behind him and Nora hurried forward.

The rain came down harder. She walked onto the deck still looking for Mason. Along the way, Nora disposed of the time travelers into waiting time warps she silently conjured. She couldn't get rid of them fast enough. They only seemed to multiply. Nora decided to give up on that idea and find Mason before it was too late.

A flash of lightning parted the sky, illuminating the ship. It was so unsettling that some of the time travelers and pirates hesitated to wait for the earth cracking thunder to shake the earth and plunge them back into the night. The powerful rumble vibrated the entire boat.

While everyone was momentarily distracted, Nora spotted Mason on the quarterdeck holding his own with a robust time traveler. The clap of thunder came to an end, and the pandemonium continued.

She ran forward, but a hand shoved her to the ground, and the unmistakable sound of two swords meeting rang above her ears.

"Mason!"

He turned at the sound of his name forgetting that he was in the middle of a battle for his life. Mason's eyes were wide in fear recognizing her voice amid the chaos. He found her crouched under a pair of blades. "Nora, don't move!" he ordered. "I'm coming!"

"Go, Nora!" one of Mason's men grunted, trying to prevent the sword from decapitating her. "Run!"

And she did. She ran to the steps that overlooked the main deck. Mason did the same a flicker of relief crossing his eyes. He was half way down the steps when a time traveler caught up to him, gripped his shoulder, and ran his sword straight through Mason's chest.

Nora awoke with a jolt, wrestling away the blanket and gulping for a new breath of air. It had been so real as though she was reliving the night all over again. She remembered how the salty water prickled her skin like sandpaper, the aches in her muscles after hours of sword training with Mason. And the pain—it was awful. It felt too real. The heaviness in her heart and the hollowness in her gut felt like it would never go away.

She closed her eyes thankful that it was only a dream. Nora didn't have to fall back asleep to know how it ended. The faint smell of blood and the sea left its mark on her. She avoided the ocean at all costs. Time hadn't healed that wound yet.

Eventually, her breathing relaxed, and she eased back into bed. Mason was still fast asleep beside her. Nora examined him up close. She traced his chest where the blade from the past cut through.

His skin was smooth to the touch. It was foolish of her to think she would find anything at all. He wasn't the other Mason.

Nora turned to lay on her stomach and shoved her face into her pillow, pushing away the last of the memory. She'd dealt with all sorts of heartbreak, but none compared to losing a time marker. His brutal death was her failure.

In the dark, she shifted onto her elbows and glanced over at Mason again. Knowing him as she did now, Nora couldn't imagine keeping away from him. Much less loosing him.

Chapter 22
Time Ascending

Nora's initial plan was to wake up early and sneak Mason out of her room. The indigo sky beyond the window meant they could spare another hour or two before the first light of the day drove them apart. She figured it was best to have him return to his bedroom in case Hogan or Angeline planned to wake soon. Mason, however, had other plans on how the morning should go. He had her beat with a series of hurried, lustful kisses savoring each one to take with him. The thought of casting him out began to slip further and further away from her mind.

Mason pinned Nora onto the mattress. His hands slowly traveled from her waist to her rib cage. She held her breath at his touch, then exhaled when his hands fell back to the outer curves of her body. Nora cradled his face in her hands and they kissed. Unlike him, she wasn't in a dramatic rush. The flow of energy between them was like a steady electrical current fueled by the need to remain close, even just for a few more minutes.

She rotated her hip until she was able to move herself and Mason in one fluid movement. He landed softly on his back with a mild look of haughty amusement. Nora intertwined her fingers through his, pulled him up to sit upright, and continued kissing. Chuckling, his hands wrapped around her hips as she dragged her fingers along the nape of his neck. Her touch reached the grooves of his muscles, the very same ones she traced hours ago.

A harsh, loud pounding on the door made Nora pull away. Mason sighed irritably behind her as she squirmed in his arms. She tumbled out of his lap landing on the foot of the bed ready to leap at the nearest article of clothing in case the door was to burst open. The knocking came again, this time faster and demanding. Nora jumped out of bed and pulled on a gray pair of legging. When she noticed Mason wasn't moving, she threw him a stern look that meant he ought to be doing the same. In a silent huff, he swept after her looking for his sweatshirt.

"Hold on," she half shouted, shoving Mason his jeans as he tied on his shoes.

"Nora," came Charlie's voice. He sounded worried. "Hogan and Angeline are gone."

Nora pulled a purple sweater over her head. "Okay, I'm coming!"

Fully clothed, Mason hurried to the window with Nora right on his heels almost pushing him along. He climbed out and took off back to his room. Once he was gone, she raced to the door and flung it open.

"Hogan and Angeline aren't in their room," Charlie explained. "They aren't anywhere on the property."

"What do you mean they aren't here?" she asked, rushing passed him. Nora walked fast down the hallway to the living room. It wasn't like them to run away. They *always* stayed put. She refused to believe the pair of them would simply vanish. Angeline was the first to remind Nora of the reason why the three of them walked the earth. And Hogan was all else but neglectful of his duty.

Wesley was up too. He stopped pacing the living room floor when he saw Nora and Charlie coming. She didn't slow down, Nora headed straight for the door. He hurried to follow them. "Angeline doesn't ever just bail," Wesley said as they reached the spot where Hogan's junker had been. "Not without good reason."

"Hogan too," Charlie added.

"Nobody bailed," Nora said sharply. Her mind raced searching for possible explanations. "They're around here somewhere."

The sound of crunching gravel made them all jump. Instinctively, Nora took a few tentative paces to meet the vehicle first. The familiar beat up truck rolled in with Angeline behind the wheel. A look of concern flashed through the windshield when she noticed the three of them standing outside. She cut the engine, jumped out of the pickup balancing a tray of coffees, tugged a paper bag off the passenger seat, and strolled over to meet them with a bright smile.

Her smile faded as she approached. "Hell," Angeline muttered under her breath, but then lifted the coffee tray like a peace offering. "Did I miss something while I was gone?"

Wesley didn't look pleased. The firm line on his forehead only deepened when Charlie helped himself to one of the steaming cups. "You should have said something, left a note at least," Wesley spit out reproachfully.

Angeline didn't look bothered by his reprimanding. "I was hoping to be back before you all woke. I ran patrol among other things. Besides, you can't be too angry with me I come bearing coffee and prepackaged drugstore provisions to last most of the morning," she said, weighing the bag in her hands.

Without a word and chewing the inside of her cheek, Wesley took a coffee. He turned to walk back into the boardinghouse. A second later he turned back around, snatched the bag of food, and lumbered back to the door.

"And Hogan?" Charlie asked.

"He did leave," she told him. "I'm to inform you that he's stepped out for the day scouting abroad and he's to return by nightfall." Angeline then addressed Nora next as Charlie followed Wesley. The girls fell back a few steps behind. "If it's all right with you, I'd like to take my leave tomorrow."

"Take the day," Nora replied, catching the door before it closed. "I still have to make certain arrangements before I go."

Angeline let slip one more dazzling smile in gratitude and crossed the threshold to help Wesley spread the contents of the breakfast haul on the coffee table. Nora approached the promising table of food. She squatted low appreciating the fact that Angeline got breakfast that morning. It had a healthier variety than usual and a pop of color with all the fruit. She picked up a bagel with plenty of cream cheese packets, a cup of assorted fruit, and an oatmeal cookie. Nora then took the open love seat. As she plopped a blueberry in her mouth, Charlie neared handing her a coffee.

"I think I owe you one for waking you at the crack of dawn," he told her. "I'm not quite sure how you take it, but any coffee is as good as any, right?"

"For future reference, she likes mochas."

The two of them looked up. It was Mason. They hadn't heard him enter the living room. He clutched the top of the seat, hopped over the couch, and landed next to her. His easy morning smile fell when he saw Nora throwing him a menacing look to stop talking. "What?" he asked. "You do, don't you?"

She ignored him. "Any coffee will do at this hour," Nora told Charlie, taking the cup. "Thank you."

Nora spread cream cheese onto one of the bagel halves. Charlie leaned on the wooden pillar fishing out a juicy green grape at the bottom of the fruit cup in his hand. He ate his breakfast on foot attempting feeble small talk with them. Mason did his best to keep the interaction afloat. Unfortunately, the two had little to talk about, and the conversation ended. Feeling pity for the two of them, Nora jumped in to spare them the awkward silence.

"Get dressed," she instructed. "If I'm up this early, we may as well do something. Bring Wesley."

The three time markers and Nora met by the back door fifteen minutes later. Angeline shooed them to go on without her. She pulled out a sleek silver laptop from a tote meaning she was about to plot a course for tomorrow's travels. The few hours alone suited her fine while Nora kept them busy.

She ushered the boys out the door. Nora trotted ahead to the dirt trail to find the tallest, strongest trees. The time markers weren't climbers in any sense of the word. It wasn't that they lacked skill; they mostly didn't find an interest in the activity as she did. Most of the time Charlie didn't see much fun in the it and Wesley who had seen her climb dozens of times gave up on the hobby when he realized he wouldn't be able to beat her. Mason was the only one with current experience, yet he did little to keep up with her.

The sparse forest and frigid morning jarred Nora awake. The excitement from earlier only faded now replaced by eagerness to get up in the branches before the sun rose. Her favorite part of climbing before sunrise was soaking up the warmth and light of a brand new day.

The allure of trees and climbing was something special to Nora, like a peculiar second home each and every lifetime. She had no place to call her own, yet among thousands of branches across time she found something entirely her own. To lose herself in the rough bark under her fingers as well as the strain of gravity trying to pull her back to earth felt like home. A part of her liked that she was still capable of defying physics outside a time warp.

Charlie, Mason, and Wesley caught up to her as she studied a long line of oaks picking out those with the lowest hanging branches. Charlie cracked his knuckles in apprehension as if regretting his decision to tag along.

"Tree climbing," Wesley said, amused. "I forgot this is what you like to do."

She turned around to face them. "You can't back out."

"I'm not," he replied.

"Good," Nora said briskly. She spun around ready to match the time markers with an appropriate tree. She strode over to a handsome thick tree with countless dark branches. The overgrown limbs were barren of any leaves. At a glance, he would have the greatest visibility to the top. It was best suited for Wesley who lacked current experience. The extra branches would provide more foot and grip support.

"This one is for you, Wes," she told him.

Next, she dashed over to the tree across from it walking through a pile of withered brown leaves. This particular oak was just as enormous with the exception of the occasional flutter of dead leaves to the ground. Under the shade of the tree, the early morning sky was blotchy, hard to see it as it was. Nora knew Charlie was more than able to tackle it. Out of the three, he displayed the most effort.

Nora patted the uneven bark. "Charlie."

Finally, the last acceptable tree was a bit further back in perfect view of the water tower. It had less branches and several empty nests scattered throughout. The driest leaves clung tight refusing to let go. Mason did his fair share of climbing with her, most of which occurred in this life when he tried to find common ground with her. She also knew he was never one to back down from her challenges.

"And I take it this one's for me?" Mason asked, standing beside her. He lay his hand on the trunk and glanced up at its branches.

Nora backed away. "Think you can handle it?" she asked.

He glanced over his shoulder at her. "Easy."

"Great. I'll see you guys at the top."

She took off in a trot to a tree just beyond the one she picked for Mason. It was a stockier tree with thin drooping branches. It looked fragile enough to be snapped in half by a thunderstorm. It was her best chance of a thrilling climb. With ease, Nora leaped to reach the first branch. She dangled for a moment, gathered all her strength, swung her legs to gain momentum, and landed in a low crouch on a steady branch. Careful not to hit her head, she took a tentative step forward to reach the next branch. Nora straightened and threw her leg over the coarse bark. She pulled herself up.

"I feel like I'm at a disadvantage," she heard Mason say. "Charlie's a psychic and Wesley has years of practice."

Somewhere a branch snapped.

"It doesn't work that way," Charlie said defensively.

"That doesn't mean I'm any good," Wesley offered up.

She stood up again and reached for a branch. "It should be all muscle memory."

"Muscle memory?"

Nora nodded even though they couldn't see her. "It's a subconscious mechanism to help you all survive different reoccurring circumstances. You've all done this enough times to retain some ability in climbing."

"So you're saying we're cheating?" Mason sounded a little lower than the rest of them.

"She means we're all evenly matched," Wesley retorted.

Nora kept going ducking among the branches. She knew where to place her feet and hands. The monotonous drill of find, hand, foot, lift, and repeat produced a calming effect. Once she was well above the others, Nora stopped a moment to watch the time markers struggle below.

Wesley wasn't too far behind. He stopped as well to take a glimpse at the incoming sunrise. Charlie was a little lower catching up fast. Mason hung back the most. The uneven placement of the branches and tricky grips proved to slow him down.

The sound of cracking wood and a sharp yell almost made Nora fall off her perch. Her hand flew to her sundial as she searched for the source of the problem. The time key pulsed against her hand as if ready to catch anyone in a time warp if need be. It was Charlie. He had lost his footing. Instead of reaching above, he let himself drop to a lower branch, scratches forming along his cheeks.

She relaxed. "Will you be okay?" Nora called out to him.

"Yeah, fine."

She waited for him to begin again. It was best to stop going easy on them and really cut out the lead. From above, she would be able to do something if anyone else took a misstep. By the time she made it to the top, Mason had passed Charlie and was neck to neck with Wesley. Both of them were close to finishing. Wesley lagged behind not daring to go any higher.

Nora stood on one of the last fat branches she could find that didn't threaten to snap under her weight. It wasn't until then that she noticed how close the treetops were from one another. If she wanted to, Nora could hop over and climb down a different tree.

A few trees over Mason tried his luck on a thin branch tugging on it once, but decided to stay where he was when it broke away from the trunk. He threw it aside. He stayed put, glancing around at the surrounding treetops in uncertainty.

"Make room. I'm coming over," Mason said after along period of silence.

"Are you insane? Did you not see Charlie almost fall to his death like ten minutes ago?" Nora demanded.

"I didn't think I would be up this high."

"Stay where you are," Nora ordered. "I'll talk you through it—"

Mason jumped. Nora screamed in horror. With a fistful of leaves around a wispy branch, she stretched as far as she could to catch him. His hand closed around hers. The sudden weight dragged her down. Nora swore under her breath. The branch she clung to sliced into her palm. It would be useless in a matter of seconds. Praying that they wouldn't fall to their death, Nora let it go to hold him steady. Slowly, she lowered him, struggling to keep herself from going headfirst into a complete dive. Mason found his footing below allowing her to shift back into place. Once Nora was sure that he was in a good position, she crouched down letting go of his arm.

He was so close Nora felt his cool breath on her lips. Suspended in the air, a part of her wanted to throw him off herself. She was furious that he even made such a dangerous attempt. Another part of her was still recovering from fright of having him so close out in the open with Charlie and Wesley in sight.

"Good catch," Mason whispered with a hint of relief. When she said nothing in return, he added: "Sunrise."

The morning sky began to change before their eyes. The gray patches nearest the horizon blended into a swirl of purple, pink, and yellow. It lasted only a minute. The colors then faded and turned to a translucent morning blue.

Chapter 23
Muscle Memory

The rustle of leaves over her head told Nora the time markers were on their way down. As she waited, she sat under the shade of the tree she had climbed tossing broken twigs into the grass. She wondered what was taking Mason so long, he wasn't too far behind her. Nora heard Wesley and Charlie talking their way down, but up above had gone strangely quiet. Curiosity getting the better of her, she looked up. Small pieces of bark fell in the grass as her hand flew to the sundial around her neck again.

Mason jumped down landing inches from Nora's outstretched feet. Somewhere in the distance two more similar thuds meant Charlie and Wesley made it to the ground without a problem.

"Sorry."

"Was that really necessary?" she asked, pulling her feet toward her.

Mason offered her his hand. "Maybe."

"That wasn't funny. It was dangerous."

Nora let him pull her to her feet. He yanked her up with such a force that it made her fumble forward. She gave him a playful shove, still wanting to be angry with him. Without warning, a vicious shove caused Mason's hand to slip right through her grasp. He toppled back, the shock disorienting him. Someone shouldered passed Nora heading straight for Mason.

"Wesley!" Nora shouted.

"Don't you touch her!" Wesley fumed, propelling Mason further away. "You almost got her killed. Or worse, yourself! How much of an idiot can you be? You go, and the rest of us go too. You may be ready to die, but I'm not!"

Mason returned the shove. "Drop it, Wes, before I choose to forget who you are right now."

"You choose? You have no other choice, but to forget!"

"Wesley!" she rounded on him.

"Like you haven't done anything that would get us all killed!" Mason yelled. "I'll die and forget this ever happened. You on the other hand will have to remember all your stupid mistakes!"

"Mason!"

Nora swooped in between them as Wesley advanced ready to throw a punch. Mason stepped up too. His arm twitched at his side, his knuckles turning white. It was taking all that he had to keep him from throwing her aside and lunging. The murderous look in his eyes meant he was seeing red.

"Nora, move!"

"Walk it off," she ordered. "Both of you!"

The two of them didn't move a muscle. The changing atmosphere around them crackled with out of control energy. Time clashing with one another was not a new concept; it's what drove time to be an ongoing current. But open hostility between the time markers was unheard of. It was a first in their history that they disagreed with one another. It made Nora nervous. Strong emotions coupled with close proximity was bound to make their souls burn brighter.

When neither of them moved, she gave them a dangerous glare. "Now!"

Out of the corner of her eye, Nora saw Mason breathe and relax. When she didn't meet his eyes, he backed away. He turned, jogged over to the dirt trail, and disappeared. Charlie muttered something about following so he wouldn't turn back. The uncomfortableness in the air dwindled away, but the tension still hung tight.

Wesley kicked the dirt in frustration. "He's so reckless and you let him get away with it. Mason could have killed you! Damn it, why didn't you say anything?" he demanded.

"Because you didn't give me a chance," she fired back. "You swooped in and told him off. All you did was rile him up."

"It didn't look like you were going to!"

Nora took a step toward him. Telling her how to handle Mason was where he crossed the line. "You're not a time guard, Wes. Stop acting like one," she warned. A flicker of shock crossed his eyes, like her words hit something in him. Clearly, no one had spoken to him like this before. "When you cool off, come back to the boardinghouse." She shouldered passed him heading to the opposite path skidding around the property line. After ten seconds, Wesley began to follow.

She walked fast in hopes to put distance between them. He caught up in long easy strides. The anger he radiated disintegrated. Nora let him match her pace in order to get a glimpse of him. Wesley's expression was calm. It made her question what he was thinking. She also wondered if she had gone too far calling him out the way she did. It was unfair of her; he was only looking out for himself.

They reached the clearing on the far left of the boardinghouse. Mason waited out on the patio pacing over the slab of concrete. He looked up when he noticed them approach. Behind her, Wesley hesitated.

"Get inside," Nora told him. "Don't confront him."

Mason glared after Wesley, but didn't make a move to follow. Instead, he took a seat on the bench. He didn't meet her eyes, at least not right away. He looked to the old water tower before stealing a glance at her as if to access the damage. She neared crossing her arms.

Nora wanted to have a valid reason to be angry with Mason, but couldn't find one. She saw him up in the branches. He calculated his steps, measured the risks; the jump was minimal compared to the other dumb ideas he had in the past. It was an easy leap. Should he have done it? No. Should she strangle him for his actions? Although she wanted to, she wasn't going to.

"Are you mad?" he dared to ask.

"I want to be," she replied.

His expression turned to confusion. "Why aren't you?"

Nora shrugged. "Because you're an arrogant show off and a hot head. I don't know what you were trying to prove and Wesley—"

Anger propelled him off his seat. He was so quick she didn't have a chance to recoil. "Are you defending him?" Mason scowled.

"No," she shot back holding her ground. "I know what you're like. I know what I'm getting into with you. He doesn't, so explain to me why you pulled such a dumb stunt back there!"

He let out a breath. It came out white in the cold. Mason diverted his gaze, as if it bothered him to say it. "I don't know, because I wanted to," he admitted. "I wanted to be out here in the open with you, to share that stupid sunrise even for a second." He paused to look at the door Charlie and Wesley crossed. "When Wesley came between us like that, he hit something I didn't even know was there." Mason touched his head tenderly, feeling for the memory in his skull that caused the sudden impulse. It was a gesture Nora recognized that *something* was coming through. "I wanted to hurt him … over and over again. And I didn't want to stop."

"You have to play it cool around him," she told him.

"I don't think I can."

"Let's get you away from here for a bit."

They walked to the end of the property. Lumina wasn't any kinder to Mason today compared to the day before. His first several attempts knocked him off his feet in a matter of seconds. Surprisingly, that didn't discourage him. He kept at it with little protest. Nora saw him struggling to keep himself here. Beads of sweat began to pool at his temples. His knees tried to refrain from buckling. He even tried to shut his eyes to keep himself from watching what was shone to him. The rough pattern of collapsing, dragging, and repeat lasted for hours. She was sure he would catch up to the progress they made yesterday.

"Wait, wait," she said aloud, stopping Mason from crossing into Lumina. "This isn't working."

He looked exasperated at her remark. "Should we stop?"

Nora shook her head. "We have to try something different," she said. "Yesterday, you were on the cusp of breaking through your time read when you spoke to me. How?"

"How am I supposed to know?"

She took a moment to think glancing around. Using their surroundings like the water tower or boardinghouse wasn't enough to ground Mason. It meant too little to him, no history. It was a temporary place in his journey. Perhaps, he needed to think of a place that was more meaningful.

"Okay," Nora said, turning back to him. "Think about your home, your friends, of anything that belongs in your time."

"All right."

Mason slowly walked backward out of Lys Gate. She watched him go paying close attention to when the time read whisked him away. Several steps in his eyes began searching behind her looking through all the layers of time. There were fractions of a second his brown eyes stilled. He was fighting to get back, but to no luck. Mason staggered back arms flailing in case he needed to catch his fall.

"Nora?"

"I'm right here, follow my voice back to your time," she said stepping closer.

He took another step back. "I can't pull out of the time read."

"Yes, you can, Mason. Think of the house you grew up in, the life you have here."

The time read had a tight grip on him. It leveled him to his knees a guttural sound escaping from his lips. It reduced to him to all fours. Mason spat onto the grass and shuddered, suppressing the urge to throw up. He wasn't going to be conscious much longer. Nora rushed forward to keep him fighting.

"Come on, Mason, I'm right here. Get out of there," she coached, kneeling.

Another shudder passed through him, and he squeezed his eyes shut. "I'm in too many versions of this place. I can't."

"Yes, you can! Focus!"

Something in Mason forced his eyes open to witness the time read. Although he was looking right at her, Nora knew he wasn't entirely there. A disgruntled sound grew in his chest; he was trying to steady his breathing. His head jerked in an effort to shut his eyes again. Under his eyelids, the movement beneath them slowed. She waited to see what would happen next.

Mason's eyes flickered open blinking hard. He fixed his gaze on her. He wasn't looking beyond her anymore, not through her, but right at her. The familiar burn of his soul made his brown eyes glow. He pulled himself free of the time read. As soon as the glow faded, he lost control and his body gave way into her arms.

Nora hauled him back to Lys Gate. He looked worse than before, he looked close to passing out. Mason sat with his head in between his knees for a long time. He only raised his head when she crouched beside him to offer him a drink of water.

"I saw you this time," Mason said after draining half the bottle. "I saw you here."

She nodded. "I know you came back to me for two and a half seconds," Nora said. "Do you feel comfortable trying again?"

"No way," he said at once and laid back on the grass.

"We only have today and tomorrow to get you in any condition to move," she told him, pulling him to his feet. "We're going again."

He let her position him along the boundary once more. He let out a shaky breath checking on Nora over his shoulder. She urged him to go. With his back toward her, he stepped into Lumina. Ten paces in Mason buckled under the weight of the time read. He kept himself upright as long as he could.

"Focus, Mason, you can do this."

He lurched forward as though someone pushed him. "No, I—can't."

"Remember *your* time, this is where you belong."

Her words did nothing. Mason still fell onto his hands and knees. His shoulders shook as he coughed up the air in his lungs. He tried to get up from the ground, but it was no use. The time read kept him down.

"I can't," Mason said, shaking his head. "I can't."

Nora swept into Lumina. "Yes, you can," she demanded, pulling him up by the wrists. Mason flinched caught off guard by her arrival. She knew she was being rough with him, the abrasive approach could work since all else failed. "I've seen you do it hundreds of times in Iran. Come back!"

Suddenly, everything shifted. The time read sucked her in. They were rooted to the spot unable to move within the multiple folds. Everything around them remained in motion. The scenery peeled itself away like a flipbook revealing its pages. It was fast and in no particular order, which was in large part of the confusion. It was impossible for Nora to tell in what time they were in. If she was looking at the past or future, all of it indistinguishable. Different stages of the boardinghouse stood behind them, neglect fading in and out. Other layers revealed a pastured meadow, a barbed wire fence to hold in a small amount of cattle, and a cottage. The houses in Lumina blinked out various times, replaced by a lone road.

Mason looked around in wonder, taking in all the sights. He couldn't get enough of what he was seeing. He was so absorbed in the time read he failed to notice that Nora joined him along for the ride.

"Mason?"

The time read shook. It flickered like a frozen screen pressed on pause. The disruption loosened the hold the time read had on them. With the connection severed, it allowed Mason to pry them out.

Her grasp on his arm began to slip. As they exited, the last image Nora saw the boardinghouse consumed in flames. They arrived back to the present. Mason hit the ground first. She helped him up. With his arm draped over her shoulders, she led him over the property line. "That was much, much better!" she said, her voice full of pride. Nora dragged him all the way to the water tower, lowered him, and set him on the ground. Her own legs were wobbly too, and not because she had dragged his weight for the hundredth time that day. "That's enough for now. Well done!"

"I felt stronger this time, more in control," Mason told her, although his breathing was a bit heavy. "I think you tagging along helped."

"We'll test that theory tomorrow."

"You sure?"

Nora clapped him on the shoulder. "Positive," she replied. "Let's get you back inside. And maybe some food."

Chapter 24
Time Spent

Crossing the threshold into the boardinghouse, Mason lost consciousness. He slumped into Nora almost causing her to collapse under his weight. Charlie and Angeline rushed to help her move Mason further inside. They got as far as the living room lowering him onto a couch. Angeline came forward to hand over a blanket. Nora draped it over Mason although the room was plenty warm.

"What's wrong with him?" Charlie asked.

"Exhaustion," Nora replied. "Freeing himself from a time read drained him. He'll be all right in a few hours."

The rest of the afternoon Nora remained at his side to keep watch as he slept. She tended to the fire keeping the room nice and cozy. Her lunch consisted of leftovers from the day before. With the cold and hunger she had, the meal was more than satisfactory. The next several hours were quiet. Nora spent it on her tablet ironing out the details of her scouting trip in less than two days.

Charlie and Wesley sat on the floor around the coffee table playing dominos. Apparently, one of them supplied the entertainment. A white backpack rested on a love seat was densely packed with games of every variety: miniature puzzles and board games, pocket-size word search books, a bag of marbles, a deck of cards, and a plug-in console of arcade games. It was an impressive choice of items and in Nora's opinion not very practical. "You want to keep us sane, don't you?" Wesley challenged when she voiced her concern. "It's the only thing that doesn't make us feel like we're prisoners."

Angeline used her time walking in and out of the room packing a bag for her departure in a few hours. She sat on the floor, weighing items in her hands, tossing aside the heavier of the two. The real entertainment was watching her choose traveling attire. She swapped through all her articles of clothing that had been so meticulously organized in her suitcase.

"No to the cloak," Nora teased, resting her legs on the coffee table. "This isn't the witch trials."

She snapped the dark fabric like a cape. "It may as well be the way we're being hunted," Angeline shot back and unfastened the cloak from her neck. She stole a glance down the hall to make sure the time markers wouldn't overhear. They had retreated to their rooms early. "He's never struggled like this before."

Angeline didn't have to spell it out for her. Her concern for Mason's time reading worried her too. Nora leaned forward to push his hair away from his forehead. "I don't understand what's wrong either," she admitted.

"Do you think something's changed in him?"

She shrugged.

Under her fingertips, Mason began to stir. He groaned complaining about a pounding headache. Nora knelt at his side helping him sit up as Angeline hurried over. It took him a moment to realize they were inside.

"You look better," Angeline said, gently feeling his forehead. "Do you want something for that migraine?"

He shook his head, shaking the sleep away. "It's passing."

"Anything else, then? Water?" Regardless, she handed him a water bottle.

He accepted it. "Lunch sounds good."

"Dinner," Nora corrected. "It's dinnertime. You've slept through the afternoon."

"I don't think we have much left," Angeline told him apologetically. "I'm sure Nora can run out and grab something for everyone."

He got to his feet and stretched. "I'll go. Fresh air will do me good."

Angeline insisted he remain behind and fully recover, but Mason refused. He promised that the fainting spell was long gone, that it wouldn't happen again within the confines of Lys Gate. Nora stayed at the margin of the debate not wanting to side with one or the other. Angeline only agreed to let him go when he swore they'd return in less than half an hour. Once they had her approval, Mason dragged Nora out the door.

He let her drive his car knowing very well Angeline was watching from the window. Nora didn't venture him out far. They picked up a dozen cold sandwiches from a shop near a closed post office. In addition to the foot longs, she ordered salads and wraps and all else from the menu. Mason directed her to a convenience store down the block to load up on snacks and water.

The clerk was kind enough to let them take the red plastic grocery basket after they approached the counter with so much food. They would have cleaned out the store if Mason got his hands on a cart.

Hand in hand, they walked back to the car. For a brief moment Nora thought she caught a glimpse of another Mason, one that reproachfully accompanied her to the market with a wooden bucket. It infuriated him to no end that she did all the bartering while he carried the items like a mule.

Mason let go of her hand to fish out the keys from his pocket. "Stop looking at me like that," he warned, unlocking the door.

She blinked. "How am I looking at you?"

He placed the basket in the back seat. "Like you're remembering another version of me. Or like you think I'm going to die," Mason told her. He reached for her and Nora stepped into his waiting arms. She felt guilty of thinking about the past. No two versions of him were ever the same.

"It's nothing," Nora lied.

He pressed his lips to her forehead. "I wish we didn't have to go."

"You'll come by tonight, won't you?" she asked, looking up at him.

Mason hesitated thinking his words wisely and pushed strands of hair behind her ear before answering. "It's not that," he muttered. "I wish I didn't have to die."

"You'll come back again," she reminded him. "I'll find you, I always do."

"I mean, I don't want to forget this," Mason explained, looking passed her before studying her puzzled expression. "I won't remember you or what we lived through. To me, it'll be like it never happened. I'll be a blank slate. I'll forget how hard it was to win you over. I'll forget your touch, your voice. All of it. It scares the hell out of me."

Nora didn't reply. She understood his fear. It often meant her time to go was close, her soul would follow his as it always did. All the progress they made would disappear. But if things got worse, like they tended to, she preferred death take him than time travelers. And if that was the case, it would give them a chance for a do-over.

"It's almost seven o'clock. Hogan will be waiting."

"Let me drive you to the train station," Mason said. A part of him relaxed that she diffused the tension. "I owe you."

She pulled away from him. "I'll find my way. Go back the boardinghouse. Let Angeline know what's going on."

"It'll just worry her."

Nora gave him a look that pleaded for him to pass on the message. Angeline needed to know they received a distress call from Hogan during their time in the sandwich shop. When she picked up the call, Nora was greeted with the sound of muffled gunfire and the jostle of the phone. Gunfire exploded into her ear, then Hogan called out in Mandarin. The call ended with more movement from the other side.

"Fine," he said.

When she was alone in the parking lot, Nora grasped the sundial. Her eyes swept to the entrance and exit hoping no one noticed the jagged six foot dark entryway opening behind her. With a tentative step backward, Nora disappeared into the darkness to let it guide her where she needed to go.

The patrol itself lasted an hour. She stopped by a few reoccurring locations that time travelers landed in: there was the city park in

Lumina, the basement of a Greek restaurant in Santa Luz, the workshop classroom at the high school in Torch Crossings, and there was an overpass on Interstate 5, where she used it as a travel point on farther excursions. Her last stop was a quiet train platform in Valo. The empty railroad meant it had stopped running for the night.

She opened another time warp and stepped through silently, telling it to take her to the location Hogan was to arrive. It spat her out on a rooftop she didn't recognize. Nora walked to the ledge to get a better look around. Treetops covered most of her view, catching glimpses of two more buildings farther away in the night. The shadows of a smaller structure caught her eye. There was a weaving paved, narrow path piecing the buildings together. Squinting, Nora was sure she saw a large clearing with posts, stadium lights, and massive set of bleachers.

Nora raced to the other side. Down below she saw a familiar structure a short open building with beams and no walls. A pavilion.

She was back on her college campus.

"A little help?"

At the sound of a new voice, Nora whipped around.

It was Hogan. He hobbled over dropping his backpack on the ground. His long sleeve shirt was scorched along his shoulders and down his back. The right sleeve was torn hanging by a few dozen threads. His left shoulder was dislocated. It hung limply at his side in a way that made Nora's own arm ache in sympathy. His jeans were splattered with dry blood under a knot of cloth below the knee.

She rushed over to help him. "Lay down," Nora ordered, kneeling. "I can fix your arm. This might hurt."

Hogan collapsed to the floor not feigning the pain he was in. He only flinched when she took hold of his wrist and aligned his arm. "You say that a lot," he grunted.

"That's because I end up as your nurse a lot."

Nora popped his shoulder back into place so fast she didn't give him a chance to brace himself. He howled and swore so loud it echoed over the campus. "What the hell, Nora!" Hogan gasped through clenched teeth.

"I didn't say you were a good patient," Nora replied. "What happened to you?"

"Time travelers were waiting for me in Johannesburg," he told her, sitting up to rotate his arm. "They know we're on the move. It won't take them long to zero in." He got to his feet still stretching. "Shall we leave? I want to see Angeline before she goes."

Securing an arm around Hogan and his other arm draped over her shoulders, they hurtled off the roof. The wind whistled in their ears as they plummeted to meet the ground. Their reflections on the dark windows told Nora there was less of a chance to be seen by someone inside. They landed hard on the grass, their feet sinking into the dirt. The impact made Nora's legs buckle. Hogan swayed, but she kept him upright.

"That's much faster than the stairs," he joked. "Where are we?"

She wiggled her feet free. "It's the college campus Mason and I went to before going into hiding. Let's go, I can't be seen here," Nora replied.

"And how do you propose we do that?"

Nora looked around the deserted campus. Late hours were the worst time to travel in a place she knew so well. During the day, she was able to distinguish faces and knew what places to avoid. At night she couldn't say who prowled the landscape. They couldn't risk taking a car from the parking lot, the university police patrolled the dorm lot ticketing students who didn't have parking passes. And the school didn't offer busing away from the campus.

On foot would have them arrive at the boardinghouse well past midnight. Asking for a ride was out of the question too. There was no one she trusted enough on campus to take her anywhere. Then her eyes landed on a bike rack beside the Arbor building. Some of the dorm students used it to get around right after breakfast. They used the rack like a parking garage.

"How do you feel about bikes?" Nora asked.

Hogan followed her gaze. "I prefer ones with a motor."

"Not tonight you don't."

She led the way across the quad. Nora served as look out as Hogan picked a lock the old fashion way, using a paper clip. It took him less than half a second to set free a sleek black road bicycle. "You're not the only one with useful gadgets," he told her, handing her the thin piece of steel.

"This is primitive," she replied.

"Don't discredit my tech just yet."

He waited for her to pick the lock of a deep teal mountain bike. The dented wire slid right into the lock. Nora fumbled with it for a moment hoping to trip the lock mechanism. She paused. Nothing happened. Between her fingers, she felt the paper clip grow hot. The metal chinked reaching the tiny gears inside, willing it to open. With a gentle click, the lock opened.

She handed it back to him. "Not bad."

"I can make you one while you're gone," he offered. "Easier to carry around than a pen."

They wheeled the bikes away from the rack and peddled out of campus. Nora led the way through the few blocks of university housing. The neighborhood eventually thinned out to marsh fields. They pulled aside of a highway ramp. If her calculations were correct, they were twenty-five miles out. It would be a two-hour bike ride. Hogan and Nora pushed off the ground and eased onto the main road.

Drivers honked in mockery when they changed lanes to zoom on ahead. She glanced over to Hogan who didn't seem to mind that they obstructed traffic. He stood on his pedals gliding smoothly beside her. His blond hair was a pale gold under the streetlamps. Nora kept a look out for squad cars. Coasting along six miles an hour on bicycles was the perfect way to end up on the side of the road being questioned by the cops. Luckily, they made it to the exit without a problem.

Once they made it onto a two lane road again, Hogan called for a stop to catch their breath. Nora's legs ached, and she was sure they'd be sore in the morning. She didn't even trust herself to walk the side of the road like Hogan. He paced back and forth checking his phone for the time.

She did the same, one text glowed on the screen from Mason hours ago letting her know he made it.

"Is Angeline still waiting for me?" he asked.

"I'd bet she is," she replied. "I'm under the impression she'd like to see you before leaving."

He nodded and got back on the bike.

The last stretch to the boardinghouse went by rather quick. They skid around the outskirts of Lys Gate before the shape of the dark house became clear. Nora hopped off the bicycle the instant they arrived on the gravel driveway. Hogan did the same. Coming from the front door, a bobbling lantern came toward them. It was Angeline. She was dressed in a thick plum-colored parka with matching boots and her hair tucked under a winter hat.

As she neared, Angeline's face relaxed. The two girls met first, clasping hands.

"You're becoming quite the delivery girl," Angeline grinned.

Nora smiled. "Make it brief."

She kept walking to give them a moment alone. She propped the bike on its peg on the back patio, then wiped the cold sweat from her forehead.

With great effort, her wobbly legs took her all the way inside to her room. She didn't have to turn on any sort of light to know that Mason wasn't there. At first Nora was a little disappointed, but reconsidered when her eyes drooped lower and lower. Yawning, she undressed and pulled an oversized nightshirt over her head. The last thing she remembered was shutting her eyes in the comfort of the warm, cozy bed.

Chapter 25
Anchor

Somewhere outside her dreams, Nora heard knocking. It came in a peculiar sequence, a deliberate rhythm of two intervals. The familiar sound touched memories deep in her mind. The more she heard it, the more she was sure it was an encoded message for her to solve. Slowly, she began to visualize the rigorous tapping.

Short long long, short long, long short long, short. Short short long, short long long short.

The message was loud and clear: wake up.

Her eyes flew open as she hastily threw aside the blanket. She sat up, straining to listen when it had gone quiet. There was nothing behind the window and silent behind the door. Nora stood in the middle of the room waiting. She was convinced it wasn't a trick from her dream. It had been real, someone coded that message.

She snatched the duffel bag off the floor to rifle through it. She pulled on a warm pair of black leggings, a beige long sleeve wool sweater, and a comfortable pair of ankle boots. Stumbling into the hallway, Nora picked up her hair in a ponytail.

The large living room was just as cold and vacant as it had been the night before. The fireplace was out, a pile of ashes in its hearth. Beside it, the neat stack of firewood was down to the last of the logs. The awful draft in the boardinghouse was worse in the mornings, when no one tended to the weakly glowing embers. Seeing as she was the first to awaken, Nora neared to relight the fire for the day.

The knocking sounded again.

Long long, long long long, short long short, long short, short short, long short, long long short. Morning.

Nora whirled around to find Mason knocking on a wood panel at the end of the hallway. He smirked, pleased to see her awake. He double-checked the hallways before he strode in and pulled her close for a kiss. Her fingers tingled remembering the words and phrases she'd spell out during class periods to communicate with Mason and their friends. They would count the taps on their desktops differentiating between long and short.

"We haven't used coded messages in ages," Nora muttered, pulling away.

"Not since high school."

"You picked it up so fast, I didn't think you'd remember," she admitted.

"I had to learn it fast. I wanted to know if you were talking about me," he said with a chuckle. He spelled out his own name on her lower back. It sent a shiver up her spine. "It was probably one of the quickest things I've ever learned."

She knocked on his head playfully. "At least that meant you were serious about me."

"I've always been serious about you," Mason replied, lacing his fingers through hers. "Even when you weren't ready."

Nora brought a finger to her lips signaling him to keep quiet. She led him to the couch nearest the fireplace. Mason wasn't able to hear the soft click of a door shutting or the shuffle of feet against wood. But he caught on by her worried expression, letting go of her hand to walk ahead and tend to the hearth.

Hogan arrived soon after fully dressed and stifling an enormous yawn. "Morning," he greeted. "Rest well?"

"More or less," Nora replied. "You?"

He stretched his neck. "Less rather than more." Hogan glanced around the room. A flicker of surprise crossed his eyes when he saw Mason by the fireplace sweeping a pile of ashes into a bin. Nora recognized that fleeting analyzing look of his. It was the same perplexed expression she wore for years trying to figure Mason out. She wondered what part of him Hogan was trying to piece together.

"You any good with an axe?" Hogan finally asked, directing the question at Mason.

He glanced over his shoulder at them when it had gone quiet. "It can't be too hard."

"There's an axe in the tool shed," Hogan told him. "Do you mind?"

Mason took the hint. He straightened, muttered something about grabbing a sweatshirt, and disappeared down the hall. Hogan and Nora watched him go.

She gave Hogan a weary look. "He's going to chop off a finger."

Hogan dismissed her remark with a wave, not worried about Mason's woodwork. "I won't take long," he told her. "I want to know what kind of progress there is with Mason's time reading."

"I don't know what's keeping him from grounding," she told him, scratching her head sheepishly. She preferred Hogan not know how unprepared Mason was. They were down to the last twenty-four hours. "There are moments he almost makes it back, but he struggles. He only managed a way out when I guide him."

His eyebrows shot up in interest. "You witnessed the time read?"

The back door to the boardinghouse opened, making Nora jump. Mason slipped outside without a word. They heard him rummage inside the tool shed that was attached to the back wall. A moment later he crossed the patio in the direction of the trees with a rusty axe and a burlap sack.

"It was more like I interrupted it," Nora answered, drawing her attention back to Hogan. "I only catch glimpses, then we're gone."

He crossed his arms now. "Focus on that this morning. Tomorrow is your turn to scout. Are you prepared?"

"I know where I'm going,"

He nodded in approval, then jutted his chin to the door. "Go, help him. Make sure he doesn't lose a hand."

Nora headed outside. She started toward the path that led to the water tower. Behind her, the rumble of Hogan's truck started. She turned around long enough to see him get on the driveway and lumber away.

The usual path to the water tower was empty. Nora trotted along the grass to make sure she hadn't missed Mason. She returned to the clearing in front of the house with a slight panic rising in her throat. She decided to circle the property in case he wandered somewhere else.

She took to the edge of the woods where the distant rush of cars from the interstate was almost visible. Unlike the opposite side she had walked with Wesley, there was a questionable murky creek, one that was surely much larger in the past. The last of it was reduced to splotchy patches of rain water.

Beyond the creek was a cluster of fallen trees that she hadn't noticed before. She climbed over them brushing away pine needles that poked her palms. By the way each was cut down and shaven of its branches, Nora knew all the lumber was supposed to be used, whittled into furniture or something else. Yet the trees lay there untouched and abandoned without a purpose.

As she jumped down from the trunk of a thick cherry tree, she spotted Mason standing over a tree hacking away at its trunk. He managed to cut a slice and chop it into small logs ready to burn.

"Better your stance," Nora instructed. "It'll make it easier to raise the axe."

Mason glanced at her over his shoulder. "Yeah, yeah," he huffed. "I've chopped wood before."

"Yeah? When?" she asked, crossing her arms.

"Shut up."

Regardless, Mason adjusted his feet beneath his shoulders, with a grunt hoisted the axe as high as he could, and brought it down in one clean swipe. He kicked each new log toward the burlap sack. Nora crouched low to gather them in the bag. When he finished, she straightened to jostle the bag and make room for the remaining pieces of wood. Mason walked over to help pick up the load.

It took Mason two attempts to throw the bag over his shoulder. "Do I make one hell of a lumberjack or what?" he asked.

She laughed. "More like a lumberjack imposter."

"Whatever."

"Very brutish in style—"

"All right, all right," he said with an amused scowl. "Quit hassling me."

Nora rewarded him with a kiss. His pleased smile told her Mason would gladly tolerate the playful mockery as long as he was well compensated after. He swayed inward. The weight of the bag and the axe kept him from prolonging the kiss when she pulled away.

"Enough," she told him. "I leave tonight, and we have work to do. We need to have your time reading down, so when you practice with Hogan or Angeline tomorrow you can manage."

Mason dropped the axe and firewood at the base of the water tower. He walked over to meet Nora waiting in the neighboring county. She held out a hand when he lingered to cross.

"I'll bring you back when you can't find your way," Nora promised.

With a shaky breath, he stepped over the property line. Mason tried to move fast before the time read took over. It stopped him dead in his tracks tampering with his ability to see Nora standing feet away. His head snapped up to the sky while his eyes analyzed every inch of the skies over and over again. Struggling to relax his breathing, Mason shouted out in frustration.

Nora took extra steps back. "I know you think you need me," she started. "But you do most of the work. I'm only there for the ride."

"No," Mason said at once, surprising her. His head snapped low and eyes shut. "You're … you're not. Just a … a passenger." He shook his head roughly, forced himself to rush forward, and took hold of her wrist. "You're an anchor."

His voice faded as she was pulled through the rapidly unfurling layers. Nora found herself in the middle of a storm, her feet submerged in muddy water up to her ankles. But it was gone in a blink of an eye.

The next layer had her mesmerized by the inky red sunset beyond the mountains. It changed again now under the watchful eyes of the stars.

Mason's attention was on the boardinghouse behind her. Still holding his arm, Nora turned wondering what he was looking at. Through the layers, much of it looked the same. At times the back door was open or the white curtains billowed from the kitchen on the second floor. The changes were so subtle and unimportant.

Then the boardinghouse was gone. A thick blanket of fog almost concealed the piles of rubble that stood in its place. The sparse trees were dark, darker than they ought to be. The grass was still and white with ice. Mason stepped forward in confusion and a bit of disappointment in his eyes.

Nora tugged at his arm not letting him go further.

He looked at her as though he wasn't quite sure he wanted to leave.

"Mason, take us back," she prompted.

With the time read disrupted, Mason returned them to the present. The last thing Nora saw was the gray sky and the halo of the moon behind the mist. Upon arriving, she caught him before he hit the ground.

"That felt different," Mason panted after she hurried him back to Lys Gate.

She was a little winded herself. "No kidding. You took your sweet time on that exit. You need to be quicker."

Their luck seemed to be turning. As long as Nora was within reach, Mason was able to free himself of the time read. His collapses became less frequent, and the waves of nausea were reduced tenfold. His eyes flickered in and out of the time read when it tried to sway him back in. It came to a definite stop as soon as Nora cut the connection.

With each passing success, Nora felt Mason's control grow stronger. The struggle within him didn't rage as it used to. He was able to keep himself in the present with a stubborn force. It made grounding much easier. After a while, Nora was stopped from intruding any further like the severed connection affected her as well.

It was ten passed noon when Mason walked back to Lys Gate on his own. He shook off the time read in record time. He paced the grass waiting to fully recover.

"What if I screw up after today?" he asked.

Nora placed her hands on her hips. "Hogan's methods are much less gentle than mine. And Angeline doesn't accept failure," she told him. Mason stopped in front of her. "Tomorrow would be the wrong day to loose focus."

"That's what a guy like me needs to hear."

She rolled her eyes. "I'm serious. Whatever progress we've made it'll have to be enough for us to run when I get back."

"I get it," he said. Mason was close enough to make Nora shift in her spot, the proximity between them potentially compromising. If he drew any closer, her heart would have started racing. "I won't slack off."

"Hey, there you are!"

Mason stepped passed her continuing to pace. Nora turned to see Hogan jog over to them. His gaze went from Mason to Nora and back again knowing full well he had interrupted something.

"Came to collect the firewood," he said, nodding to the sack on the ground. "The others have been complaining about the draft in the house." He rubbed his hands together. "It's chilly out here too. When will you be coming in?"

"Now I hope," Mason said at once. "She's been working me like a dog."

"I have not."

Hogan chuckled. "There's take out by the boardinghouse."

Mason heaved the bag onto his shoulder and headed back to the boardinghouse. With his back to them and out of ear shot, Hogan plucked Nora by the elbow before she could move to follow. "You and Mason. When did it start?"

A load roar in her ears, a tight knot in her throat, and the sudden heaviness in her chest made it hard to breath. Her whole body went cold watching Mason go. She fought to keep the heat of embarrassment from rising to her cheeks. Somehow, Nora kept herself from hyperventilating out loud. Instead, she dropped her gaze to the ground in case Mason decided to look over his shoulder.

"It's not—"

"I hate it when you think you can lie to me!" Hogan hissed and shook her arm roughly, then tightened his hold on her joint. Nora flinched. "Time shouldn't tamper with these matters, but to our misfortune it might." He paused easing his grip and let go. "Love can't be tamed or imposed, Nora, I trust you know that more than most. Don't let this go to waste."

Chapter 26
Timeless

Hogan knew.

That was the clearest thought in Nora's mind. With one look, he pieced together what was going on between her and Mason. And what troubled her above all was his lack of fury. He had been angry, but it had nothing to do with her questionable ethics as a time guard. To add to her confusion, he encouraged her to pursue the very thing she was supposed to be ending.

As soon as they came in that afternoon, Nora used the preparation for her trip as an excuse to avoid Hogan. She took a nap while the others lunched down the hall. Every ounce of rest mattered when she would be spending the next twenty four hours running. When she woke up a quarter passed six o'clock, cold slices of pizza and a boxed salad waited for her on the night stand.

Nora stood at the foot of her bed staring at the items laying in front of her. The empty backpack sagged over a pillow. Her thoughts kept returning to Hogan and his words. She wondered if it were true, if time was incapable to interfere in the most intimate aspect of their lives because for eons that didn't seem the case. They were agents of time, tools of order and progress.

She rummaged through her things deciding what would be of most use to her in five different locations she was to visit. Nora dumped the contents of a duffel bag to see if it had anything good to offer. It contained an array of clothes, some suitable for travel and others not so much. She found a good pair of shoes under the bed and packed those as well.

A sharp knock at the door made Nora drop the flashlight, lighter, and an empty canteen on the floor.

"Come in."

The door opened and Hogan came into the room. "I see you've begun to pack," he noted. She picked up the fallen items one by one, tossing them into the bag. He came in holding a neon green knapsack. He set it beside her own bag. "I recommend you take your lock opener and any other tech you have."

She gave a nod.

Hogan was unusually awkward, that wasn't like him. He was often direct and business like when discussing delicate matters. She would have appreciated the sentiment more if their conversation was likely to end in a berating lecture on her rule breaking.

Nora let out a breath, she didn't want to beat around the bush any longer. "Listen, about earlier, Mason and I are—"

"You don't have to explain," he interrupted. Hogan pressed his lips together in a thin line perplexed, wrestling with the idea he was about to say. "He looks for you," he went on. "Although we are always the ones searching, Mason looks for you too. *Something* draws him to you.

"I've seen it more than once, but I dismissed it thinking he recognized your familiar soul or that he suspected his true nature. Do you remember that moment we crossed paths in a town square outside Rome? It was a brief encounter, the sack of flour spilled all over the garden of some uptight aristocrat. His wife was furious."

"The one with an artist for a son," Nora remembered, making a face. "He threatened to gift my blood in a dozen bottles of red paint."

Hogan smiled a little. "Mason covered the damages. When he turned to look for you, you were long gone. We were only meant to be passing through, but I couldn't talk him out of leaving. It took him weeks to give up his search for the kitchen maiden. Whatever drew him to you, I suspect time had nothing to do with it."

"I find that hard to believe."

He looked at her thoughtfully, the way he often did when he was going to tell her that she was overthinking. "Time can't be that cruel," Hogan said at last. "I refuse to believe it."

He wasn't assigning blame; it was quite the opposite. He was telling her no one was at fault. There were things that time had a say in like where the time markers landed in each cycle and the course of their lives, but who they came to be was up in the air. And who they came to love was just as unprecedented.

"The others might not think the same," he added. "They still believe in the old ways, that there's no greater force than the power they cannot see, even when it's right in front of them."

She took his hand in gratitude.

Hogan spoke out of experience. The safety of the three time markers would always be top priority; however, his love for Angeline surpassed that any day. He wasn't guaranteed a perfect beginning or an easy job. His reassurance lay in girl thousands of miles away doing the exact same thing and loved him in return.

With the tender moment fading, he left her to finish packing. She went through the bag he brought in. It contained left over items from his own journey. He salvaged things like a thick coarse rope, a climbing harness, thermal mittens, and a bizarre looking oxygen mask. Nora added them to her backpack.

Heeding Hogan's advice, she checked her briefcase for any gadgets of the future to bring along. Nora pocketed her lock opener to keep it close. In a small box, she packed three sea-blue marble-size balls that burst into water when chewed. There were also gas pellets that emitted a loud bang before releasing a cloud of black smoke.

Dressing for the departure was one more thing Nora had to master. She was meant to dress for all sorts of climate conditions. Too much, and it felt like an oven. Too little, and she was certain to freeze to death. Her best hope was that she didn't have to stay in each place for long. The stockings under the leggings and jeans made her legs itch while the five layers of various tops kept her toasty. Nora disliked the feeling of being swaddled in cotton. Moving around felt less than graceful. Pulling on a hat, she was ready to go.

She shouldered the backpack and walked out to meet Hogan by the back door. He put down the newspaper he was reading when she approached.

"Angeline will be under the water tower in ten minutes," Hogan told her.

"I'll be gone by then," she replied.

"Make sure you see her coming."

"I will."

"Is there anything you want me to tell Mason?" he asked.

"Tell him that I'll be back soon," she said, cracking her knuckles. "That I won't take as long."

Hogan opened the door for her. "I'll keep him safe."

Without a word, she crept out the door to the patio. A wispy cloud formed when she breathed out. She hurried across the concrete until she heard a pair of feet land in a thud. Nora turned around to see Mason closing the window.

"What are you doing up?" Nora demanded.

"You were asleep when I sneaked into you room earlier," he said, walking over. "I wanted to see you off." Mason kissed her before she could shove him away. She kissed him feeling herself melt in the inside, her worries momentarily gone. Nora pulled away to rest her chin on his chest. He looked at her right in the eye. "Don't make me wait."

They hugged tight, Nora burying her face in his chest for a long minute and took off to the water tower.

Nora spent the first twenty-five minutes of the night running ten miles in the direction of the mountains. She mustered all her agility in order to move at the speed she was going. It didn't register how fast her feet carried her until she avoided being hit by a red car. The driver and passenger screamed in terror. Nora slid over the hood and kept running.

The sky above was full of stars. She looked to Polaris to guide her north. It was the same star Hogan used to smuggle African slaves up into Canada from New York and the only compass available to Angeline when she crossed the Middle East. Nora came to a stop under an overpass to catch her breath. Her calves burned as every muscle rejoiced at the opportunity to rest.

"Don't time jump yet!" Angeline had shouted, running over and pulled off the light brown hijab she must have picked up along the way. To Nora's relief, she returned with minimal injuries: a bandaged arm, a scrape on her temple, and charred sneakers. Soot peppered her hair and dry mud crusted the knees of her jeans. Angeline stopped in front of Nora. "Wait until you get further out. I couldn't shake the time travelers the last bit here. I'm almost positive I wasn't tailed. Go, run!"

Angeline was shivering in the oversized sweatshirt. The parka and backpack with all her supplies she had left in were missing. As she urged her to get inside, Nora's stomach tightened, getting back wasn't going to be easy.

She dug through the numerous layers of clothing to pull free her time key. She clasped it tight feeling the gentle hum against her palm. A rip in the air darker than the night widened by the second until it looked like an opening. The whistle of the wind hurtling inside sang to her like a lure.

Nora concentrated hard picturing her first stop. Her memory of Toronto came in pieces. It was vague, her trip years ago had led her someplace else. She remembered a cobblestone boulevard with its lush rows of trees casting shade over parked cars. There was a bakery and a record store across a deli and a small boutique. A clear memory of a sign popped into her head: it pointed to Elmwood Square.

A flickering light from within the darkness beckoned to her. It came and went like a lighthouse cutting through fog. Nora stepped into the time warp. The usual feeling of suspended gravity lasted a blink of an eye before the darkness whisked her right out. She skid out tripping on the uneven surface.

Cobblestone.

She heaved herself back onto her feet. If it weren't for her scraped palms, Nora would have thought she went back in time. The street hardly changed. It had upgraded to present day standards like streetlights and stop signs, but the brick buildings were still in place. Newer cars lined both sides of the street. The bakery and deli looked well kept and operational. Above the shops were small quaint apartments. It looked so unbothered, or rather untouched, by the fact that time had passed.

She looked down at her phone. It was three thirty in the morning. Nora knew she had to keep moving. Keeping a careful track of how much time she spent at each location was vital for a successful scouting trip. Stalling would be wasting precious seconds. She set a timer for forty-five minutes. It was enough to patrol the area and look around.

Under the streetlights, the shops and homes above them looked well lived in. The pots on the balconies and the cluster of bicycles on the stoops made the neighborhood feel safe. Nora hurried onto the sidewalk heading for the nearest intersection.

She turned the corner and that's when she saw it. Five blocks away in the middle of the town square was a clock tower. It was three stories high with a glowing white face. A tingle of pleasure swept over Nora. An open place like a central plaza was bound to be a magnet for the homeless crowd. It was the perfect place to start for anything unusual.

To her disappointment there was no one in sight. As she crossed the square, Nora took note on how dated the town actually was. It wasn't just out of date; it was old like original European architecture old. This part of town had to be well over three hundred years old. The columns and curving arches were enough to make her think twice as to where she was.

Nora stopped in front of the clock tower. She ran her fingers over the rough bricks. There were few clock towers left in the world. She wondered how it managed to be so well kept. She ducked under the arches to find a way to the top. Nora aimed her phone at the low ceiling. A wooden door with a hatch like an attic door was over her head. With a short hop, she was able to grasp the cord and tug the door open revealing a ladder. She began to climb.

From a window halfway up, Nora got a view of the town. Toronto was a lot smaller than she remembered. Lake Ontario in the south was like a dark ocean with glittering lights in the distance. She guessed central Toronto couldn't be too far, but liked this area more for Mason. The faint sound of echoing laughter from the street caught Nora's attention. Squinting in its direction, in the morning quietness movement came from closed skate park. A cluster of kids disappeared into a tunnel, the laughter dying with them as they went.

If anyone would know about suspicious activity in the area, it would be the local riffraff running amok at this hour. She decided to investigate there first.

About ten minutes later Nora found herself at the entrance of the skate park. She grabbed the chain link fence, pushed off the ground, and climbed it easily. When she reached the top, Nora noted the layout of the park. The worn out ramps were on the far right side with a pair of low grade metal half pipes. Farther along were the bigger half pipes for the more skilled skaters as well as the cemented bowl. It led into an underground tunnel looping beneath the whole park and opened again at the entrance.

Nora jumped down and walked to the rim of the bowl. The kids she had seen were gathered at the mouth of the tunnel staring up at her in distrust and hushed whispers. The oldest, an auburn haired girl in her midteens, stood at the opening with a set jaw under her tight frown. Her short choppy cut reminded Nora of her own short hair at her age. The girl nodded to the others, she didn't want an audience in case it got ugly. They scrambled back inside.

Nora slid down.

"You lost?" the girl called out.

"Not exactly," Nora replied, trying to sound friendly. "I'm passing by. My name's Nora. This seems like the only place with people up."

She narrowed her light brown eyes at Nora. "Yeah, so?"

"I was hoping for a bit of shelter before I keep moving. Can I find that here?"

"Are you a cop?" the girl asked.

"No."

"You one of those welfare workers? Are you looking for someone?"

The girl was protective, Nora anticipated that. "No, listen, I'm not that much older than you," she told her. "I just want to know if this is a safe place."

The girl's eyes landed on the backpack on Nora's shoulders, and her angry expression softened. "My name's Cassia," she said. "Come in."

Nora followed hanging behind a few steps. She wondered how well she would be received among Cassia and her friends. She didn't want to scare them off with her invasive questions, although she suspected they would willingly answer with the right incentives.

They reached the center of the tunnel where twelve or so other kids sat huddled around a fire. The boys and girls talked and ate together. Some struggled to keep warm in their tattered bedding. Two of the younger girls shared a sleeping bag as another boy yanked at his blanket in apprehension at the visitor's arrival. Nora recognized a nest when she saw one, the kids were homeless.

Cassia invited Nora to sit with them offering a stale sandwich. She declined the kind gesture, they needed it more than she did. "This is the only safe place around for kids like us," Cassia said. "If that's what you're looking for."

Nora decided to remain standing. She was on the clock and couldn't stay long. "I need to know if any of you have noticed sketchy adults wandering around here, people who shouldn't be here," she said, crouching to see all the kids in the fire light. "People that look out of place. They'll travel alone or with a partner."

The children exchanged looks. Most looked to Cassia questioning if they were allowed to answer. She gave a permissive nod. In a mumble, they gave Nora a unanimous no, they had seen nothing like that. She knew what she was asking sounded a little far fetched, but kids on the street were much more intuitive with strangers on their turf. The ins and outs of most towns were well known by the lost, unwanted, and undetected.

"Like a social worker?" Cassia asked.

"Not exactly," Nora replied. "These people will try to blend in and ask a lot of questions."

"Questions about you?"

"They might."

Again, the children shook their heads.

Nora straightened. She was going to trust them. She didn't take street kids as very good liars, especially ones so young. "That's all I need to know for now," she told them. Nora turned and walked in the direction of the exit. The concerned whispers of the children faded, and the glow of the fire dimmed the closer she got to the opening.

"You're bailing? I thought you needed a safe place."

Cassia ran to catch up to Nora outside the tunnel.

Nora gave a nod. "I do."

"Then why are you leaving? Who are you running from?" Cassia asked. "We can hide you."

"I'm more of a body guard," Nora told her, unslinging her backpack. "I'm here because I want to keep someone safe. If anyone comes looking for me …" She reached in to look for a pen. "You notice anything out of the ordinary in the next twenty-four hours you call me. It's really important that you do, and if I don't answer you leave a message. Can you do that for me?"

With a Sharpie in her grasp, Nora scribbled Mason's number on Cassia's sleeve. "It's important that you help me because this person is important. And if you let me, I can help you keep your friends safe," she went on. There was one other thing she had pulled out of her backpack. It was a money clip she kept hidden in a secret pouch. In total, there was probably three thousand dollars all together. It was meant for extreme emergencies and this was as good as any. "Cassia, I need to know you can do this for me."

Surprise glossed over her eyes at either seeing so much money at once or that Nora possessed it. The shock passed, her expression changing to a mixture of yearning and need. The wad of cash looked appealing. The way the girl's eyes darted back to her friends Nora knew all those kids weren't in the best of shape to be on their own. They needed food, warmer clothes, and a shelter, especially with winter right around the corner. Nora knew what it was like to live day by day trying to survive each moment at a time. She only hoped Cassia accepted the help.

Cassia raised raised her hand, not reaching for the money quite yet.

"All I have to do is call this number?" she asked.

"Or a text, which ever you prefer."

Cassia took the money.

Chapter 27
Time Jumping

Nora stood under the clock tower as it struck four in the morning. Every chime made her skin vibrate. She waited until the last hour struck to pull out her time key. Tracing the numbers with her fingers, Nora wondered how she got so lucky to land in a safe place on her first try. She hoped Toronto remain that way. Nora stepped out into the square and headed back to the boulevard.

The brisk walk to the street she arrived in was different. The town was beginning to stir awake. There was movement beyond the windows from the apartments over the shops and light flooded onto the sidewalk. Nora avoided the pools of light by walking in the middle of the road. She hurried to the next intersection not wanting to be spotted.

A time warp was waiting for her. The flicker of light from within meant the darkness was ready to whisk her away to her next location. She touched her time key hoping for her luck to continue. Nora strode right in, the town just outside Toronto disappearing behind her.

The blinding light turned out to be snow, a bunch of it. Her feet sank crunching the smooth blanket of snowflakes. The morning sun and clear blue sky caused a blinding reflection along the white plateau. The cold was sharp and angry on her face. Her breath came out as a thick cloud fading into the air in slow motion.

Nora stared out into the frozen tundra. Pulling a pair of gloves from her pocket, she began to walk toward the snow dunes. Beyond them, she spotted smoke, a sure sign that she landed in the right place. A small settlement of Inuit people wasn't far. She read about it twice—once in the 1950s and a few nights ago on the internet. It was supposedly so small that newcomers were unheard of. And it was so remote no one outside the community bothered to find it.

She stopped amid the snow dunes. Nora's ears perked up. The shift of feet over snow made a gentle squeaking noise catching her attention. She wasn't alone.

Three men burst from the snow dunes with a startling cry. By the way they rushed her, she knew they were going in for a tackle. Nora threw herself into the air rolling over the first time traveler's back, then quickly catapulted over the second. They rushed by, unable to stop.

The third time traveler didn't follow his comrades' mistakes. He grabbed Nora by the scruff of the neck slamming her to the ground. To her dismay, the icy snow cushioned her fall. Her ear went numb, and her arm was crushed under her own body weight. She yanked away just as his fist crushed the ice where her head had been seconds ago. Still suffering from whiplash, Nora jammed her elbow into his jaw, opening an opportunity to land a kick to his gut.

"Enough, Alphonse!" one of the men shouted. "Kill her!"

The man named Alphonse unsheathed a dagger and took aim without hesitating.

Nora rolled to one side, colliding into his waiting knee. She recoiled in the opposite direction just as the dagger sank into the snow. Instinctively, she drew her legs close to her chest, wrapped her legs around his middle, then with as much force Nora swung her hips upward, tossing Alphonse off her. As he flew over her head, she took hold of his arm until it popped.

He shouted out in pain, and the dagger in his dislocated arm dropped.

"No!"

She scooped up the dagger, turned to the incoming time traveler, and threw the blade. It plunged into his chest right above his sternum. Nora only enjoyed her first defeat for a moment. A sharp pain in her leg made her suck in a breath, swearing with gritted teeth. She looked down. Alphonse stabbed her ankle with a spare dagger. In return, she kicked him in the face knocking him unconscious.

A thick arm wrapped around Nora in a headlock she wasn't prepared for. The harder she struggled to fight for air, the more constricting it became to breathe. In a matter of agonizing seconds, her sight became spotty, and her body was beginning to give way. She mustered all her draining energy to execute a halfhearted elbow to his hip bone. It was enough to force him to drop her.

Coughing, she staggered to her feet. Nora launched herself again this time wrapping her legs around the time traveler's middle and drove the last available dagger straight through his chest.

Nora tumbled onto the snow with the body. The shooting pain returned flaring up her leg. She glanced down to assess the damage. Blood poured into her shoe making her sock wet. With effort, she rolled over another flare of pain shooting up her leg. Nora untied the black scarf around her neck, dabbed at some white snow to clean her wound, when that didn't work she wrapped it around her leg in a firm knot. It would have to do until she fully healed in a few hours.

She limped around studying the mess she had made. The snow was soaked with time traveler blood. It would take hours for the members of the settlement to find them. She had to get rid of them.

She hobbled over to Alphonse and bent down to rifle through his pockets. All she found was a wallet with a fake identification card inside from 1910. It read Alphonse Gerard, a twenty-seven-year-old from New Orleans.

"Looks like you came all this way for nothing," Nora said, snapping the laminated card in half and tossed it back to the senseless body.

Nora willed a time warp to open as she rolled the bodies into one big heap. It unfurled over a large patch of blood stained snow. Gingerly, she threw in one body at a time. When the last time traveler was swallowed by the darkness, the time warp billowed in protest sending red snow up in the air like a frothy geyser.

She looked at her time key. It was a little passed eight o'clock. She was good on time. Nora shoved the black sundial under her shirt and and jumped into the time warp.

It deposited her right onto a sidewalk. Her backside and palms were scorched by hot sand. It was twice as worse than landing in a snowbank. Nora looked around and noticed she arrived in the middle of a sunny bus terminal; however, there were no buses idling or passengers waiting along the curb with suitcases in hand.

Nora got to her feet dusting herself off as she walked to the nearest bench. Instead of sitting to rest, she propped her leg up on the seat. The pain had subsided to a minor ache. It was much more bearable compared to a few minutes, or rather, hours ago in the Arctic. Wincing, Nora loosened the crude bandages to reveal a mostly healed wound. She stuffed the bloody cloth in a garbage can.

The sun over her head was hot, comfortable enough to shed a layer or two of clothes. She shrugged off her jacket, folded it into her backpack, and rolled up her sleeves. Its position was off center casting Nora's shadow due west. It was three o'clock. The latest time jump really cost her valuable hours.

The bus terminal was abandoned. It hadn't been that way when she visited in her previous life. Nora wondered what happened to revert this place so desolate. She decided to check the ticket kiosk in case she landed someplace else.

She almost hoped to see people in the short hallway, anything to indicate that she hadn't walked into a trap. Sunlight poured in to display the condition inside. The cracked floor was peppered with broken glass, and the linoleum-tiled walls were coming apart. A previously hung clock was smashed to pieces on the floor, the hand no longer in the center. At the end of the hall, a man and woman in black-and-white suits came to meet her with guns in hand.

They shouted something in Arabic, then opened fire.

Nora threw herself out of the way as the round of gunfire flew passed her. It lasted twenty long seconds before it went silent again.

Hurried footsteps rushed her way. She took this chance to hide. Running to jump the fence wasn't an option. By the time she made her first attempt to pole-vault over, they'd gun her down. Instead, Nora wedged herself in between the awful-smelling dumpster and the bus station.

Scrambling to get out of cover, Nora's breath caught in her throat with pain. She felt like her skin was on fire. Looking down her arm, she saw that the layers of clothing had been torn. Two bright red streaks pierced her skin. Graze wounds.

"Come out, girl!" the man jeered. "We know you're a time guard. Our friends in Aleppo said you would be here."

Syria, she thought at once. She was right where she ought to be, although she didn't anticipate the welcoming committee. When she didn't reply, bullets clattered like a hailstorm, making her wince.

"Stand down!" Nora shouted over the gunfire. Her Arabic was a little rusty.

She could take on two travelers easy, but two with heavy ammunition was another dangerous story. There was no way Nora could get up close to kill them. Weapons like guns never last through time despite all the damage they caused. Execution by hand to hand combat was the only method that ensured time travelers wouldn't cross her path again.

This was a battle she had to abandon. Nora willed a time warp to open. The pull of the darkness welcomed her. The familiar gust of air tickled her back. She took a step back ready to be swept away. Before she had a chance to step through, a hand sprang out the darkness, took a fistful of hair, and pulled Nora in.

The girl cried out in surprise when Nora's aura of light blinded her. She struggled to keep a grip as she tried to shield her eyes. Nora pulled free, whirled around, took the girl's arm, and slammed her elbow into her forearm. A bone chilling crack echoed through the time warp like a drop of water. For good measure, she took the girl's knife and drove it into the arm she injured.

Nora kicked her away. She floated into the darkness, her painful screams fading fast. The moment she became a spec, images began to whirl beneath the dark sheets of protection. The coastline of a beach shined its way to the top. Nora reached for it, her hand phasing through, and the rest of her followed.

She dropped onto a beach. Nora fell face first into cool, white sand as the time warp behind her shut. She sat up to see the ocean twenty feet away, sending gentle waves to meet the land. The rolling breeze whipped her hair in all directions. She looked around, relieved to see she was in fact alone.

The pastel sun sank into the watery horizon. Time was dwindling, Nora had to move. She scrambled to her and dashed over to the road. Old pickups sped along, with music blaring. Sleeker cars coasted by, not all bothered by the stranded tourist. She hailed a cab that dropped her off at the next town over.

The driver dropped her off in the middle of a small sea porting town with cramped streets and low, solid buildings in rich earthy hues. Motorbikes wove through the street honking as they went. People of every shape, size, and color walked and gathered at hot spots all over town. The smell of something sweet like fresh fruit caused a wave of hunger to roar in her stomach. The familiar sound of their colloquial Spanish made Nora feel out of place as though she were a real tourist.

Nora walked into the local tavern called *La Alma Negra*. She didn't want to linger out in the open where everyone could see she was a foreigner. The place itself was no bigger than a small garage. It was a miracle they dared to fit as many tables as they did. By the looks of it, she had arrived for dinner. Everyone was either placing an order or waiting on food. She moved amid the noise and bustle to the lone stool by the bar.

The woman behind the counter was pretty. Her smooth cocoa skin and bright grin gave her an ageless quality Nora rarely saw. Her hair was clipped short, but it didn't take away from her feminine features. On the contrary, it added to her soft, youthful appearance.

"*Buenas*," she greeted in Spanish over the noise. "What can I get you?"

"*Una agua fresca*, please," Nora replied.

The woman grinned pouring her a tall glass of lemon and raspberries. She also moved a bowl of peanuts her way. "Ah, American!"

Nora shifted in her seat. Spanish, that was easier than Arabic, but still not fully in her repertoire. "English," she lied.

"Is this your first time to the Dominican Republic?"

"Once before. Years ago," Nora told her. "I take it this isn't much of a tourist town." She took a sip of the drink, a burst of tart sweetness filled her mouth.

The woman shook her head. "Many Americans pass through here, but not all stay the night," she replied. "Local fishermen is all we get."

"At least it keeps the town authentic and beautiful."

"I'm glad you think so. My hometown is just as gorgeous, if not more."

"What part of the island are you from?"

"A northern village closer to Haiti called *Arroyo Claro*."

Nora choked on her drink. She set down the glass coughing into her fist. Her throat struggled to bring down fresh air as it tried to expel the liquid from her vocal cord at the same time. It had been ages since she heard that name. Memories from her first journey to the island swept her away: masts from a ship, the coarse rope on her right arm like a leash, a white villa near the ocean, and the rowboat out at midnight.

"*Ay mi cielo, que te pasa, mi niña!*" The woman's voice brought Nora back to the present. She walked around the bar counter in concern. As soon as Nora quieted from her coughing fit, the woman pressed a hand to her forehead, then to her flushed cheeks. "You went awfully pale. Perhaps, you ought to lie down."

"I'm fine, really."

She stared at Nora hard like she didn't believe her. She raised her from the stool. "I insist, please, we have an inn out back. It wouldn't be right if you didn't see a doctor in the morning."

The bartender led her past the counter and kitchen and through a screen door. The back porch was covered with white tarps to provide shade over a dozen hammocks. Additional sheets were hung like canopies surrounding each hammock to ensure some sort of privacy. They doubled as mosquito nets for the sleeping guests. Hammocks one, three, and four were occupied, Nora could tell by the dangling feet gently rocking and soft snores accompanied by the lull of rustling waves.

"You can have hammock five," the woman whispered. She drew the curtain for Nora to see inside. Her hammock was sunshine yellow. In the small space was a wooden chair and a short stack of old wine crates acting as a stand. Each crate held items: a blanket, toiletries, a water bottle, and a flashlight.

"There's a bathroom off the corridor behind the kitchen and a landline near the bar if you need to make a call locally," the woman advised. "If you feel faint again, look for me. I'm usually up front. Otherwise, I'm right up stairs." She pointed to second story over the restaurant. "I'm Maoli Torres, by the way, at your service."

Torres. That was another name she hadn't heard of in a long time. "Thanks, I'm Nora."

The two women shook hands. Maoli smiled, stepped out drawing the curtains to a close behind her, and walked back to the restaurant.

Nora lowered into the hammock. It was the most she could do when her mind was full of nostalgia. With a leg on the ground, she used her heel to begin an anxious swing. She spun the timepiece in her hand, thinking. It had to be a coincidence that Maoli had Clara's last name, the one Clara adopted soon after Mason began using it as an alias during his time in the Caribbean. On the other hand, it couldn't be a coincidence that Maoli came from the only place on the island Nora helped build centuries ago. What were the odds that what she was thinking was true?

She closed her eyes, a flash of guilt hitting Nora. She left Clara all alone. After Mason was killed on the ship, she fled to America. She could only imagine the worry they put her through when they didn't return. Clara was the closest thing Mason had to a mother then and by extension an authority figure for Nora. She had children of her own—that Nora was certain of. Clara mentioned as a slave she had a boy and a girl. By the time she met Mason, she had given up searching for them. She hoped the woman who loved Mason like a son continued to live as a free woman on the island.

Time travelers didn't have to appear to tell Nora the Dominican Republic wouldn't be an entirely safe place for Mason. It wouldn't take long for someone like Maoli to take notice that long ago there was a rogue pirate of the same name had founded her hometown. And Nora's name was bound to surface, too, along with Clara. They couldn't run the risk of being recognized.

Nora opened her eyes. It was dusk. There was more dark than light out. She shuffled through her backpack to leave a well earned tip. She hid it under the flashlight and got to her feet. She peeled off the rest of the layers she wore leaving on the leggings, sweatshirt, and a jacket. After emptying the sand from her boots, Nora shoved them in her backpack too and swapped them for sneakers.

She slipped out of the canopy, walked across the wooden porch, and trotted down the creaky stairs. Nora found herself on a beach again. The patch of sand was small unlike the one she arrived in. The dark water was feet away.

She forced a time warp to open. The black door grew into existence in front of her. The swooshing of the dark void and the quiet rush of the waves overlapped one another. Without thinking, she stepped into the time warp letting it lead her to the last stop of her journey.

Chapter 28
Buying Time

In the precise moment she landed, all Nora saw was the unclear bottom of a ravine. She gasped and backed away until her right foot gave out from under her. Her stomach slammed onto the floor boards hard. The wooden bridge rocked back and forth as though someone gave the ropes a giant push. Nora shut her eyes not willing to look at the abyss below. Once she stopped moving, she got to her feet. The bridge was ten yards long suspended between a pair of cliffs. She took a few tentative steps toward the closest ledge. When it didn't break, Nora rushed across eager to feel solid ground again.

Every inch of distance between herself and that chasm made Nora feel at ease. Just thinking about how deep the canyon could be sent a jolt up her spine. She walked fast following the narrow path that led downhill. Although it was hard to tell, she landed somewhere well above ground level. The air was thin making her ears pop much like if she were on an airplane.

As she hurried on, Nora pulled out a flashlight from her backpack. She cast the light around. It was a rough patch of land full of rocks and dirt. Short, brittle bushes that looked more like ferns sprouted from the dry earth here and there. The whole place had gone untouched by water for what looked like months.

A storm was brewing far below. Clouds gathered over a hillside village. Rain and wind pelted a handful of houses. One powerful gust of wind threated to knock them all flat. Lightning parted the sky in two, then thunder echoed up to her in a great cacophony of rumbles.

The final clap of thunder made the ground vibrate under her feet. Her knees would have rattled together if she hadn't quickened her pace. She may have been too high up to feel the full effect, but she recognized a time quake anywhere.

She stopped walking.

"You're as good as dead. Come out now."

"Very well," a voice from behind told her. "I suppose I have nothing to lose."

Nora turned around. Russell approached, stepping into the vicinity of the flashlight. He changed since she last saw him. His face was gaunt: his eyes had dark circles under them wrinkling at the corners, stumble grew along his cheeks, his once well kept hair was now dull and dry with flecks of gray at his roots, and he lost a quarter of his weight his cheekbones now prominent.

She eyed the sword that clung to his tattered belt. On a reflex, Nora grabbed her time key tugging the sundial, the black chain digging into the back of her neck. Russell's hand hovered over the hilt, at least he had the courtesy to fear her.

"Have you been waiting long?" she asked him.

"I only just arrived," he said.

Quickly, she swept her gaze looking for additional company. They seemed to be alone.

"This isn't your first time here," Nora said. "A younger version of you came looking for me days ago demanding I help you. How long ago was that? Five, ten years? I'd be willing to guess more."

A flicker of recall crossed his eyes. Russell let out a fake almost wistful laugh. "Oh, I remember," he mused. "Mason was very protective of you, more so than usual."

"You gave him a reason to be."

He raised an eyebrow. "I distinctly remember hitting a nerve. Mason always had a certain fondness for you like he did back home, even though you *choose* not to see it." When that didn't get a rise out of her, Russell corrected himself feigning apathy. "Sorry, I mean you didn't return his affection. Surely, that isn't the case anymore."

"Why are you here, Russell?" she asked, exasperated. Nora could only take him in small quantities, and she'd had enough of him for one lifetime. "Are you looking for an apology or to settle the score?"

Russell clutched the hilt. "Neither."

In the split second that it took for him to unsheathe his sword, Nora dropped the flashlight and drew her own weapon. With a rough tug, she yanked her necklace off her neck. The thin black chain grew cold, rigid, and heavy in her hand. It expanded to a seven foot rod. The sundial fastened itself on one end. Carvings were imprinted on the blunt side of the pole, the markings of a time seal. If she hoisted it in reverse, it resembled a giant stamp. She twirled it once like a deadly baton.

When their weapons clashed, a shower of yellow-and-orange sparks exploded into the night like a stray firecracker. Each burst of light flashed across his aged face. The clatter mimicked the thunder going on down below.

To her knowledge, Russell was no swordsman. He was the son of a prolific barter of livestock not a warrior. He was cunning and had a sharp tongue. His father taught him in the art of manipulation and deceit. It was how he coaxed Mason into having Nora give him a time key. His best trick of all was disappearing. She was willing to bet he never raised a sword in his life. His lack of ability and age proved it. All he had was blind hatred on his side.

With a staff in her hand she could only act defensively blocking jabs and deflecting swipes. Her heels dug into the dirt. It was all that kept Russell from slicing her skull open. Nora flicked her wrist, letting the staff move beneath, then over the blade. It flew passed her shoulder away from them.

She swiped the staff across his legs, and he toppled over. Behind him, a time warp began to open.

Nora poised the staff over his body. "You're not worth this much effort."

"Then shame on you for bothering with me," Russell said breathlessly. He dared to sit up, raise his hands in surrender, and drop them to the ground at his sides. He patted the ground on his left as if inviting her to sit with him. He looked unbothered at his easy defeat, pleased he still had her talking. "Hello, darling, does the word decoy mean anything to you?"

She reaffirmed her grip on her staff and wedged it into his chest above his heart. "You're stalling," Nora caught on. "You have allies. Where are they?"

He smirked. "By now that boardinghouse I hope. I told them to burn it to the ground time markers and all."

Russell's hand closed around something. It wasn't until the click and the light in her eyes that she understood why he had been groping the floor. He was searching for the flashlight she dropped earlier. Hastily, Nora took several steps back, trying to get the brightness out of her face.

She heard him scramble to his feet moving away from the time warp. Nora ducked away from the beam in order to see Russell catch himself on a thorny bush. She threw her staff at him, using it like a javelin. He leapt out of the way, freeing himself in the process. The staff soared over his head and the time warp. It went dark again. Russell's fall sent the flashlight down the hill.

Her eyes adjusted to the darkness fast. At her feet was the sword she won from him. Somehow she managed not to step on the blade when he blinded her. Nora snatched it up and took off running.

She tackled him in hilt first making sure it made contact with his gut. The force of it pushed him in. The absence of gravity kept them from hitting a landing. The sword in Nora's hand wrenched free shooting into the dark. She held on tight to Russell's collar, she didn't need a weapon to finish him off for good.

"This is where I leave you," Russell muttered. He pulled out something from his pocket, reached for the darkness below him, and sank away.

She dove after him only to keep endlessly falling. "Damn it!" Nora said aloud, slapping the nothingness in front of her. It was useless, she couldn't even see where he had gone. Wherever he disappeared to, Nora wasn't following.

Completely alone now, she glided forward. She was stuck in the time warp with no way out and unable to navigate. She was as useless as any time traveler without a time key. Nora needed to get back into the present. Outside time was passing by, and the others were about to be ambushed.

"Halt!" A staff poked her in between her shoulder blades. "You are trespassing, time traveler!"

Nora raised her hands showing that she was unarmed. She looked over her shoulder to see an eleven-year-old girl standing behind her in a silky white chiton and a gold belt around her dainty hips. Her skin was the perfect shade of cocoa, which shined thanks to her brilliant gold aura. She wore her black shiny hair in a sophisticated braid laced with strands of gold threads. Her beautiful dark doe eyes were mean, but softened when she recognized Nora.

"It's not like you to linger," the girl said slowly, not letting down her guard yet.

"Cut it out, Elian, I know you were watching," Nora demanded. "It's me. I'm stuck here. Help me!"

Elian frowned. "Where is your time key?" she asked.

"I lost it in the fight. I'll go back and get it later, but I need you to put me back in. The others are going to get killed. Elian!"

Finally, Elian withdrew her staff to her side, allowing her to turn around. Elian's staff was identical to Nora's apart from the pearly white rod and timepiece. It towered over them at an impressive nine feet. The time key's power radiated like a furnace, pulsing in waves. Despite its size, she maneuvered it with ease. An image erupted out of the darkness—the grainy picture was of the boardinghouse in the morning hours of the next day. Nora could tell by the orange-and-purple streaks filling the horizon.

Elian shifted her staff into her other hand. In her now free hand, she clutched something. It was Nora's time key back in its necklace form.

"Never leave your time key unattended," she told Nora, watching the sundial shoot toward the time guard like a magnet. "Listen, closely, I cannot interfere, though you must know Russell Durand does not operate alone. He never has."

All the stolen moments he crossed her he acted alone. Perhaps there was more to his agenda than she thought.

Nora clasped the necklace back on, then shoved it under her shirt. "You can't tell me anything more?" she asked.

Elian shook her head. "Go," she said urgently.

Nora raised a hand. The ability to shift and move in the darkness came back to her. She sank through the layers and left the time warp.

Chapter 29
Time Keys

Nora skidded onto the gravel driveway. The sharp morning air and unearthly stillness bothered her, as if the world was holding its breath. Something about her arrival didn't feel right. She looked around wondering if she was too late. Up ahead, the boardinghouse showed its first signs of distress.

The front door was blasted apart, and a tall pillar of smoke was coming from the back. And with the bits of plaster scattered across the lawn, Nora knew a wall had been taken down. On the second floor the old siding had a neat circle the size of the cannon ball showing the kitchen inside. Rapid gunshots sounded from the back.

"Shit!" she gasped.

She ran up the driveway, the sinking feeling weighing heavy over her heart.

"Nora?"

She came to a grinding stop.

Mason and Wesley dropped from nearby trees. They were both in pajamas. They looked disheveled, obviously having no time to swap clothes. There was a long tear on Mason's sleeve while a bruise formed under his chin. Wesley's pants had grass stains, but otherwise seemed unharmed. The two of them looked relieved to see her.

She ran over.

"Where's Charlie?"

"With Hogan and Angeline," Mason told her.

Nora looked to the boardinghouse. Muffled voices came from inside. "Are they still in there?"

"They might be," Wesley replied, wiping his face. "I don't know. We managed to escape using the cellar. They were supposed to be right behind us." Another set of gunshots went off behind the house. Both time markers flinched at the sound.

"I need to get in there, I need to help!"

Mason grabbed her arm. "We should run. We can't stay here."

A series of loud booms made the three of them jump. Nora's hair stood on end. It wasn't another wall being blown to pieces or shingles flying. It sounded an awful lot like a detonation, a big one.

"Get down!"

She pushed Mason and Wesley down hard as the boardinghouse exploded. The immense impact knocked her to the grass too. Nora covered her head with her arms, but that didn't stop the deafening boom from leaving a loud ringing in her ears. The strong gust of wind whipped her hair forward, the heat burned her back. Bigger chunks of debris crashed around them bouncing off the ground. Bursts of embers and splinted wood peppered over them like smoldering hail.

She waited until the roar of the flames turned hazy in her ears. Smoke filled Nora's lungs when she tried to call for Mason and Wesley. Instead, she raised her head to look for them in the dark fumes. Her eyes watered, the smoke stinging like needles.

The boardinghouse was a skeleton in flames, engulfing what was left of the building. Large sections of the walls had caved in while other portions flew onto the lawn. It was a miracle any of it didn't crush them. Items like bedding, tables, chairs, and couches that had caught fire hit nearby trees.

With difficulty, Nora pushed herself off the ground tears rolling down her cheeks both from the smoke and dread. She staggered only to fall down again. Fear closed in on her chest. *They can't be gone*, Nora forced to tell herself, *I can still find them.* She refused to come to terms with the fact that she may be the last time guard left.

Nora somehow got to her feet. "Go," she croaked, wiping her tears. She almost fell over Wesley on all fours gagging. She helped him to stand, then Mason. They were both coughing, struggling to get any clean air in their lungs. "Go. Hide. Run far and fast," Nora told them, shrugging off the backpack to hand to them. "Don't use any landlines or cell phones. Keep running and stay hidden. Whatever you do, don't look back. We'll—we'll catch up. I'll find you."

"What about you?" Mason asked. "Look at it. Do you really think anyone survived?"

"I have to see for myself."

"Mason," Wesley said, shouldering the backpack. "Let's move. Now."

"Go," she urged. "You can't stay here. I have to make sure the others—" Her voice faltered. "Go, now."

Wesley didn't need telling twice. He jogged off without a word. With a pleading look from Nora, Mason followed.

She ran up the rest of the driveway. The wildfire made it impossible to get close enough to see past the blaze. Black clouds of smoke spiraled into the sky and flared covering the back of the house like a dark fog. The eruption was far worse than she imagined. It came from the cellar taking out the den and leveling the first floor almost completely. Furniture and broken couches slammed into trees knocking whole branches off. Among the rubble and growing fires were bodies sprawled over the grass. Nora ran to the nearest body and turned it over.

It was a man, or rather what was left of one. His chest and face were charred beyond recognition. And his arm was bent in an odd angle exposing bone that had ripped through his skin. Little tuffs of black curls remained on his skull. It took all Nora had to not gag at the smell of burnt flesh. She gingerly placed him the way he was not wanting to see more.

Nora straightened. "Charlie?" she called out, walking fast. "Hogan! Angeline!"

She ran further onto the grass. The madness of the boardinghouse fire hadn't caught up to it yet. In a few hours, that could change.

A hand grabbed her shoulder. Fingers dug into her muscles sinking into a pressure point right above her collar bone. Stinging pain shot down her arm. She dropped to her knees. Blindly, Nora reached behind her, took a handful of fabric, and heaved the person over her shoulder. As they hit the ground, she pulled off her necklace bursting into the black staff. She drove it through the red head's chest.

Up ahead, Nora heard voices coming her way. Her staff retracted to its sundial form and threw it around her neck. She sidestepped behind a tree, crouching low. It was two women, they rushed passed talking in a Slavic language. She couldn't listen in to what they were saying, because two more time travelers were closing in to join them.

Nora backed away careful not to be spotted. She moved across the field backward until water splashed her shoes. She made it to the creek. It looked safe. It seemed no time traveler was paying attention to the property line. She stayed low; from there it was easy to see that the property was crawling with time travelers. Most of them arrived in time warps, surely to replace the first group lost. They all headed in the same direction: the water tower.

She followed several yards away from the last time traveler. The chatter grew louder. Nora knelt behind a tree watching them gather. Three or four dozen time travelers had shown up. They formed a tight perimeter around the base. The first line held eight men with poised arrows aimed at the water tank. A second line stood waiting. At the foot of the ladder two men lay still. Everyone watched muttering with enthusiasm. Nora shut her eyes, concentrating hard drowning out the extra noise.

"Three time markers in one place," said a gleeful, boyish voice. "These time guards are losing their touch."

"Pray that the others died in that fire."

A gruffer, more demanding voice caught her attention. "I want someone to bring that water tank down. And I want someone to cut through the steel and forge an opening. I want to know who's in there."

"They think a time marker locked himself in."

"Why doesn't someone go up there?" asked a woman's voice.

"Because no one is dumb enough to go up alone in case its not."

It gave her an advantage if the time travelers were running scared. If she played her cards right, Nora could cut down a fraction of their forces. How she would deal with the rest of them, well, she'd figure that part out later.

Nora rose to her feet. She needed distance to scheme the best angles of an attack. A hand touched her arm. Caught off guard, she slammed backward jabbing her elbow straight in their gut. Whomever it was anticipated Nora's move. They pinned her arm to her back so effortlessly she swore she almost forgot about the excruciating pain in her shoulder. She went to grab her time key. A blade dug into her hand clasping the sundial.

"Stop!" hissed a voice in her ear. "Stop, it's me!"

The dagger dislodged and blood trailed down her fingers.

She turned around. It was Hogan. He was still covered in ashes, but looked whole and unscathed apart from healing scratches and bruises.

A wave of relief washed over her despite the pain. "Damn it, Hogan," she scolded. "I was ready to snap your neck." Nora swore again and hugged him tight. He wrapped his arms around her too. Underneath the smell of burning wood, she smelled traces of his clean spring water fragrance and citrus. "You won't believe the crap day I've had."

"I'm sure I can picture it well."

More shouting came from the cluster of time travelers. Hogan gestured for her to follow. He led her away from the property to the open field next door. The tall grass was high enough to hide them as long as they knelt. Hogan parted the grass like blinds. They had a clear view of the water tower.

"Who do you suppose is up there?" Nora asked, after she bandaged her healing hand.

"Angeline. I saw her climb up. Charlie ran east."

Another wave of relief washed over Nora. "I found Mason and Wesley out front, I sent them away from here."

"Great," he muttered. "While you fetch Charlie, I will help Angeline."

"And how do you plan to do that?" she demanded. "You need my help to get her out."

He acted like he didn't hear her. "I'm going to clear a path for you," he went on evenly. "You'll have a minute or two to find Charlie." Hogan pointed beyond the water tower. "Bring him back. If I can manage to make a crack in their defenses Angeline will emerge and join the fight."

Anger swelled in her. "Hogan—"

"Find Charlie."

"I will, but—"

"His safety is essential."

"Hogan," Nora said again, her voice betraying her this time. "We can't lose you, not now."

Hogan's lips almost turned into a smile. "You won't lose me."

He reassured her with a tender stroke of his hand brushing strands of hair behind her ear. Hogan reached into his pocket and pulled out a thin, black, sleek pocket watch. With a flick of his thumb, the plate opened revealing the face of a clock. The small disk like watch expanded in his palm growing the size of a large garbage can lid. Engraved on its curved surface were carvings in white. It depicted glowing Hebrew numerals, giving the rest of the shield an intimating aura.

The dark shield had saved her lives countless time. If he said he could hold a line, she had to believe him.

Chapter 30
Yielding

Gunshots propelled Nora to her feet.

The diversion had begun. She waited, watching Hogan run into the center of the battlefield. The line of archers turned to him releasing poised arrows as other time travelers advanced firing rifles. The black shield swung to deflect the incoming harm. Bullets and arrows ricocheted to the ground.

While they reloaded, Hogan took to the offensive. The shield ripped through the sky and came down spinning fast, like a massive blade. Time travelers dived escaping certain death by inches. Someone shouted for more weaponry. Hogan beckoned the shield to return with his arm. He brought it over his head spinning slowly. With a flourish of his forearm, the shield went flying shoveling time travelers out of the way.

That was her cue.

Nora ran to the path he cleared for her. She didn't go unspotted. Arrows flew over her head missing her by centimeters. She heard the whoosh of the shield as it came to protect her from another barrage of bullets. She pushed to run faster.

The sound of the battle faded. Nora ran onto the next plot of land. The dirt field was nothing like the surrounding areas. It offered no places to hide, the open space was for all to see. No time marker could have gotten far. She slowed down turning on the spot to scan the morning landscape.

"Charlie!" Nora shouted, tugging at her sundial.

Nothing.

"Charlie!" she called again. "Charlie, come on, it's me!"

"Look out!"

It was Charlie's voice, but he was nowhere to be seen. A searing pain in her spine caused Nora to fall over. Brief seconds of numbness swept over her body. Her legs felt unattached like they were no loner hers to control. The pain intensified when who ever stabbed her in the back plunged the arrow further into her vertebrae.

"Try healing from that, time guard!" a voice snarled in her ear.

A kick to Nora's side made it hard to stay conscious. Getting up wasn't an option. Her legs would remain as they were until the arrow was somehow removed. Painfully, Nora rolled onto her side and reached for the arrow.

"Ah, ah or this poisoned arrow goes right through your heart."

Nora looked up to see who momentarily put her out of action. It was a woman passed her forties with black curls and green eyes. She wore a white cloak over clothing making it hard for Nora to tell when and where she came from. Nothing about her was familiar except for the second arrow ready on her bow.

"Ah, ah," she repeated when Nora reached for her sundial. "Where are the time markers?"

"Ashes. Under the boardinghouse."

"I saw them run."

Nora shuttered involuntarily. The shooting pain in her back was like a hot knife spreading fire up and down her torso. Her legs beneath her wouldn't cooperate no matter how hard she wanted them to. She needed to get the arrow out. On the ground, there was little she could do to help anyone much less defend herself.

From the corner of her eye, an uneven patch of dirt stirred. Jeans and brown hair became visible, lumps of rocks tumbled to the floor. Charlie had hidden in a narrow trench. He was feet away from Nora and the time traveler who granted temporary mercy.

Her mind raced a mile a second trying to think of something to keep the cloaked woman's attention. Nora huffed, ignoring the pain as she moved. She sat up right supporting much of her weight against her arm.

"Looks like Russell let's anyone in his ranks," Nora baited.

The woman's nostrils flared and brought the arrow an inch from Nora's throat.

"Talk."

"I'd rather you shoot that arrow," Nora challenged, yanking the bow closer until the tip was hairs away from her skin.

She flinched. She hadn't anticipated a time guard encouraging to finish her off, to welcome death as Nora did so frankly. She recovered from the initial shock fast, nocked her arrow further.

"Suits me just fine."

"Wait, don't hurt her!"

It was Charlie. He emerged from the trench hands raised. His wide eyes told Nora how scared he was. He looked to Nora and the woman, unsure with how to approach. He did anyway causing everything to go out of the control.

The arrow the woman released soared passed Charlie's head. He ducked out of the way. As she reached for her quiver to replace it, he swept in to try and stop her.

"No!"

Nora ripped off her necklace letting the staff explode in her hand. The pain in her back shot up her spine again almost propelling her to the ground. Charlie and the woman turned into blurs and noise. Their intertwined bodies wrestled up close, then away.

"Nora!" Charlie warned.

With the help of a final burst of strength, she lifted herself and the staff. Charlie tackled the woman as hard as he could straight into the dark pole. Nora held on tight until she heard the sound of skin puncturing open. Warm, sticky blood poured onto her hands like an open hose. The body stopped moving. Once it had gone quiet, Nora threw aside the skewered woman.

"What do I do?" she heard Charlie say, his voice rising in panic. "What do I do?"

"Get my staff!" Nora practically shouted. She heard him dislodge her staff in one quick try and felt him return to her side. "And get this arrow out of my back. Make sure—"

"Right, okay."

He didn't hesitate, he pulled free the arrow from her back. She didn't even get a chance to finish her thought. All Nora remembered was the splitting pain and the decrease in pressure. The feeling in her legs hadn't returned yet, but at least now she would properly heal. She sat up easier this time.

A loud cry from the water tower made them jump.

"You need to go," she told him, taking the staff.

"Where to?" he asked.

It finally hit her that she didn't even know where Mason and Wesley were running to, or if they would remain together. They couldn't have gotten far. Nora thought for a long moment. For the first time in a while she was at a loss for instructions. There wasn't ever going to be a good enough answer except for far and fast. She needed to give him a solid reply in case things didn't go as planned. And the way he looked at her, Charlie counted on her for guidance and to get through this ordeal alive.

An idea came to her.

"Find Heywood Park," she said at last, wincing using the staff to stand. Her legs tingled at each movement, regaining feeling. "Follow the path to the amphitheater. Hide there. If we aren't there within the hour, go. Use any means to get there." Nora handed him her phone.

"Mason and Wes—"

"Will be there," she finished with certainty. She was sure Mason would be there. It's where she would be if she wanted him to find her. It was the first place that meant something to the both of them, the first place he kissed her. "Hurry!"

Charlie nodded. He straightened and made a large arc to the front. The faint blue light of her phone blinked on across the road taking him away from the boardinghouse. Nora watched him go before fumbling forward. Leaning on the staff for support, she made her way back to the others.

The time travelers were putting up a good fight; despite, their numbers being drastically cut in half. The center of the fray was in two areas. One was over by Hogan where he raised his shield in defense blocking four swords at once. A small group of archers sent repeated volleys at the water tank. Up on the stand, Angeline had come out from the water tank to aide Hogan. The unwanted bath in the old tank made her look menacing, her pajamas were crusting with mud, and the blond ponytail was coming undone with every movement. Her black bow was drawn. She crouched low as flaming arrow missed their target. Once the last arrow flew passed, Angeline hurried forward and drew the bow string back holding nothing but air. As she released it, dark jagged bolts flew toward awaiting time travelers hitting them squarely in the chest. They evaporated in puffs of dark smoke. Angeline was taking them down in waves with her impressive bow. She was giving Hogan a run for his money.

A lone time traveler saw Nora approaching. In a less than graceful motion, she used her staff to draw him close picking up an abandoned machete as she went. She moved the blade across his neck.

Next, a woman with a katana rushed to meet her. The girl had an advantage: her blade had a farther reach, and her health was in better condition. Her moves were quick and lethal, unlike Nora who had to move in the defensive to remain standing. The tip of the sword pricked patches of exposed skin it could reach. The shrill whistle of Hogan's shield hurtling toward them made the two duck. Distracted, Nora backhanded the sword away from her hands and plunged the staff in her lower stomach.

A hard shove sent Nora face first into the ground. She rolled out of the way as an axe sank into the earth where her shoulder had been. The staff in her hand spun hitting the man once, twice, then a third time across the skull. He fell beside her.

"We got a runner!" Angeline shouted from atop the water tower.

The young archer ran to the fields. With all his comrades gone, he didn't plan on sticking around and Nora didn't blame him. With a hard flick of his wrist, Hogan's shield went spinning in his direction and Nora staggered forward throwing her staff. The shield hit him first knocking him clean off his feet. The staff clamped down over his trench coat keeping him in place. Before he could register what happened, a single dark flare hit him on the leg, and he disappeared.

⏳

"How did this happen?" Mason asked hours later. He faced the heaping piles of gray ashes. Black trees formed a new forest where the old one once stood. They reminded Nora of dark needles poking the earth like a scorched cushion. Any greenery left was completely gone, disintegrated by the fire. Thankfully, the last of the fumes were lost in the midmorning fog.

The time markers and time guards gathered near the water tower. Angeline volunteered to fetch the boys as soon as they cleared the grounds of the fallen time travelers. It also gave Hogan and Nora the chance to clean themselves up after the surprise attack.

Hogan nodded for Mason to rejoin the others in the circle. He didn't need to look at that anymore.

"They knew we were on the move, about the boardinghouse ..." Nora told them. "Russell must have tipped them off. Two different groups of travelers were waiting for me outside the country. Somehow he—well, another version of him—found me on my last stop. He came to stall. I just didn't know it then."

"We took precaution in your absence," Angeline said, shoving her hands in her sweater pockets to keep warm. "With our rotten luck abroad, we packed and moved the vehicles to safer locations."

"Russell and I fought ... I wanted to get here in time—"

"You did," Charlie said at once. "You got us all away from here."

Nora shook her head. It was all she could do to resist the urge to kick the dirt. "Russell knew everything, he set us up." She looked to Angeline and Hogan to relay the message. "Elian warned me he isn't working alone."

Hogan's eyebrows raised. "Elian left her post in the Passage?" he asked seriously.

Nora nodded.

"Elian?" Charlie asked, puzzled.

"The fourth and final time guard," Wesley muttered when the time guards didn't reply. "She protects the Passage of Time, the space outside a time warp where one can travel from the past to the future. She's the only true immortal being amongst us."

"She left her post to deliver this message?" Angeline asked.

Nora nodded again.

Elian's words weren't meant to be taken lightly. She only intervened when she knew a certain event was about to obstruct the natural order of time in the Passage.

Wesley balled his fists. "We have to go after him."

"He got away. I don't know where he went," Nora replied.

Angeline shifted in her spot. "He won't stay hidden for long," she said.

The words hung in the air, longer than they ought to. They all understood what this meant. Charlie, Mason, and Wesley especially knew what that information meant. They weren't out of danger yet. It was also a daunting reminder that time used them as malleable, almost expandable characters in the greater scheme of things. The souls within them would move on, but they would not.

"Will you stay behind to assure we aren't followed?" Angeline asked Nora.

She nodded.

Immediately, Angeline turned to Hogan. He drew her in close wrapping his arms around her tight. He whispered something in her ear, and her shoulders began to shake. Nora stepped away from them to give them a moment. It would be quite some while until they met again. The most she could do for them was spare one more minute.

Nora gathered the time markers. "Have Hogan reteach you your strengths. You're an excellent carpenter and a talented pathfinder. Things will come to you with practice. Don't let the abilities you've gathered go to waste," she urged Charlie. "And, Wesley, your mortality shouldn't be a bother. Enjoy what you have now in this moment.

You'll only live through it once. Also, don't let Angeline drag you to another French colony. Explore the old and the new world."

"What foolish things are you telling *my* time marker?" Angeline demanded playfully. She strode over looping her arm through Wesley's. "I'll have you know we don't always stay in former French countries. We *are* civilized." With her free arm, she extended it to Nora with a smile.

The girls clasped hands in goodbye.

A second later they let go. Angeline and Wesley departed first moving swiftly to the road. They turned to wave once before continuing on in a light jog.

Hogan approached next. He drew Nora close too, but not in the way he did with Angeline. He pressed his forehead to hers, his hand on the back of her neck. The gesture was familiar and still very much intimate, a farewell between close friends. He took a step back as soon as she opened her eyes.

Nora climbed up the water tower to stand on the platform. Mason followed. Elevated, she was able to see Angeline and Wesley had gained distance heading in the direction of the over pass. After several long minutes, they were far enough to send the others on their way. She signaled them to depart.

"Come, Charlie," Hogan said. He led the future time marker east.

She sat on the ledge with her legs dangling. Below, the others kept growing smaller as they went. The fog added to their concealment making them look like fuzzy creatures in the haze. Instinctively, Nora took the sundial in her hand. The pendant was cold and quiet.

Behind her, Mason circled the water tank once, then stared out for several minutes. Finally, he sat next to her. "What are you thinking?" he asked.

"That we ought to move," she said with a sigh.

Mason gave her a quizzical look. "And why aren't we?"

Nora shrugged. It was the most she offered him when she was so exhausted. Looking around at the misty grounds, her mind found it hard to piece together all that had happened in the passed twenty-four hours. It came in fragments, then all at once, catching up, making her legs twitch.

Sitting on the water tower with Mason felt like the right place to be, even if it was for a few more minutes. The unfamiliar calmness before beginning anew was a forgotten memory in Nora's head. It was a long ago concept she knew so well, yet fresh in every way. It pushed her to keep pace with the universe when she wanted to slow down.